Taste

Special Edition

Melanie Harlow

USA TODAY BESTSELLING AUTHOR

Cover Designer: Janett Corona

Editors: Nancy Smay, Julia Griffis

For readers of the Frenched Series...
who'd have thought?

I've been doing a lot of thinking.
And the thing is, I love you.

NORA EPHRON

CHAPTER 1
GIANNI

I didn't have to go through the tasting room at Abelard Vineyards to get to the kitchen—in fact, it was out of my way—but I never missed an opportunity to mess with Ellie Fournier.

Sure, she was the boss's daughter and our moms had been best friends forever, but I'd been pushing her buttons since we were six years old and didn't see any reason to stop just because we were now adults and co-workers.

If anything, it was even *more* fun now that the restaurant her parents had hired me to open at their winery was up and running. Since she was in charge of the wine list and worked the floor as sommelier, she had to put up with me every single day.

Believe me, I made the most of it.

And I *always* got a rise out of her. You'd think she'd just ignore me by now, but no—she consistently gave me the satisfaction of a scowl, a dirty look, a barb hurled in my direction. But I couldn't help myself. There was just something so irresistible about getting under her skin—I was a kid in a candy store around Ellie Fournier.

I took the steps down to the lower level and found her in

the light to ensure they were each *perfectly* clean. It was Monday morning, which meant the tasting room and restaurant were closed. Although I loved a crowd, the quiet was kind of nice. Even in January, weekends here were jam-packed. Etoile, with only eight tables, was booked out every Friday and Saturday night for months. We had phenomenal reviews for everything from the food to the wine to the setting to the service. I'd like to take all the credit—and sometimes around Ellie, I did, just to bug her—but the truth was, much of it had to be shared with her.

She was fucking dynamite on the floor every night. Smart and energetic and approachable, with an innate talent for pairing food and wine. And she never came off as stuffy or snobby like a lot of sommeliers did—she was genuinely friendly and welcoming to everyone.

Except me.

"Morning, princess," I called as I approached the bar. Since it wasn't technically a workday, I was surprised to see her wearing charcoal dress pants and a black blouse that tied in a bow at the neck. I swear she had that blouse in every color of the rainbow—she never wore anything low-cut. Her long, reddish-brown hair was neatly pulled back into a ponytail, the way it always was on the job.

"Could you please not call me that?" She frowned at a smudge on the glass in her hand and set it aside. "I'm not a princess."

"But you *were*." When we were kids, Ellie used to compete in pageants, and I never got tired of teasing her about them. "And old habits are hard to break."

"Try, please."

I could tell from her tone and expression she was already in a mood. "What's the matter?"

"Nothing."

the weather forecast."

"What about it?"

"They're predicting a ton of snow later tonight." She picked up a white linen napkin and rubbed the rim of a glass. "Like a solid ten inches."

"Really?"

"Yes. They're calling it the blizzard of the century." She put the glass in a quilted storage box. "How have you not heard about it? It's all over the news."

"I never watch the news."

"Why not?"

"Do you ever feel good after watching the news?"

She thought for a second. "I guess not."

"That's because it's all bullshit created to scare you into watching *more* news, so they can solve the problems *they* made up in the first place."

One of her brows peaked. "Says the guy who starred on a reality TV cooking show called *Lick My Plate*. Talk about bullshit."

"Hey, I'm not saying *Lick My Plate* wasn't bullshit, but at least it wasn't pretending to be anything but entertainment." I took a sip of my coffee. "And I was very entertaining. My tagline was 'too hot to handle.' And whenever I was onscreen, they played that old song called 'Fever.'"

"I wouldn't know," she said, turning away with a shrug. "I never saw it."

"Really? Because your mom told me you guys never missed an episode."

She picked up another glass and held it to the light. "I *may* have been in the room when it was on a couple times."

My grin widened at the lie. "Anyway, what do you have against getting a solid ten inches tonight? Sounds like a good time to me."

She set the glass on the bar with a clank and glared at me. "This is serious, Gianni. If I can't get to Harbor Springs tonight, I'll lose my opportunity to meet Fiona Duff."

Something about the name was familiar, but I couldn't place it. "Who's Fiona Duff again?"

"She's the chief editor at *Tastemaker* magazine, and she's married to Malcolm Duff, some big-shot ad executive who's also a wine collector. They hired me to do a tasting at their vacation home tonight."

"They did?"

Ellie sighed. "I've been talking about this for weeks, Gianni. You don't listen."

"Sorry," I said, because it was true that listening was not a great skill of mine. My mind tended to wander—usually to food or sex. But in my defense, Ellie could talk the hind legs off a donkey, and it wasn't like she often stopped chattering to ask my opinion on anything.

Plus, her face sometimes distracted me from what she was saying.

Ellie was beautiful, with an awesome curvy body she usually kept fully covered with those librarian blouses and dressy pants. She did sometimes wear fitted pencil skirts that came down to her knees, and even though I consider myself more of a miniskirt man, I had to admit I liked the way they clung to her hips and thighs.

Her grown-up hotness had sort of surprised me, because as a kid, she'd been short and scrawny, with curly pigtails that begged to be pulled, know-it-all eyes, and a pouty round mouth—which she used to tattle on me *all* the time.

Although, to be fair, I *was* a little shit.

I'd steal the perfectly sharpened colored pencils from her desk. I'd take one bite from the cookie in her lunch box but leave it in there. I'd chase her on the playground while she

drove her nuts.

But she was just such a perfect little goody-goody—she never did *anything* wrong. Teachers adored girls like her, and I was constantly in trouble. My mom was always saying shit like, *"Why can't you be more like the Fournier kids?"* because they were all so well-behaved, and my younger brothers and I were fucking devils.

By high school, I'd let up on Ellie somewhat—I was more interested in girls who let me put my tongue in their mouth or my hand up their shirt, and it was crystal clear she was *not ever* going to be that girl—but I can't say I ever missed an opportunity to torment her.

Or to fantasize about what her mouth might feel like on my lips or my chest or certain other parts of my anatomy.

It was like a perfect, luscious little plum.

I tore my eyes off it and forced myself to focus. Setting my cardboard coffee cup on the bar, I perched on one of the stools. "Tell me about it again."

She closed her eyes briefly and took a deep breath, like she needed it for patience. "Someone I went to Michigan State with works as an assistant editor at *Tastemaker*. The offices are in Chicago, and she texted me that she heard my name being tossed around in a meeting as a possible candidate for one of the 30 Under 30 spots, and it was right around the time I got hired to do the tasting."

"Don't get mad, but what's 30 Under 30?"

"It's a feature in the magazine. Every year they name 30 people under age 30 who are doing cool things in the food, beverage, or hospitality industry. Evidently, they heard about the thing I did with the QR codes on the labels."

"Oh yeah? Congrats." Ellie had convinced her dad to add QR codes to Abelard's wine bottle labels, which directed people to a landing page where they could learn more about

recipes, and a video featuring Ellie herself giving tasting notes alongside an ASL interpreter.

"It's too early for congratulations, but *if* I got a spot," she went on anxiously, wringing her hands together, "the media attention would be great for Abelard, and for Michigan wines in general. There are small wineries doing such great things here, and no one knows about them. We spend too much time fighting the misconception that we make mediocre wines rather than talking about what really matters."

"I hear you. Kind of like when I was featured in *People* magazine's special issue: The Sexiest Chefs Alive. Everyone knows that what really matters is how sexy a chef is."

"Gianni, I'm being serious." Her voice took on a desperate tone. "They usually feature people working for big-name wineries or Michelin-starred restaurants. I just want a chance to have that kind of reach. To be seen and heard by a wider audience. But it won't happen if I can't get there."

"Who's doing the food tonight?" I asked out of curiosity, picking up my coffee and taking a sip.

Ellie shrugged. "I assume Fiona. She loves to cook and throws fabulous dinner parties."

"Why didn't they ask me?"

"I don't know. Not everything is about you, Gianni."

"Yeah, but the food's better when it is."

She rolled her eyes and picked up another glass, getting back to work. "I don't know why I bother talking to you about this stuff. You don't understand."

I was going to argue with her, but she looked so upset I decided against it. Maybe she was worrying for no reason—it wouldn't be the first time. Ellie liked everything *just so*. Setting down my coffee cup, I pulled out my phone and checked the radar app, prepared to tell her she was making a big deal out of nothing, just like TV news people did.

grayish white moving across the upper Midwest on the screen made my gut a little uneasy. "I don't know, Ell. I'm not sure you should be on the road tonight."

"You sound like my dad, who's texted me twice already from *France* telling me to cancel."

"That's probably a good idea. This storm looks big."

"Didn't you just say the news was full of made-up problems?"

"Yeah." I flashed the screen at her. "But this isn't a made-up problem. This is a polar vortex."

She lifted her chin. "I'm not canceling."

"Ell, I get that the opportunity is important to you, *and* that you love to disagree with me whenever possible, but it's not worth spinning out on an icy highway or sliding into a ditch."

"I'm *going*." Her eyes blazed with determination. "The snow isn't supposed to start until ten or so anyway, and the tasting is at six. I'll probably be back home in my pajamas with a cup of hot tea before we get an inch or two. I don't even know why I mentioned it."

But I heard the shaky note in her voice and looked at my phone again. According to my weather app, Ellie was right and the worst of it wouldn't reach northern Michigan until later tonight—but that could change. Weather was unpredictable. "I still think you should reschedule."

"Well, you're not the boss of me." She folded her arms. "And if something was this important to *you*, I know you'd find a way to get there."

"It's really that important to you?"

"Yes!" She threw her hands in the air. "I can't explain it, but I just know that somehow, tonight will change my life. Look, I know this place doesn't matter to you like it does to me, and Etoile is just a temporary diversion for you while you

want to give it everything I have."

"Abelard matters to me too," I said defensively. "Just because I don't want to spend my life or career in one place doesn't mean I don't care." I made a split-second decision. "I'll take you tonight."

The scowl was back. "No. I don't need a babysitter."

"I'm not letting you drive more than a hundred miles north in a blizzard tonight by yourself, Ellie. In what car?"

"Mine."

"Your little Honda? That thing looks like a toy. I had Matchbox cars bigger than that."

"Not all of us can afford a fancy new SUV."

"My SUV isn't new or fancy, but it does have good snow tires. I'm driving you." I stuck my phone back in my pocket like the matter was settled.

Ellie continued to glare at me. "This is you not listening again, Gianni. I don't need you to protect me."

"Yes, you do. Remember Tommy Tootag from grade school?"

"What about him?"

"He stole your Scholastic book fair money in third grade."

"Gianni, *you* stole my Scholastic book fair money in third grade. Then you gave it back to me because I threatened to tell on you."

I shook my head. "The money I gave you was mine. Tommy Tootag took yours."

She looked at me skeptically. "Why didn't you say anything?"

"Because Tootag was a fifth grader and he was fucking huge—he had a *beard* already." I shrugged. "And you were crying. I felt bad."

Her expression softened—slightly. "Well, thank you for

When she turned around like the matter was settled, I changed tactics. "Stop being so selfish."

She whirled to face me again, her mouth agape. "Selfish!"

"Yeah. Tonight is my night off, you know, and I had plans with my dad. But how am I supposed to enjoy them when all I'd be doing is picturing you shivering beneath an overpass, wishing you'd have listened to me?" I gave her a little performance just for fun. "Gianni . . . Gianni," I moaned pitifully, "why didn't I believe you? I'm sorry . . . you were right all along."

"That is ridiculous." But her lips were dangerously close to a smile.

"No, it isn't. And I'd feel terrible. Your parents would never forgive me. In fact, I'd probably lose my job, and soon I'd be poor and homeless. Hot girls wouldn't go out on dates with me, I'd never have sex again—for fuck's sake, I might as well join the priesthood at that point. No one would ever taste my cooking again. And it would be all your fault, which is why I will cancel my plans in order to chauffeur your ass safely to Harbor Springs and back."

"Give me a break. You would never join the priesthood."

"What if you got a flat tire?" I persisted. "What if you ran out of gas? What if you were driving perfectly safe but someone skidded out of control and hit *you*?"

She chewed on her lip, and I could see her resolve start to melt.

"It's safer to go together," I told her with finality. "You know your dad would feel better if I took you. Go ahead and text him right now. See what he says."

She didn't even get her phone out because she knew I was right.

"I'm not asking you to do this," she said quickly. "Just so we're clear."

"Sorry. I guess I'm not used to your gentleman routine. And *one* good deed in twenty-three years doesn't exactly make up for all the other mean shit you did."

"Come on. I wasn't mean, Ellie. I was . . . playful."

"Playful? You called me a shrimp. You pulled my pigtails. You drew mustaches on my favorite dolls." Her eyes narrowed. "You pinned me down, sat on my chest, and let drool ooze out of your mouth until it almost hit me before you sucked it back in."

I laughed. "Fuck, I forgot about that. How about I let you sit on me right now? Can we call it even? I won't even mind if there's saliva involved."

"And let's not forget the Cherry Festival."

"Are we *still* talking about that? Ellie, for fuck's sake, it was six years ago. We were seventeen. And it's not my fault you got assigned to the dunk tank—that's where the reigning Cherry Princess has to sit. And it's the God-given right of the townspeople to come and dunk their princess." I could still picture her sitting in that dunk tank in her crown and sash, her smile big, her bikini small. The memory made me warm all over.

"You didn't have to come back fifty times," she seethed. "You humiliated me over and over again on purpose. Then instead of using the photo of me from *before*, when my hair was dry and my makeup was pretty, the newspaper used the one of us from *after*—I was plastered on the front page looking like a wet raccoon."

"And I had a face full of whipped cream, since you got back at me for the dunk tank by throwing eight pies in my face."

"You deserved it. And you got back at me later that night, didn't you?"

For a moment, we continued to stare at each other, both of

That dark room. The door closed. The clock ticking.

"I got back at you? Is that really how you think of it?" I asked her.

She started polishing a wineglass again. "Actually, I don't think of it at all."

"Me neither," I lied.

"It's ancient history."

"My point exactly. Maybe as a kid I *sometimes* did my best to antagonize you, and *possibly* there were some shenanigans that got out of hand when we were teenagers, but ever since I moved back here, I have been nothing but nice. Can't you forgive and forget?"

"You get me to Harbor Springs and back in one piece tonight, and we'll talk."

"I will. Trust me."

"Trust me, he says," she muttered, zipping up the storage box.

"Yes, trust me." I puffed up my chest, a little insulted. "My dad taught me to be a man of my word."

"I do like your dad," she conceded, as if that was the one thing I had going for me. "I guess I could trust you for a day."

"Thank you."

"Should we leave at two?"

"Sounds good. I'll pull my car up at one-thirty and help you load it."

"I don't need your help."

I shook my head. "Why are you so stubborn?"

"Why are you so bossy?"

"Because it's fun." Grinning, I slid off the stool and headed for the door, but at the last second, something made me glance over my shoulder. When I caught her staring, she stuck her tongue out at me.

"You're going to miss me when I'm gone," I told her with

She squawked with laughter. "Fat. Chance."

Whistling "Fever," I turned around and headed for the kitchen.

CHAPTER 2
ELLIE

I watched Gianni leave the tasting room, refusing to look at his butt in his jeans.

Okay, I looked.

But in my defense, Gianni's backside is one of the best parts about him. It's round and muscular and looks like it might be fun to grab onto—not that I'd ever thought about doing that.

Much.

But if I can see his butt, he's probably not talking to me, and that's when I like Gianni best—when he's not talking to me. Actually, if he would just not speak at all, I'd like his face more too. I'd never tell him this, because he's cocky enough as it is, but Gianni is undeniably, *unreasonably* hot.

It's infuriating. Truly.

When we were in grade school, I didn't think he was cute at all. He was tall and wiry, his dirt-brown hair was usually a mess, and his nose was crooked because one of his brothers broke it during a fight. His pants always had holes in the knees, his sneakers were always filthy, and he had this way about him that always made me think he was laughing at me.

And nothing was safe around him—not your fresh box of

which he'd take from your desk and hold over your head so high you had no chance to reach it. I couldn't stand him.

But he grew up to look a lot like his dad, whom I call Uncle Nick and have always had a bit of a secret crush on. He'd gotten his dad's strong jaw and sculpted cheekbones, the dimple in his chin and those thick black eyelashes. The only difference was that Gianni had his mom's blue eyes, while his dad's were dark.

I'd actually had a super sexy dream about his dad once as a teenager, which I'd never told *anyone* about because it was so embarrassing. For like a year afterward, I could hardly look him in the eye. But I blamed Gianni for that, since it was right around the time of the Cherry Festival and that stupid game of Seven Minutes in Heaven the summer after our junior year.

That night had messed with me. Badly.

Maybe it had messed with him too, because after that, he seemed to lay off me a little. We spent our senior year mostly ignoring each other, and then he'd left almost immediately after graduation for New York City, where his dad—who was also a chef—had gotten him a job washing dishes in some famous restaurant kitchen.

Of course, I loved his cooking, but who didn't? Gianni talked a big game, but he had the talent to back it up. And he hadn't ridden on his dad's coattails—he'd made his own way, worked his way up from the lowest jobs in the kitchen, impressing even the most tyrannical chefs with his talent, his work ethic, and his tenacity. Occasionally his big mouth got him in trouble—I was pretty sure he'd been fired a couple times for insubordination—and he still loved to break rules, but at twenty-three, he was already making a name for himself in the industry. Mostly because of that ridiculous show, but there was no denying he'd been the standout star.

Okay, three times.

I'd also read all his press, which was how I knew so much about his career over the last five years and how in-demand he was. In fact, I'd been shocked when he returned to Michigan last summer and then accepted the job offer from my parents last fall.

I'd sulked like a toddler at the prospect of having to deal with him, his ego, and his constant poking at me day in and day out. But my parents had been thrilled, not only to have his name attached to the opening of Etoile and his expertise in the kitchen, but to have someone they considered family at the helm.

"This is better than we could have hoped for, Ell," my dad said while I pouted. "Beyond Gianni's skill and name recognition, he's someone we trust. That means everything when you're investing in a new business."

I'd had no choice but to accept their decision. And since my parents were now empty-nesters—my older brother Henri was in grad school and my younger brother Gabe was a freshman at college—they'd decided to spend some extended time in France, where my dad had been born and where they'd met. Living there had always been their dream and I was happy that hiring Gianni had allowed them the peace of mind to achieve it, but he still drove me nuts.

And I'd be trapped in a car with him for *hours* tonight.

How the hell had I let him con me into that?

I was still brooding about it when Winnie MacAllister popped into the tasting room. Winnie, who'd been my best friend since kindergarten, had taken over for my mother as guest services manager and event planner at Abelard, and I loved working with her—it almost made up for the fact that I was stuck with Gianni Lupo too.

Right behind Winnie was her older sister Felicity, who'd

"Morning," Winnie said brightly.

"Good morning," I said, smiling at them both. "I didn't know you were working today, Win."

"I'm not. I'm just showing Felicity around." Winnie glanced down at her sweatpants and sneakers, then touched her messy bun. "Can you imagine if your mom saw me at the front desk in this?"

Laughing, I set the final storage case on the bar and unzipped it. "She's in Paris. Even Mia can't see sweatpants across an ocean."

"Doesn't matter. I feel like she'd sense it in the ether that I was not perfectly put together."

I snickered. "Yeah, and she'd give you that look I got during my rebellious phase when I tried to sneak out of the house on a school morning in ripped jeans." I imitated my mother's voice. "Ellie, you have a closet full of beautiful clothes. Do you have to dress like you just rolled out of bed or put your pants in the blender instead of the dryer?"

"Oh, I remember that phase," Winnie said with a grin. "It didn't last long."

"Nope. Which Mia was quite relieved about. Although she still loves to blame my teenage years for her seven gray hairs and two wrinkles. And probably the worst thing I ever did was get a B on a French test!"

"You got a B on a French test?" Winnie asked in surprise.

"Once." I shook my head, angry at the memory. "Fucking *subjonctif plus-que-parfait*."

Felicity laughed. "Were your parents that strict about your grades?"

"They weren't strict exactly, they just had high expectations. I felt like I had to be perfect—I mean, I felt like I *wanted* to be perfect." I placed two more wineglasses into the box. "I liked the way it felt to bring home good report cards or keep

"Really?" Winnie blinked at me. "I've never heard you say that. I always thought she drove you crazy."

I shrugged. "She drives me crazy because she's perfect. She's never made a misstep in her life. It's like she made a list when she was young—go to college, start business, find soul mate, fall in love, get married, have three children, build dream home, never look a day over thirty—and she just keeps checking all the boxes."

Felicity laughed. "I'm sure she'd tell the story differently."

"Maybe, but sometimes I feel like I'll never live up." What I didn't say was that I had my own list too—I'd inherited my mother's obsession with them—and so far, I'd only checked off one box: graduate college. Next on the list were things like, *eliminate chemicals from our farming methods, grow brand awareness for Abelard, increase retail sales, prove to my parents I could run this place when they retired . . .* At some point I was hoping to meet the man of my dreams and have a family too, but I wasn't in a rush. I was only twenty-three, and I figured that could wait until I was closer to thirty.

That's why it really wasn't *too* worrisome I hadn't been on more than a handful of dates in the last six months, and all of them had ended with me alone on my couch in my pajamas, eating M&M's off a spoon I'd dipped in peanut butter, and watching reruns of *Friends*.

"Anyway, how was your dinner last night?" I asked Felicity.

"Oh, it was amazing—thank you so much for getting us in."

"You're welcome." I smiled at her. "I'm happy you enjoyed it."

"The food was just incredible," she gushed. "The friend I was with is a pretty influential food blogger and photographer, and she was really impressed."

"Oh my gosh! I've seen it—she takes gorgeous photos."

"Doesn't she?" Felicity laughed. "It's like food porn. I don't know how she makes broccoli look sexy, but she does."

"I didn't realize she was from around here," I said.

"She's not—she lives in Chicago, but I begged her to come up and take some promo photos for me."

"Lissy is starting her own food blog and catering business," Winnie said proudly, putting an arm around her sister's shoulders.

"Really? That's great!"

"Thanks." Felicity pushed her glasses up her nose. "I'm still in the early stages of putting a business plan together, but I'm excited."

"What's your blog going to be called?"

"I want to focus on plant-based recipes, so right now my favorite is The Veggie Vixen."

I laughed. "I like it. You went to culinary school, right?"

"Yes. And I worked as a sous chef in Chicago for a couple years before veering sideways into food science. Which was interesting—I liked the test kitchen, and I learned a lot—but I missed being in a *real* kitchen, creating food from *real* ingredients that people would enjoy eating just for pleasure. Beyond that, I discovered that I don't love working for a big corporation. I'd like to work for myself."

I smiled. "I don't blame you."

"But that sort of means starting from scratch," she said with a laugh, self-consciously tucking her straight dark hair behind one ear. "So here I am, age twenty-seven and living at home again, saving up money and trying to get a business off the ground."

"I think it's awesome," I said. "And don't feel bad. I still live at home too." When I'd first moved back last year, my parents had let me stay in one of Abelard's guest cabins,

guests. Last fall, I'd moved back into my former bedroom in the main house, which I was trying to view as a smart financial decision rather than a backward move.

But it was so convenient—I worked a lot of late nights, didn't have to drive home, and with my parents in France and my brothers away at school, I had plenty of privacy . . . not that I used it for anything fun. But a long dry spell was perfectly normal when you worked as much as I did, right?

"I told Felicity she could stay in the second bedroom at my place, but she turned me down," Winnie said.

"Um, and listen to you and Dex going at it on the other side of the wall every night?" Felicity laughed and shook her head. "No, thanks."

"It's not every night." Winnie blushed. "Just . . . most nights. But he and I could always stay at his place."

Felicity poked her sister's shoulder. "From the stories you've told me, I'd probably still hear you."

I laughed—Winnie had fallen in love with the guy who'd moved into the condo next to hers last summer, and they were disgustingly crazy about each other.

"So will you work out of the kitchen at Cloverleigh Farms?" I asked Felicity. Their dad had been CFO at Cloverleigh Farms for as long as I'd known their family, and their stepmom's family owned it. Like Abelard, Cloverleigh was a winery and an inn, although it was much bigger, with a large restaurant and bar on the premises, and soon they'd be opening a spa.

"In the beginning, yes," said Felicity. "I have an arrangement worked out with Alia, the head chef there—I'll use the kitchen during the hours between lunch and dinner at Cloverleigh for now, since I don't want to step on Alia's toes. But speaking of chefs, Gianni Lupo is incredible."

when he came over to the table to chat with us."

That was something Gianni did at the end of every night, and I found it a bit show pony, but customers seemed to love it. I had to admit, Gianni could charm the fuzz off a peach. Many of our best reviews raved about the way he took the time to talk with people and ask about their dining experience. In a place as tiny as Etoile, it was possible to greet each table personally.

"His family is still here, right?" Felicity asked.

"Yes," Winnie said. "I'll have to take you to his dad's restaurant too, Trattoria Lupo. It's *so good.*"

"So is Gianni back in this area to stay?"

I crossed myself. "God, I hope not."

She laughed. "You don't get along?"

"There's some . . . history," said Winnie with a grin. "Gianni was sort of a rascal growing up."

"Yes, and since our mothers have been besties for a hundred years," I said irritably, "I was forced to spend time with him."

Winnie's blue eyes gleamed. "And when we were seventeen, they spent seven minutes in a closet, but neither of them will admit what happened in there."

Felicity's jaw dropped as she looked back and forth between Winnie and me. "What happened in there?"

"We don't talk about it." I sniffed, carefully lowering another glass into the box before changing the subject. "How did you like the Pinot Noir Reserve last night?"

"It was delicious. And you were right—it paired perfectly with the mushroom risotto."

I smiled, zipping up the last box. "Good."

"Ell, what are you packing up for?" Winnie said, eyeing the storage boxes.

"My tasting tonight in Harbor Springs. The guy's a wine

"Oh right, the editor's dinner party," she said, because she *listens* to me when I'm talking. "I hope the roads will be okay. Your car can't be much better than mine in the snow—Dex is already on me to get better tires."

"Dex is on you every chance he gets," I teased. Not only was Dex a former Navy SEAL, but he was a firefighter, dad to two young girls, and a dozen years older than Winnie, so protectiveness ran through his veins.

Winnie blushed. "But seriously, want me to ask him if he'll drive you? He's off work today and tomorrow, and the girls are with their mom. We could take you up there."

"Thanks, but I actually already have a ride."

"With who?"

"Gianni." I frowned. "He was in here bothering me already this morning, and when he heard I was planning to drive up there alone, he went all Italian caveman and insisted that he needs to drive me."

"That was nice of him," Felicity said.

"I know. I'm highly suspicious."

"Oh, come on," Winnie scolded. "I know you two bicker like cats and dogs, and he does have a bit of an ego—"

"A *bit* of an ego?" I shrieked. "Has he told you about his *Lick My Plate* tagline—*too hot to handle*? Or how they played 'Fever' any time he was onscreen? Or perhaps you've seen him featured in *People* magazine's Sexiest Chefs Alive issue?"

"Okay, but at heart he's a decent guy." Winnie wouldn't give up. "He offered to drive because he cares about you."

"He didn't offer, Winnie—he *informed* me he would drive. He was bossing me around."

"You could have said no," she pointed out.

"I *did* say no!" Then I hesitated. "At first. But he scared me with all these terrible things that could happen, and I thought about being alone out there on the road in the freezing cold

"I mean, he's not wrong." Felicity lifted her shoulders. "It will definitely be safer if you're together."

"Maybe it'll be fun." Winnie's voice was full of optimism. "Maybe you guys can work through some of the tension in your relationship."

I shook my head. "The tension in our relationship stems from the fact that he walks around here like he owns the place, and he knows it makes me crazy."

"That's the thing," Winnie said. "You make it so obvious that he gets to you. Why can't you just ignore him?"

"I don't know!" I threw my hands up. "I tell myself that *all* the time. I wake up and say, I will *not* give him the satisfaction today, and somehow I forget that once he's around me, and I end up all . . ." I fidgeted, trying to think of a word for the way Gianni could make me feel—something close to the truth without being the actual truth, which I didn't even like admitting to myself.

"Hot and bothered?" suggested Winnie.

"Let's stick with bothered."

"Wow, he's really got your number," Felicity said.

"He does," Winnie confirmed. "And personally, I have always thought all that heat and friction between them would make for a good time, if you know what I mean."

"Not even if it was the end of the world and he was the last man on earth," I said, grabbing one of the storage boxes. "Now you can make up for putting that horrible thought in my head by helping me carry these upstairs."

Winnie giggled and grabbed one of the boxes. "I'm just saying, it's kind of a shame all the sparks that fly when you're in a room together can't result in something other than frustration. Maybe if you guys just went at each other one day, you'd get along better."

"She might be right," Felicity said, taking the third box in

his hands."

"Yeah. Just ask him," I muttered, leading the way out of the tasting room.

But truthfully, I did like Gianni's hands. After his butt, they were probably my favorite part of him.

For a moment, I imagined them skimming across my stomach or sweeping down my hip or sliding up my inner thigh.

A memory gripped me so tightly it stole my breath.

"Ellie?"

I opened my eyes and realized I'd stopped halfway up the stone staircase leading from the cellar and tasting room into Abelard's lobby. "Sorry."

I started moving again, offering no explanation and doing my best to shove the memory and the thought of Gianni's hands on my skin from my mind.

It could never happen again.

CHAPTER 3
GIANNI

nside the small office off Etoile's kitchen, I took off my coat and sat down at the desk. Leaving here by two o'clock meant I had a lot to get done in the next few hours—check yesterday's sales and time sheets, do inventory, place orders, help Ellie load the wine and glasses she was taking to Harbor Springs into my SUV. I also wanted to run home and change clothes, just in case Ellie needed a hand pouring or the hostess needed help serving.

Anything I could do to increase Ellie's chances of snagging that 30 Under 30 spot, I'd do it.

But before I did anything, I had to call my dad. We both had Monday nights off and usually spent them cooking together at my parents' house, trying new ingredients, testing out recipes, coming up with fresh takes on traditional favorites, giving my mom a hard time, making her taste everything and tell us whose dish was better (she would never choose).

I wasn't sure I'd ever get married—and it wouldn't be until I was much older and too tired to do anything else—but if I did, I wanted the kind of marriage my parents had. It wasn't that they always got along perfectly, like Ellie's

usually it was them against me and my twin brothers, who were two years younger and ten times as rowdy. My poor mom had to put up with a lot of shit when we were kids, and my dad worked crazy restaurant hours, so she had to wrangle us on her own most of the time and take care of our baby sister too.

My dad knew it, and the only time he'd ever really get mad at one of us was if we'd done or said something that upset our mom. He was a guy's guy, and he could be a real dick in the kitchen if things weren't done exactly the way he wanted them, but he was madly in love with my mother and always had been. He said he knew he'd marry her the first day they met.

That was why last summer, when she was diagnosed with breast cancer, he'd asked me to come home from L.A. and run the kitchen at his restaurant, Trattoria Lupo, for a few months. *Lick My Plate* had already finished filming, but I wouldn't have hesitated anyway—I jumped on a plane, rented an apartment not far from the restaurant, and dedicated myself to his kitchen like it was my own.

Luckily, the cancer was non-invasive and treatable, but it was still a rough time. She'd needed surgery and radiation in order to lower the risk of recurrence. My dad wanted to focus solely on her, and she was overwhelmed trying to manage her health and get my younger sister—her name was Francesca, but we always called her Chessie—ready for her freshman year at Kalamazoo College.

Since my mother would have been livid if she'd known he asked me to come home—she didn't want anyone to know about her diagnosis—I never said a word about it to anyone. I just said I was taking a break after the show wrapped in order to consider my next move. The offer from Ellie's parents—who I called Uncle Lucas and Aunt Mia—to open Etoile had

could only commit for six months, I decided to take it.

Although, if I accepted the new reality show I'd been offered, I'd have to get out of the contract at least a month early—that was one of the things making me hesitate about the contract. I didn't want to go back on my word.

"Hello?"

"Hey, Pop."

"Hey. We still on for tonight? I'm gonna kick your ass with a duck breast."

I laughed. "You probably would, but I can't make it tonight."

"Scared I'll beat you?"

"Listen, old man, I had a prawn and chive dumpling with sake butter and ponzu planned that was gonna make you weep."

"Damn. That does sound good. Why can't you make it?"

"I have to take Ellie up to Harbor Springs. She's doing a private wine tasting at somebody's vacation home, and she was planning to drive alone."

"Tonight? There's a huge storm coming."

"I know. Believe me, I tried to talk her out of it, but she wouldn't listen." I explained who the host and hostess were and why Ellie was so determined to get there and impress them. "She's convinced that somehow, tonight is going to change her life."

My dad laughed. "Yeah, you can't talk to a woman when she gets that in her head. Well, be careful. Leave early, go slow, and get off the road if it gets bad."

"I will."

"You give any more thought to that other TV offer yet?"

"Some." I hesitated. "It would be a hard thing to walk away from."

It was another cooking competition show, where experi-

be judged by a panel of experts. It was called Hot Mess, and as ridiculous as the concept was, it would probably be a huge hit.

But the offer was to *host* the show, not appear as one of the mentor chefs or judges, and I wasn't sure I wanted to move in that direction—away from the kitchen.

And contrary to what Ellie implied, I loved Abelard and enjoyed working here. I'd had a lot of input into the kitchen design, the hiring, the menu, and the methods. I was proud of the way it had turned out. But I'd never planned to stay forever.

I never planned to stay anywhere forever.

As a kid I'd been restless, never wanting to sit still or do what I was told. Fragile objects tempted me to smash them, rules dared me to break them, every hill had to be climbed and conquered—boredom was the enemy. As an adult, I still had that burning desire to go everywhere, do everything, fuck shit up. I never wanted to stop moving or settle down or even grow old. The question was always, what will my next adventure be?

I wasn't positive another TV show was the answer, but I'd told Spencer, my agent, I'd decide on the network's offer this week. For a second, I thought maybe I'd talk to Ellie about it on the ride to Harbor Springs. She was smart and ambitious too, so maybe she'd have some advice. Granted, she was likely to give me some shit about cutting out of Etoile early, but maybe she'd be so eager to get rid of me, she'd encourage me to take the gig.

Then she'd watch every single episode and lie about it, I thought with a grin.

"I agree, it would be hard to turn down," my dad said. "But ultimately, is another show what you want to do? Is that the direction you want to take with your career?"

matter. I like cooking for people, learning new things, coming up with new ideas. I don't even think I'd be in the kitchen much on that show they're pitching. I'd be the host. Fucking window dressing."

"It's a bitch to be so good-looking."

I laughed. "Yeah." I tried again to put my finger on what was holding me back and heard Ellie's voice in my head. "Do you think it's just bullshit? A joke?"

"Nah. People like to be entertained. Those kinds of shows are an escape."

"So I have to decide if I want to be an escape or a chef."

"Being an escape pays better," my dad pointed out. "You could take the paycheck and do something more worthwhile afterward."

"True."

"When do you have to give them an answer?"

"Next week. And then I'd have to talk to Lucas and Mia about leaving Etoile before my six months is up. I'd have to be in L.A. by the first of April."

"I'm sure they'd understand. And that's almost three months away, but the sooner you tell them, the better. They'll need the time to find someone to replace you."

"I know." I glanced out at Etoile's kitchen, torn between staying and going. "I do like it here."

"But it was always temporary, right?"

"Right. You know me—no standing still."

"I'm just glad I don't have to get the phone calls from the principal anymore."

I laughed. "Me too. Later, Pop."

We hung up, and I looked at the radar again. Once more, the giant gray and white cloud heading our way gave me pause. But it was still a little ways off and likely wouldn't be an issue on the drive there, as long as we left on time. And

Setting my phone aside, I got to work.

By two that afternoon, my SUV was loaded with cases of wine, boxes of stemware, and an insulated cooler bag with the ingredients I'd need to plate the prawn and chive dumplings with sake butter I'd prepped. It meant I hadn't had time to run home and grab a nicer pair of pants, but I figured we could swing by my apartment on our way out of town.

"Ready?" I asked Ellie, who stood at the back of my car looking over everything. She was all bundled up in her winter coat, mittens, and snow boots, as if we were walking to Harbor Springs, not driving.

"Yes." She frowned at the cooler bag and pointed at it with one hand. "What's that?"

"Don't worry about it." I reached up to close the hatch, and she grabbed my arm.

"Gianni, what *is* it?"

"It's just an appetizer. I had all the ingredients because I was planning to make it at my parents' house tonight. Those are the plans I had to cancel." I paused for effect. "You're welcome."

She looked scandalized. "We can't bring *food*!"

"Why not?"

"Because it's insulting! The hostess is cooking."

"I'll just offer. If she turns me down, fine."

"What is it?"

"Prawn and chive dumplings with sake butter and ponzu sauce."

nice surprise, but if you want me to take them out, I will."

"No, it's fine. I'm sure everyone will love them, and I can pair them with the sparkling white. Just . . . just don't make tonight about you, okay?"

"It's just some dumplings, Ellie."

"I know, but you have this way of—of sucking up all the energy in a room. You're entertaining without even trying to be, so just stay in the background and don't be charming," she begged. "Don't even smile."

"I will be a bump on a log. Now will you let go of me so I can shut this and we're not late?"

Reluctantly, she took her hands off my arm, but she stayed right there while I shut the hatch, as if she didn't trust me not to add any other illegal cargo to her ship.

Once it was closed, I turned to face her. Snowflakes floated down around her. Her cheeks were flushed pink from the cold, and her skin seemed paler than usual—was she nervous?

"What's wrong?" I asked her.

"I don't know," she said, her brown eyes troubled. "I just have a weird feeling."

"I thought you had a feeling that tonight was going to change your life."

"I did. I *do*. I just . . ." She shivered. "I have this *other* feeling that something could go wrong."

"The weather?" I looked up at the gray sky. "Come on, it's barely snowing. These are just flurries." I thumped a hand on the back of my car. "She's sturdy. We'll be fine."

"Aren't you the one who said I should cancel?"

"I changed my mind." Taking her by the shoulders, I turned her around and steered her to the passenger door, which I opened for her. "I turned the seat warmer on for you. Get in and toast your buns. Leave the rest to me."

drive."

She rolled her eyes and hopped up into the front seat. "Wow. It is nice and warm."

"See? Now relax. Everything is gonna be great." I shut the door, hustled around to the driver's side, and we headed out.

Abelard Vineyards was located mid-way up Old Mission Peninsula, a narrow, eighteen-mile strip of land jutting into Grand Traverse Bay. Its gently rolling hills and surrounding waters not only gave it gorgeous views, but a microclimate that was particularly suited for growing grapes and other fruit. We passed several other wineries and farms on the twenty-minute drive to Traverse City, as well as some luxury vacation homes. Ellie seemed distracted by the scenery for a while, but the moment I exited the highway, she snapped to attention.

"What are you doing?" she asked, glancing around. "This isn't the way."

"I have to stop by my apartment real quick."

"Why?"

"Because I don't want to show up in jeans, okay?" I turned into my complex.

"Why didn't you do this sooner?"

"Two minutes, and we'll be on the road again. Promise."

She remained silent as I pulled into a spot in front of my building, arms folded over her chest.

"Do you want to come in?" I asked, unbuckling my seatbelt.

"No."

"Wait, I'll come in," she said, opening her door too. "I forgot to go to the bathroom at Abelard, and it's a long drive."

"Okay." I shut off the engine and grabbed the key fob, locking the doors behind us.

Ellie followed me into my apartment and looked around. It wasn't a big place—one bedroom, one bath, small living room and kitchen right behind it—but it was enough room for me.

"Kinda sparse," she said, taking in my couch, coffee table, and lamp, which was really the only furniture I had.

"Yeah, it's just a few things my parents gave me from their house. I didn't know how long I was going to be here, so I didn't want to buy too much." After ditching my boots, I went around the corner into my bedroom, gesturing to a door off the hall. "Bathroom is right there."

"Thanks."

Inside my room, I took off my coat, lifted my sweater over my head, and tossed it onto my unmade bed. Kicking the door shut with my foot, I traded my jeans for a pair of dress pants and yanked a clean white shirt from a hanger. After buttoning up and tucking in, I zipped up my pants and grabbed a nicer belt.

From the back of my closet, I snagged a small duffel bag and tossed in a good pair of shoes. On impulse, I grabbed a clean pair of underwear, some deodorant, and an extra pair of socks—just in case. I tossed it all in the bag, and at the last second, decided to throw in my jeans and sweater too.

I turned off the light and opened the bedroom door at the same time Ellie came out of the bathroom. We stood chest to chest for an awkward moment—or maybe more like face to chest. She'd taken her boots off at the door too, and in her

"What's funny?" she demanded.

"Your socks." They were bright aqua blue with strawberries and some kind of small animals on them. "Are those beavers?"

"Hedgehogs." She covered one foot with the other. "These are my lucky socks, okay? My dad got them for me. I love hedgehogs."

"Okay."

"What's in the bag?" she asked, pointing at my duffel.

"Whips. Chains. My gimp suit." I shrugged. "If the party gets fun, I want to be prepared."

She exhaled, her eyes closing.

"Relax, it's just my dress shoes. A change of clothes."

"Why do you need a change of clothes?"

"My mom taught me to be prepared." I sidestepped her, dropping my bag in the hall and moving into the bathroom. "Didn't yours?"

She stood behind me, watching as I checked my reflection in the mirror over the sink. "Um, only every single day of my life. I was the only kid in elementary school that had a spare raincoat, umbrella, hat, mittens, and scarf in her locker at all times."

"I think I stole an umbrella from your locker once."

"You did. It had hedgehogs on it, and it was adorable. You whacked it against the flagpole, and it got all bent out of shape."

"Sorry. I'll get you a new one." I ran a hand over my scruffy jaw. "I didn't shave today. Or yesterday."

"Too late to worry about that now."

I fussed with my hair a little and caught her smirking in the mirror. "What?"

"You're so vain about your hair."

"I am not." But I totally was. If she wasn't standing right

"You so are. I bet you have more hair products than I do." She nodded at the vanity cupboards. "Open that."

"No."

She elbowed me aside and opened one door, then burst out laughing. "My God! You have more hair products than Winnie and me put *together*! Is that *mousse*?"

"Enough." I grabbed her from behind and dragged her out of the bathroom. "We have to go. You're in a hurry, remember? Go put your boots back on."

But I didn't let go of her right away. I was bigger and stronger and felt like I had to take her down a notch by showing it. Plus, not gonna lie, her hair smelled amazing— like summer at the beach. I almost asked her what shampoo she used.

She tugged at my arms. "Let go of me, you big umbrella-bashing bully."

I held on a couple seconds longer than necessary, then released her. Back in the bathroom, I shut the door, used it, and washed my hands. Figuring she'd hear the blow dryer if I turned it on, I settled for messing with my hair with my fingers. After a quick spray of cologne, I tossed a couple products in my bag, hid them beneath my jeans and sweater, and zipped it back up.

When I opened the door, she was standing right there, a grin on her face. "Did you pack the mousse? The blizzard might flatten your 'do."

"Go," I barked, giving her a gentle nudge with my bag. "We're going to be late."

I followed her out, locked the door, and popped the hatch on my SUV. The temperature was dropping quickly, and the wind had picked up. The flurries that had been gently drifting from the sky when we'd left Abelard were blowing

"It's like we're on a romantic little road trip," I said as we headed north.

"No, it isn't—it's a work event." She reached over and poked my shoulder. "*My* work event. You're going to stay in the background, remember?"

"So, like, don't take my pants off and dance on the table?"

"I would murder you with a corkscrew. Then I'd flatten your hair in your coffin."

"Damn. I'll stay out of your way."

"Thank you." A few minutes later, she sniffed. "What is that?"

"What is what?"

"That smell." She leaned toward me, nearly putting her face in my neck. "Did you put cologne on?"

"I forget," I lied, unnerved at the way my pulse quickened with her lips so close to my skin. "I might have."

She laughed. "Why?"

"I don't know. I like to smell nice."

She inhaled once more, then settled back in her seat. "It does smell nice."

I glanced at her, surprised at the rare compliment. "Thank you."

"You're welcome."

Focusing on the road again, and the snow swirling across the pavement, I felt warm beneath my coat as I thought about my hands on her body in the dark.

CHAPTER 4
ELLIE

Jesus, he smelled good.

I'd always had a really sensitive sense of smell—and it definitely helped me professionally—but right now I wished I could turn it off.

The scent of him was filling my head and doing pleasant but worrisome things to my body . . . warming my skin, stirring my insides, quickening my pulse. It was giving me ideas I didn't want, making me wonder things I had no business wondering about—like what kind of kisser he was or what he looked like naked or whether he was greedy or generous in bed.

A guy like Gianni, who knew how hot he was and had never lacked for female attention, would probably be a selfish lover, right? Or would his ego demand that he made sure a woman never left his bed unsatisfied? As puffed up as he was, I'd never really heard him brag about the size of his dick or how many notches he had on his bedpost. He made a lot of dirty jokes and he was a relentless flirt, but he didn't boast about his sexual conquests.

Before I could stop myself, I glanced over at his crotch. One of his hands was resting on his thigh, and I got distracted

know what it looked like. The back of his hand had visible veins, and he kept his fingernails short and clean. His fingers were long, not too skinny and not too thick, and they gave his hands a sort of elegance that I secretly admired sometimes while he was plying a knife or kneading some dough or tossing a skillet. He had strong hands, but they were dexterous too. Graceful. Artistic.

Suddenly, my brain took an unauthorized turn. I imagined him unzipping his pants and reaching inside them, taking out his cock and starting to stroke it with slow, deliberate, *artistic* bends of his wrist, his flesh growing hard and thick as it slipped through his fist. Veins would appear. His breath would come faster. Maybe he'd moan softly, his voice raw and deep.

Except that *I* moaned. *Out loud.*

"You okay?"

"Huh?" I looked up, startled. My pulse was racing.

"Are you okay?" he repeated. "You made a weird noise."

"I was . . . singing." I reached for the volume on the radio and turned it up. "Any music requests?"

"You can pick."

"No, because you'll just make fun of what I like."

"That's because you like weird, sappy stuff no one has ever heard of."

"I like to support independent singer-songwriters, okay? Not every great band or musician wants to sign their life away to a giant label that's just going to take their money."

"I get that. It's the same reason I like to support local farms. But the music still has to be good."

"It *is* good! It's just not as loud and chaotic as the music you like. It's more about lyrics and mood."

"Okay, so instead of arguing with me, why don't you sync your phone and put on one of your playlists? I'm sure you

I reached over and punched his shoulder. "You said you wouldn't make fun of me."

"I would never say that. I just said I'd listen to your lonely girl music, but if you don't want to play it for me, I'd be happy to listen to you moan some more, especially if you want to stare at my crotch while doing it."

"I wasn't staring at your crotch!" I shrieked, mortification burning a hole in my chest.

He chuckled. "Sorry. I must have been mistaken."

"Why on earth would I stare at your crotch?"

"You tell me." He glanced over, sending a little bolt of lightning straight to my lonely girl parts.

"I wouldn't. You were mistaken." I reached into my bag for my phone and busied myself connecting it to his car, my heart thumping hard all the while. Damn these nerves! They were messing with me, making me think weird things.

A couple minutes later, we were listening to my current favorite playlist, which happened to be called Winter Vibes, but I wasn't about to tell him that. As we drove, the snow fell faster and the light faded. Visibility grew worse, but Gianni didn't seem worried—at least, he didn't say anything to that effect—and he was able to drive the speed limit.

We didn't talk much on the rest of the drive up, which was fine with me because I didn't want him to tease me again about staring at his crotch. In fact, the only time we spoke was when he asked me for the address so he could enter it in his GPS.

We pulled up in front of the Harbor Springs vacation home of Malcolm and Fiona Duff around five o'clock. By then, it was pitch dark and their multi-million-dollar home was blanketed with a few inches of snow.

"Nice place," said Gianni, parking on the street.

My stomach twisted with nerves, and I put a hand on it.

to play you some *good* music to get you pumped up?"

"No. I just need a second to breathe." I inhaled and exhaled, willing my pulse to slow. "I don't know what's with me today. I'm normally not so tense. This is my job. I know my stuff."

"Yes, you do." He thumped a hand on my leg. "Come on, princess. Chin up."

I gave him a warning look. "No princess jokes in there, okay?"

"None?"

"None."

He sighed. "You're taking all the fun out of this, but fine. Let's go."

We trudged through the snow covering their front walk, and Gianni knocked on the door. When no one answered after a minute or two, we exchanged a look and he knocked again. A moment later we heard a muffled yell from inside.

"Coming!"

The front door swung open and an older teenage girl wearing a huge gray hoodie, a plaid skirt, and knee socks gave us a sullen look, like we'd just interrupted her *Gossip Girl* marathon.

"Hi," I said brightly. "I'm Ellie Fournier from Abelard Vineyards. And this is—" But I didn't have a chance to finish my introduction because the girl suddenly let out a bloodcurdling scream.

"Eeeeeeep! Gianni Lupo!"

I blinked at her as she stared at Gianni and jumped up and down, the messy bun on the top of her head coming loose. Then I looked at Gianni—did he know this girl?—but he seemed as bewildered as I was.

"Hadley! Did you get the door?"

Behind the exuberant teen, a woman appeared, wearing

sively over the past couple weeks, learning her favorite wines, her pairing preferences, her likes and dislikes.

She was even more intimidating than in her photos—tall and thin, with attractive, angular features and dark hair styled in a smooth, chic bob.

"Hadley," she scolded. "Why didn't you invite them in?"

"Sorry, Mom. But look who it is!"

"I apologize for my daughter's manners," she said, motioning us inside. "I'm Fiona Duff. You must be from Abelard?"

"Yes," I said, as we stepped into the foyer. "Nice to meet you. I'm Ellie Fournier. And this is—"

"It's Gianni Lupo, Mom!" her daughter squealed, bouncing up and down again. "From *Lick My Plate*! You know —the 'too hot to handle' guy!"

Fiona's face suddenly lit up too. "Is it really?"

"Nice to meet you." Gianni held out his hand, and they both shook it, Hadley's cheeks turning pink, my stomach turning over.

"Gianni is the chef at Abelard's new restaurant, Etoile," I said, "but since we're closed tonight, he offered to make the drive with me and help out."

"How nice." Fiona smiled broadly at Gianni. "We haven't been to Etoile yet, but I've heard so many good things. And I've just started watching *Lick My Plate*. Hadley has been telling me for months that I need to binge it, and I'm sorry I resisted—I'm addicted now!"

"You are?" I couldn't help being surprised. Fiona seemed like a person who preferred Roquefort with a fresh baguette, and *Lick My Plate* was Cheez Whiz on a Ritz cracker. (Although, for the record, I loved Cheez Whiz on Ritz crackers.)

"Of course I am." She laughed. "It's such good, campy

ously. And chefs are the hottest new celebrities." She shimmied her shoulders.

"I wouldn't call myself a celebrity," said Gianni in this aw-shucks voice I'd never heard him use before. "Just a chef. But tonight, I'm only here to assist Ellie."

"I wish I'd have known you were available this evening." Fiona looked distressed. "I did all the food myself, but I'd have hired you to cook in a heartbeat."

"I did prepare something for tonight, but—"

"You did?" Fiona clasped her hands together. "Did you really?"

"It's nothing fancy, just some prawn and chive dumplings with sake butter that could work as an appetizer maybe, but don't feel—"

"I'm delighted," Fiona assured him with a smile.

"Mom, can I come to dinner?" Hadley asked in a rush.

Her mother faced her, hands on her hips. "Earlier, you said you'd rather eat dirt than attend another one of my boring Monday night dinner parties."

"I changed my mind." Hadley glanced at Gianni and giggled.

Fiona rolled her eyes and gestured at her daughter's attire. "Well, you're not coming to my dinner table dressed like that, so go clean up if you want to attend. You can sit at your father's place since his flight was delayed, and he won't make it home on time to eat with us."

"Okay." After giving Gianni one last adoring look, Hadley raced up the stairs.

Sighing, Fiona watched her go. "I thought the terrible twos were bad, but seventeen is ten times worse. She drives me crazy."

I laughed politely. "I think I drove my mother crazy at seventeen too."

will be thrilled. They're not quite here yet, but let me show you where the kitchen is."

"We have some things to bring in," I said, feeling like I'd invited myself to Gianni's job and not the other way around. "Cases of wine and glasses. Where would you like us to put them?"

Fiona turned to me like she'd forgotten I was there. "Oh! The kitchen, I suppose."

"Do you have a back door we can use? I don't want to get your floors wet." I glanced at the gleaming dark wood. "They're so beautiful—your whole house is beautiful."

"Thank you," Fiona said. "We do have a back door. Maybe you could pull into the driveway and drive around?"

"Sure." Gianni glanced behind us. "And if you have a shovel, I don't mind shoveling your front walk and maybe the steps—I'd hate for your dinner guests to slip."

Fiona laughed girlishly as she reached out to pat Gianni's cheek. "Aren't you adorable? You don't have to do that."

"I really don't mind."

"I might take you up on it since Malcolm isn't here. He'd normally be the one I sent out there in the cold."

"It's no problem at all," Gianni assured her.

She beamed. "You're an absolute doll."

I took a deep breath and counted to ten.

Fifteen minutes later, Gianni headed outside to shovel while I added flute wineglasses to each of ten place settings on the Duffs' long, rectangular dining room table. It was a beautiful, dramatic room—high ceilings, walls painted a deep gray, a huge gold candle-style chandelier, chairs upholstered in navy velvet. I'd changed from my snow boots into high heels, and they sank into the plush Persian rug under the table.

Nearly one entire wall was windows, and through them I

the Duffs' front walk, and the noise was shredding what was left of my nerves. It was obvious Fiona and Hadley Duff were completely starstruck, and I felt like a total jerk for being upset about it, but I was. He was stealing my thunder without even trying!

After I had everything in place for the first course—which would be Gianni's dumplings as well as the clam chowder with warmed radishes Fiona had made—I returned to the kitchen through the old-fashioned butler's pantry, which included a wet bar. In the kitchen, Fiona was spooning her soup into tiny white mugs placed on a cast iron serving tray.

It was a beautiful space, of course—in contrast to the dining room, it was decorated in bright colors and glossy textures. Cabinets in a pale ash color, white marble counters veined with silver, mirrored subway tile backsplash, gleaming chrome hardware. It smelled delicious too, like roasting beef tenderloin and fresh thyme, which would be the main course.

"Can I help you with anything?" I asked.

"Well, if you wouldn't mind placing these in the warming oven, that would be great. The guests should arrive shortly, and I just need a few minutes upstairs to finish getting ready. Hadley was supposed to help me in here, but she's probably tearing her room apart looking for something that doesn't look like she found it in the rag bin at a thrift shop."

"Of course," I said, unbuttoning my cuffs and rolling up the sleeves of my blouse.

"And usually Malcolm is on hand to show everyone in and make cocktails, but since the big galoot didn't fly home yesterday like I told him to, I have to do everything on my own—cook, host, serve." She shook her head. "I don't know what he was thinking trying to get out of Denver today."

"Gianni and I would be glad to serve."

"Absolutely. You don't want to be getting up and down all night. Gianni and I can take care of everything. We're used to working as a team."

"I'm just so ecstatic he's here," she gushed, untying her apron. "Usually we just talk about food and wine at these things, and the conversation can feel stale. But tonight we'll have something more fun to talk about! He's even better looking in person than he is on TV, don't you think?"

The smile was frozen on my face, but my hopes were melting. "Sure."

"And that was *so* sweet of him to bring something. I'm dying to taste his dumplings." She laughed and whispered scandalously, "I bet they're as delicious as he is."

I ignored that. "Um, other than the dumplings, are there any changes to the menu?"

She shook her head. "No, it's exactly as I emailed you. After the soup and dumplings will be the beet salad, then the tenderloin and vegetables, then the cheese—you did receive the list of cheeses I'll serve?"

"Yes. I think the wine I brought to serve with them will really complement the—"

"There you are!" Fiona squealed as Gianni entered the mudroom through the back door and stomped snow from his boots. "Are you frozen solid?"

"Nah." He brushed snow off his coat. "It wasn't bad."

"I was just saying to Kelly how excited I am that you came tonight." She sent him a dazzling smile.

"Ellie," he corrected.

She looked perplexed for a moment, then laughed and glanced in my direction. "Ellie. Sorry."

"That's okay," I said through my teeth.

"I'll just excuse myself to finish getting ready. Use

"Of course," I said. "I'll also offer them an aperitif. I brought a—"

"Thank you, see you in a moment!" she called, sailing out of the kitchen with one final smile at Gianni.

When we were alone, he looked over at me. "Is that smoke coming out of your ears?"

"Yes," I said. "I can't even finish a sentence around her unless it's about you."

"Don't worry." He hung up his coat next to mine in the mudroom, took off his boots, and dug around in his duffel bag for his dress shoes. "You're going to knock her socks off tonight."

"I think she'd prefer you to take her socks off," I muttered, sliding the tray with the soup mugs on it into the warming oven. "By the way, I told her we'd serve tonight."

"Fine with me." Gianni tied his shoes and came into the kitchen, rolling up the cuffs of his dress shirt. "I need a sauce pan to make the sake butter. Think you can find one?"

Distracted momentarily by the appearance of his wrists—he wore a watch on the left one with a large round face and black strap—I didn't answer the question.

"Ell?" He snapped his fingers in front of my face. "You with me?"

"Sorry—yeah." I located a pan for him while he unpacked the cooler bag. As he worked on the sauce, I put the dumplings on a tray and stuck them in the warming oven. I was pulling out the platter Gianni had brought to serve them on when the doorbell rang.

"You go," he said, taking the platter from me. "I can handle things in here."

"Okay." I hurried to the front door and pulled it open. A huge gust of wind brought snow swirling into the house, and the two couples on the front porch laughed along with me.

Vineyards."

"I was going to say, Fiona, you look amazing," joked one of the men as they removed scarves and gloves, unbuttoned their coats.

Laughing politely, I glanced around and noticed a closet behind me. "Can I take your coats?"

"You must be Lucas and Mia Fournier's daughter," said one of the women as her husband helped her out of a long fur coat. She looked a little older than Fiona, maybe more like my parents' age.

"Yes," I said.

The woman smiled. "You look just like your mom. Tell your parents the Kriegs say hello. We own a restaurant in Harbor Springs. We haven't been to Etoile yet, but we have a reservation next month—can't wait."

"The chef is actually here with me tonight," I said, taking the fur coat and hanging it in the closet.

"Gianni Lupo?" said the other woman, whose husband was helping her from a camel-colored wool duster I wished I could steal. "As in 'too hot to handle?'"

I set my teeth. "Yes."

The two women exchanged excited glances. "To cook?"

"No—well, he made one dish, but Fiona made the meal." I hung up the duster. "He's really only here because he didn't want me to make the drive up alone in this weather, but I roped him into helping me out."

"Is Fiona just beside herself?" asked Mrs. Krieg with a laugh. "She used to tease me for watching all those silly reality cooking shows, and then she started watching *Lick My Plate*. She adores him."

"She's, um, excited. Yes." I hung up the men's coats. "She asked me to show you into the living room."

"Can I offer anyone a drink? I have with me a spiced cherry aperitif Abelard just started making with fruit locally sourced from Cloverleigh Farms that's delicious on its own, over ice, or in a spritz."

Everyone said they'd like to try it over ice, and I perked up. But as soon as the first two couples wandered into the living room, the doorbell rang again, and I greeted three more people—a gay couple and a woman, the three of whom had driven up from Charlevoix together.

I introduced myself, and it turned out that the couple had stayed at Abelard in the past and loved the wines. The woman said she'd never tasted them but had heard great things and was very excited about the tasting. My spirits lifted even more. While I hung up their coats, they set their overnight bags at the foot of a huge staircase.

"Whew—that drive was a nail-biter," remarked the man in the dapper bow tie. "I'm glad Fiona insisted we come for the night."

"Me too," said the other guy, who wore thick tortoise-framed eyeglasses. "The roads are already awful." He gave me a sympathetic look. "Are you driving back to Abelard tonight?"

"Yes, but I'll be fine. I have someone with me, so I won't be on the road alone," I said, deliberately leaving out Gianni's name, just in case they were *Lick My Plate* fanatics too. "Can I interest you in an aperitif?"

They all said yes, so I hustled back to the kitchen, where Gianni was whisking butter into the sake. "How's it going?" he asked.

"Good. Great." Grabbing the spiced cherry aperitif from the fridge, where I'd placed it to stay chilled, I lined up seven glasses on the marble island, filled them with ice, and poured.

Gianni, who'd taken the dumplings from the oven, dipped

of these."

"I can't right now. I'm sure they're good." I ducked into the butler's pantry and grabbed a silver tray from the glass cabinet—hopefully Fiona wouldn't mind if I used it to serve the drinks. Back in the kitchen, I placed the glasses on the tray and picked it up.

"Wait a minute. Just taste this." Gianni came toward me with the other half of his dumpling, and when I opened my mouth to protest, he stuck it in there. Of course, he also slipped his thumb in too, and before I could stop myself, my lips closed around it. He paused with his thumb in my mouth for just a second, his eyes locked on mine, then slowly pulled it out, my tongue stroking its tip.

Another electric pulse went through me, just like in the car.

"You're not supposed to eat my finger," he said.

I chewed and swallowed the bite he'd fed me, trying to act cool. "Then you shouldn't stick your finger in my mouth."

"Well? What do you think?"

"Delicious. Which you already know."

He gave me his cockiest grin. "But what about the dumpling?"

"Get out of my way before I throw every drink on this tray at you."

Laughing, he stepped aside. "Can I help you?"

"No. Just stay in here until I tell you it's okay to come out."

I made my way back to the living room on trembling legs. What on earth was my problem tonight? First, I had that stupid fantasy in the car—and got caught moaning while I stared at his crotch—and then I *sucked his thumb* in the kitchen!

I managed a smile and a steady hand as I served the drinks, answered the door once more, hung up another coat, and turned to see Fiona coming down the stairs in a new outfit. She'd traded her pants and blouse for a cocktail dress and heels that seemed a bit much for a Monday night dinner party at home—and was much fancier than anything her guests were wearing—but maybe that was how she always dressed. Right behind her was Hadley, who'd swapped her hoodie, skirt, and socks for a fitted black crop top with long sleeves, baggy high-waisted jeans, and white sneakers. Her dark blond hair was long and wavy, and her eye makeup looked more professional than anything I could have done.

Fiona went into the living room to see her guests, but Hadley made a beeline for the kitchen. When I got there, she was sitting at the counter, her chin propped in her hand, watching Gianni arrange the dumplings on a platter. It was easy to imagine the cartoon hearts popping out of her eyes.

"You're, like, *so* amazing," she gushed. "And your following is so huge. I've been telling my mom she needs to put you on the cover of *Tastemaker* for months."

I sighed.

This was going to be a long night.

But just then, Gianni looked over at me and smiled—not his usual arrogant grin. The curve of his mouth was somehow kinder and more private, like he could read my mind and he was on my side.

Something rattled in my chest, shaking loose a warmth that radiated throughout my limbs and sloshed back to pool at my center. I looked away quickly, hurrying to pour another drink.

Gianni isn't just a chef, he's an actor, I reminded myself. *He was popular on the show for the same reason he's popular in real*

But it wasn't real.

I'd seen him play the game with plenty of girls in high school, one right after the next, all dying to be the one he wanted—and left heartbroken when he lost interest and moved on. He never stayed with anyone.

He wasn't cruel, but all he'd cared about was having fun.

And no matter how much I thought about him in private, I vowed back then I was never going to be one of those girls —fooled by those eyes and that smile and the promise of a good time.

It was a vow I intended to keep.

CHAPTER 5
GIANNI

I did my best to blend into the background and let Ellie shine, but it was a struggle.

It was like she was invisible.

Every time she started to talk about the wine she'd just poured, someone would ask me about *Lick My Plate*.

Every time I tried to steer the conversation back to Abelard, someone would mention a rave review they'd just read about the food at Etoile.

Every time one of the guests would compliment the wine Ellie had paired with a particular dish, Hadley would say something like, "Oh, enough about the wine already! I want to know if that chef from New Orleans was really that mean, or if that guy from Dallas really threw a pot at your head."

I grinned. "No, that was all fake drama, but Ellie here once threw eight pies in my face."

Finally, Hadley looked at Ellie with interest. "Why'd you do that?"

"Uh, it's a long story." And one she obviously did not want to tell.

"I want to hear it," the teenager insisted. "How old were you?"

"So you've known each other a while," Fiona remarked, looking back and forth between us.

"All our lives," I confirmed.

"Wait. Were you, like, a couple?" Hadley narrowed her eyes at Ellie.

"No," she said emphatically.

"We grew up together," I explained. "Our mothers are best friends, but I'll admit I was pretty terrible to Ellie when we were kids."

"Is that why she threw the pies in your face?" Hadley asked.

Ellie and I exchanged a look. "You'd have to ask her that," I said.

"I'll ask her," said one of the other women at the table with a laugh. "Why did you throw so many pies in his face?"

Ellie cleared her throat. "I threw the pies in his face because I was mad at him for dunking me so many times."

"Dunking you?" The guy with the bow tie looked intrigued. "Okay, now we *have* to hear the rest."

Ellie reluctantly told the story about the dunk tank and the pie-throwing at the Cherry Festival, and it was the longest anyone let her speak all night. They were roaring by the end, and at first I was glad I'd brought up the incident—then I looked at her face, and I knew she was furious with me.

"Oh, that's priceless." The woman who'd encouraged Ellie to tell the story wiped tears. "I can just picture you in that sash and crown, soaking wet and steaming mad."

"Good thing you got him back." The guy wearing glasses smiled at Ellie and lifted his glass in a toast. "This Riesling is divine, by the way, but I think my favorite wine tonight was the pét-nat."

A little of her sparkle reappeared. "Thank you. That's one of my favorites too. I'm really interested in natural wines, and

"Now what's the difference between a pét-nat and other kinds of sparkling wine?" his partner asked. Then he smiled guiltily. "Sorry for the ignorant question."

Ellie stood even taller, her smile genuine. "It's not an ignorant question at all. Pét-nat is short for *pétillant naturel*, which is the original method of making sparkling wine. The process involves bottling and capping wine that's not finished, allowing it to ferment in the bottle. It's a little unpredictable, but it's a really fun, refreshing, uncomplicated wine. We made ours from a hybrid grape called Melody, which was biodynamically farmed, grown without pesticides, herbicides, or other chemicals—"

Hadley blew a raspberry. "No more about wine. Mom, I think you should put Gianni on the cover of *Tastemaker*. Don't you all think she should?"

Everyone at the table spoke up enthusiastically, and Ellie deflated like a week-old balloon.

"I mean, seriously, you're always complaining that people don't read magazines as much as they used to," Hadley went on. "Why not put someone on the cover who will actually sell copies?"

"That's enough, Hadley." Fiona gave her daughter a stern look. "Why don't you go turn on the coffee pot?"

"I can do that," I offered, grateful for a chance to leave the room. Maybe if I wasn't in there, Ellie would get one more chance to talk about her work at Abelard.

But it wasn't even a full sixty seconds later that Ellie came into the kitchen carrying a few empty wineglasses, her mouth pressed into a thin line. "They want you back in there. I was asked to bring out the coffee and dessert."

My heart sank. "Fuck. Really?"

"Of course, Gianni. Who really wants to listen to me talk about wine when they have a *celebrity chef* here to entertain

"I'm sorry, Ellie." I touched her shoulder. "I wouldn't have come if I'd known it would be like this."

She glanced at my hand and shrugged. "I'm not surprised. Go do your encore so we can leave. This dinner already went later than I planned, and the storm is getting worse. I don't want to end up stranded here."

"Me neither." I grinned at her. "I don't trust that teenager one bit."

Ellie didn't even crack a smile.

While the guests drank coffee and ate dessert, Ellie and I bundled up and loaded the car. The snow was knee-deep and still falling. The wind howled out of the north. The temperature made our noses turn red with cold.

I started the car to warm it up, but I wasn't looking forward to the drive—visibility would be shit and the roads were going to be a mess. It was ten-thirty already, and I guessed we wouldn't get home until after two in the morning. I wondered how Ellie would feel about staying at my place in Traverse City, since the drive up Old Mission Peninsula would probably be horrific. I could give her my bed and sleep on the couch.

Trying to remember if my spare sheets were clean, I closed the hatch of my SUV and went back inside, stomping the snow from my boots.

"I'll wait in the car," Ellie said, slipping past me with her bag over her shoulder. "Can you get the check from her? She just went to write it."

"Sure. You okay?"

I felt terrible she was so disappointed—I'd seen Ellie mad a million times, but I didn't often see her sad, and I wished I knew how to make her feel better. It occurred to me that for as long as I'd known her, and as much as I saw her at work, I didn't really *know* her on a personal level.

What were her favorite things? What made her happy? What did she see for herself five, ten, twenty years down the road? What were her guilty pleasures? What did she think about when she was alone in bed at night?

My mind started to wander—as it often did—down a slightly dirtier path.

What was she like in bed? How did she want to be touched? Had she ever been with anyone who knew what he was doing? Given the jackasses she'd dated during high school, I doubted it, unless her taste had drastically improved in college. The side of herself she showed me at work ran cool and tart, but I had a feeling she ran sweet and hot beneath the surface.

Most importantly, why had she been staring at my crotch in the car on the ride up? I chuckled to myself at the way she'd denied it, because it had been obvious that's what she was doing. Not that I hadn't stared at parts of her body from time to time, but I'd at least been stealthy enough not to get caught. And mostly when I thought about her body, I was alone with my pants off, my dick in my hand.

I had this one fantasy of her that I loved, where she crawls across the kitchen floor toward me wearing nothing but that Cherry Princess crown and a smile. I tell her we can't, I insist that we shouldn't, I warn her if she comes any closer, I won't be able to hold back. But she refuses to accept my gentlemanly caution and confesses that she's only pretended to hate my guts all these years and she can't hold back any longer—she has to have me or she'll go crazy.

"Gianni?"

Fiona Duff stood before me holding out a check folded in two.

I realized I'd been staring at the door Ellie had just closed—and also that I'd started to get hard thinking about her. Luckily my coat was long enough to cover the crotch of my pants.

"Thank you." I took the check from Fiona and stuck it in my pocket.

"Thank *you* for coming tonight. Everything was wonderful."

"Glad to hear it." I glanced at the door. "I should get going. The drive might be a little rough."

"Of course. I'm sorry we kept you a little later than planned." She winked at me. "I added a little to the check to cover the extra time."

"Ellie will appreciate that. Thanks again." I pulled on my gloves just as Hadley burst into the kitchen.

"There you are! Did you ask him yet?"

"I was just about to," said Fiona, moving closer to me. "Gianni, I wonder if I might get in touch with you about a feature in *Tastemaker* magazine we do called 30 Under 30. We have one spot left, and I'd like it to be yours. I also think my daughter was right about putting you on the cover—that's something I'll have to discuss with my editorial team, of course, but assuming you say yes to the spot, I don't really see a reason why it wouldn't be approved. What do you say?"

"Say yes!" Hadley shouted.

My heart had lurched the moment I'd heard *30 Under 30.* "Uh, I'm not sure."

"It's a great opportunity," Fiona went on smoothly. "It's always our biggest-selling issue and our most popular online article. Tons of hits. Granted, you already have more name

cover—but I still think it would be great for you. We aim for more of a pop culture audience these days, but lots of industry insiders still read. Your name might catch the eye of the person who can rocket your brand to the next level. I'm sure you're not planning to stay at Etoile forever."

"No," I said honestly.

"So what's your next move? A Michelin Star? A James Beard Award? A line of cookware? Being on the cover of *Tastemaker* and at the top of the *30 Under 30* would be fabulous publicity—it could give you some leverage."

"Mom, those things are so boring. He needs his *own show*," said Hadley. "And, like, merch. Not just pots and pans, but like sweatpants and T-shirts and hoodies with his signature line from the show! *Gianni Lupo: too hot to handle*." She dragged her hand down the side of her leg where the lettering would go. "I could totally design it all for you. My friend got famous on TikTok and I did all his merch. Are you on TikTok?"

"Uh, no."

"Oh!" Hadley snapped her fingers. "What do you call those things you wear on your hands when you take stuff out of the oven so you don't get burned?"

"Oven mitts?"

"Yes. How cute would it be to have some made with a pic of you and *too hot to handle* on them? Your fans would go crazy!"

I had to laugh at the idea of my face on people's hands in kitchens all over America—my mother would think it was hilarious.

Ellie would not.

"Listen, this is fun to think about, but . . ." I glanced at the door again. "Have you thought about asking Ellie to be on

Hadley rolled her eyes. "*Wine* again. No one cares."

Fiona sighed. "I'll be frank. We don't have anyone on the list who'd get the attention you would—and that means better ad dollars for us. I only just started watching *Lick My Plate* in the last couple weeks or I'd have approached you sooner. And I hate to say this, because Ellie seems very knowledgeable and we always love to feature women in the industry, but I really need a *name*. What do you say? Can I call you later this week? Set up an interview and photo shoot?"

"Do it," prodded Hadley.

For a moment, I entertained the idea—being on a magazine cover would be pretty cool, and my agent would love it. Maybe Fiona was right, and the publicity would mean I could ask for more in negotiations with the network who wanted me to sign a contract with them . . . not only more money, but more creative control, more of a say in my role on the show, or maybe a different show altogether. I'd be little more than a prop on Hot Mess.

But the thought of a bunch of Hadleys running around with my name on their sweatpants was a little weird.

And accepting Fiona's offer would crush Ellie.

I shook my head. "Look, I appreciate the offer, but I have to say—"

Fiona held up a hand. "Don't answer yet. Take a few days and think about it. I realize I just ambushed you on your way out into a storm."

"I don't really need to—"

"The issue won't come out until June, so we don't have to shoot you until spring." Fiona moved past me and pulled the door open. Snow rushed in on a blast of cold air, and Hadley shivered. "Be careful out there. I'll be in touch this week."

"Wait!" Hadley ran at me. "Can I have a hug?"

I was nearly knocked over backward when she threw her

"And a selfie?" She reached into her back pocket and pulled out her phone, snapping a bunch of photos of us before I even registered what was happening. "Thanks!"

"No problem." I ducked out the door before she could ask me for anything else.

Hurrying toward my SUV through the wind and snow, I yanked the door open and slid behind the wheel. The interior was cozy and warm, and the windows were fogged up. Ellie was staring out the passenger window, arms crossed over her chest. She didn't even look at me when I got in.

I tossed my gloves in the back seat and pulled the check from my pocket. "Here. She paid us extra."

Ellie took the check from me without a word, stuck it in the bag at her feet, and resumed her previous pose.

"Are you mad at me?"

"Just drive."

"Not until we talk this out."

"I don't want to talk, Gianni. There's nothing to say, and the longer we sit here, the worse the storm is going to get."

"I can't even see," I told her, switching the defroster to blow cool air. "You're so steaming mad at me, you fogged up the windows."

"I'm not mad at *you*."

"No?" I cracked a window and she did the same.

"No. I'm just . . . mad."

"You sure about that?"

"Yes." She wrapped her arms tighter around herself as the air in the front seat grew icy cold and snow blew in. "I know you did me a favor by making the drive, I know my dad felt better knowing I wasn't alone on the road, and I know everyone had a much better time at dinner with you there than they would have had with just me. So thanks, and let's just leave it at that."

you do."

"Well, who wants to listen to me talk about wine when they can listen to you tell tales of reality TV?" She blew a raspberry like Hadley had. "*Bor-ing.*"

"I didn't think you were boring. And they loved the actual wines. That's good, right?"

"You were supposed to stay in the background!" she burst out, finally looking over at me. "It was *my* show for once, not yours!"

"I tried! Swear to God, Ellie, I tried—they just kept passing me the puck."

"And you had to shoot instead of pass it back?"

I opened my mouth to defend myself and closed it again. Hadn't I sort of done what she was accusing me of? Told all my best stories? Landed all my favorite jokes? Charmed the women and bumped elbows with the men? It was my usual way when I was in front of a crowd.

I held up my hands. "You're right. I'm sorry, okay? Once I get going, it's hard to turn it off. I don't know how to do anything else. I thought I was helping you by entertaining them."

"Forget it. Let's just go home."

I could tell nothing I said was going to cheer her up tonight, and possibly the more I talked, the more I might upset her. I didn't want to offer false hope about the 30 Under 30 spot, now that I knew it wouldn't be offered to her— although I sure as hell wasn't going to tell her Fiona had offered it to *me*. Not tonight, anyway.

Exhaling, I rolled up the windows, and slowly swung around so I could pull forward down the long drive. Snow crunched beneath the tires. At the foot of the driveway, the street wasn't visible. No other vehicles were on the road.

"Let's hope so."

My knuckles were white on the steering wheel, and I could hardly see five feet in front of us. When we reached the highway, I could see some tracks, but no other headlights or taillights. If the trucks had been here before, whatever they'd plowed or salted was buried now. "Fuck," I said, leaning forward and trying my hardest to stay on the road. It was a near total whiteout. "This is worse than I thought it would be."

"Me too."

I started sweating beneath my clothes. If it didn't let up, no way would we make it all the way back to Traverse City tonight. But I didn't want to give up yet. I switched on the radio. "Maybe this is the worst of it. Let's listen for a weather report."

But the forecast was dire—in fact, the advice for drivers was to get off the road and find shelter.

"Shit." Ellie was nervous too, her legs bouncing up and down, her thumbnail in her mouth. "Do you think we should do what they say? Get off the road and wait it out?"

"I'm not sure where we'd go," I said grimly, wiping my forehead. "Fuck, I'm not even sure where we *are* exactly." My GPS signal was weak, and I couldn't see road signs until we were right beneath them—and even then, it was tough. "We might not make it home tonight."

"Let's just get off the road."

"Are you sure you don't want me to keep going?"

"Can you see?"

"To be honest, no."

"Then get off the road."

I managed to spot the next exit at the last second and swerved to take it, the SUV skidding a little. Ellie gasped and grabbed the dash.

figure out where we are and what to do."

I kept the SUV crawling forward, my jaw clenched.

"I see a neon sign!" Ellie pointed at the passenger window. "I think it might be a gas station. Up there on the right."

I couldn't even see the road to turn right on, but I spotted the sign Ellie had seen and followed it like the North Star, praying another car wouldn't come out of nowhere and hit us.

"The lights are on inside," Ellie said with relief. "I think it's still open."

I pulled into the station's service lot and put the car in park. "I'll go in and ask what's around here."

"Okay," she said. "If I can get service, I'm going to try to call Winnie and let her know we might not be back in the morning."

I jumped out and hurried into the store. The old guy at the register was watching the news on a television behind the counter. On the screen I saw cars buried in snow, drifts that reached the tops of front doors, and radar showing that the storm was still building in intensity with no signs of letting up, from the Dakotas across the Great Lakes.

"Where's that footage from?" I asked.

"Minnesota." The guy scratched his grizzled gray beard. "They've gotten fifteen inches so far, and it ain't stopping. That's what's coming our way."

"I thought we were only supposed to get ten inches or so."

The guy cackled. "When have those idiots ever been right about anything? You can't know what Mother Nature's gonna do before she does it. She's a woman!"

I nodded grimly, eyeing the snowfall predictions that showed our edge of the state with possible lake effect snow reaching twenty-four inches over the next couple days. "Right."

He shook his head. "Best take shelter while you can, and maybe stock up on some groceries. I'm closing here soon. I just live over there"—he gestured toward the store windows—"but the walk's only gonna get worse."

"Is there a hotel or anything nearby?"

"There's a motel just up the way, but it's usually full up this time of year with cross-country skiers." He shrugged. "Worth a try, though."

"Okay." I glanced out the door at the headlights of my SUV. "You gonna be open a few more minutes?"

"Sure. Name's Milton, by the way."

I headed for the door. "Thanks, Milton. I'll be right back."

It took some effort to push the glass door open in the gusting wind. When I was back behind the wheel, I looked at Ellie. "Did you talk to Winnie?"

"I left her a message."

"What did you say?"

"That it's possible we might not be home tonight and to ask Desmond to cover my eleven o'clock tasting tomorrow just in case."

"We might not even be able to open tomorrow. I saw the news. It's bad."

"How bad?"

"Like two feet of snow coming our way bad."

"Shit! What are we going to do tonight?"

I exhaled. "There's a motel up the road, but the guy said it's usually full this time of year."

"Should we try it anyway?"

"We don't have much choice. I can't drive in this."

"Okay."

"And I think we should get some groceries. Given what's coming our way, things might not be open tomorrow. And who knows how long we'll be stuck here?"

"Me too." Groaning, she dropped her head back on the seat. "God, why didn't I cancel that stupid dinner?"

I opened my mouth and closed it again. No point in saying *I told you so*—she was miserable enough.

"And why did you have to talk so much? If you hadn't stood around regaling them with the story of how you dunked me fifty times, we'd be home by now."

Okay, fuck nice.

"Excuse me, but I was the one who said you shouldn't try to drive three hours north in a blizzard."

She fumed silently for ten seconds, but she couldn't argue.

"Come on," I said, taking the edge off my tone. "It won't do us any good to fight. Let's grab some snacks. We're both hungry and tired."

We hurried into the store, where I waved at my friend Milton behind the counter. After grabbing some chips, cookies, protein bars, a toothbrush and toothpaste, I placed everything on the counter and found Ellie in an aisle stocked with protein bars and bags of granola. She studied each package, occasionally picking one up, reading the ingredients, and putting it back, like we had all day.

"What are you looking for?" I asked her impatiently.

"I don't know. Something that hasn't been on this shelf for two years?"

"Pick something, okay? I want to get over to that motel and see if they have room."

She looked at me. "What will we do if they don't?"

"Just hurry up."

Her eyes narrowed. "Stop bossing me around. I've had enough of you."

"Well, sorry to say, we're stuck with each other for at least the night, maybe longer."

"Do you want me to buy a toothbrush for you?" I asked.

"I have one. But I need something I can wash my face with."

"Go find it."

She stalked over to another aisle, and we met up at the register, where she refused to look at me as she set her things on the counter—two protein bars, a bar of Ivory soap, and a giant bag of M&M's.

Milton eyed us with interest. "You two married?"

"No," we both said at the same time.

I looked at her. "We just work together."

Ellie stared right back at me. "We don't even like each other."

Milton chuckled. "Heck of a night to be out with somebody you don't even like."

"I'm having that kind of day," she told him.

"Well, hope your luck turns around soon."

I grabbed the plastic bags full of junk food. "You said the motel is up the road?"

Milton nodded. "Yup. The Pineview Motel. Got a big sign. Normally, I'd say you can't miss it, but tonight might be another story."

"We'll find it."

"It's run by Rose and Bob Jenkins. Good people. They'll take care of you."

"Thanks, Milton."

He lifted a hand. "Be safe."

CHAPTER 6
ELLIE

The Pineview Motel was one of those classic roadside motels with a big old sign out front boasting about its kitchenettes and swimming poo.

"I think someone stole their letter L," Gianni said as we pulled up in front of the office.

"I certainly hope so." I tried to relax—I'd been holding my breath for the entire five minutes it had taken us to crawl half a mile up the road, hazards blinking, both of Gianni's hands gripping the wheel.

He put the SUV in park. "I'll go in."

"I'll come with you."

"Why?"

"Because I don't want to be alone out here." I looked around—nothing but snow-covered evergreens surrounded the motel. "We're in the middle of the woods. Someone with an axe could jump in the car and abduct me."

He laughed. "The way you jabber, they'd bring you right back."

We got out of the car and entered the lobby, which was small and shabby, but clean and tidy. It even smelled nice, like hot chocolate. The grandmotherly lady behind the desk

"Cancel?" I glanced back at Gianni, but he looked as confused as I was.

"Are you the Witherspoons?" she asked.

"Depends," Gianni said. "Does that mean we could have a room for the night?"

"Two rooms," I put in. I wasn't about to spend the night in a confined space with Gianni Lupo.

"Oh, dear. We definitely don't have two rooms," said the woman, whose name tag read *Rose*. "In fact, an hour ago, we were totally booked. But we just had a cancellation."

"We'll take it." Gianni pulled out his wallet. "You take credit cards?"

"Of course, dear." Rose tapped a few keys on her computer. "How many nights?"

"One."

"Dreadful storm, isn't it?" Rose clucked her tongue. "I hear we might get two feet of snow! Of course, sometimes they say that, and we barely get anything at all."

While Gianni arranged the reservation, I wandered away from the desk and checked out the photos hanging on the lobby walls—groups of smiling cross-country skiers captured in black and white, families enjoying lunch at picnic tables, kids splashing around in the shallow end of the swimming poo, squinting in the sun. Shoving my hands into my coat pockets, I shivered.

Gianni came up behind me. "You cold?"

"Yes." I turned to face him. "It's freezing in here."

"Yeah, Rose said they're having a slight issue with the heat."

"Even in the rooms?"

"I think so."

"Great."

"Also, the television in that room doesn't work." He

"Do we have a key?"

"Yeah. We're number thirteen," he said as we headed for the door. "I think that means I'll get lucky tonight."

"Think again," I told him.

We got back in the car and drove to the end of the single-story building. A minute later, I stood shivering while Gianni tucked his gloves between his knees and fumbled with the lock on the dark green door to room 13. "Hurry up," I said. "My toes are already numb."

"Sorry. This thing is sticky." But then it clicked—Gianni pushed it open and gestured for me to go in first.

The room was dark, so I couldn't see anything until Gianni shut the door and switched on the light.

"You've got to be kidding me." I stared at the lone bed opposite the door, sandwiched between two small tables in a room that could generously be called *quaint*.

Gianni stood next to me. "Damn. That's a small bed. Is it . . . a queen?"

"Not even. I think it's a full."

Gianni looked around. "There's no couch."

My eyes wandered over the rest of the room. Pretty much everything was pine—the furniture, the walls, the floor. The bed was made up with white sheets, with a thick buffalo plaid blanket lying across the foot. Above the headboard was a window covered with curtains that matched the blanket. Along the wall on the right was a tiny two-burner stove, a small sink, a mini refrigerator, and about two feet of counter with two drawers and open cupboards beneath it. A second window looked out onto the parking lot, and in front of it was a tiny table with two wooden chairs. But no couch or anything one of us could sleep on.

We'd have to share the bed.

"I'll sleep on the floor," Gianni said.

and share the bed."

"Can we cuddle?"

"*No*." I shivered again. "God, it's fucking arctic in here."

"I can try turning up the heat." Gianni tossed his gloves on a small table to the left of the door, set down his bag, and looked around for the thermostat.

Leaving my snow boots by the door, I wandered to the left and pushed open the door to the bathroom. Flipping on the light, I half expected to see a knotty pine toilet seat and tub, but it was the usual tiny motel bathroom—everything that was once white was slightly yellowed with age, but it appeared to have been freshly cleaned. The towels hanging on the bar weren't thick, but they were bright white, and when I sniffed, I could smell bleach and—what else?—pine-scented cleaner.

Wrapping my arms around myself, I went back into the room, where Gianni was still bent over the thermostat. "I turned it up, but I think this might be as warm as it gets in here," he said. "We might freeze to death after all."

Suddenly all the shitty things that had gone wrong tonight hit me with the force of the storm outside. I dropped my face into my mittens and, to my utter humiliation, started to sob.

"Shit, I was only kidding." A moment later, Gianni's arms came around me, both of us still wearing our winter coats. He rubbed my back. "We're not going to freeze, Ell. Don't cry. We'll be fine."

"It's not that." Under normal circumstances, I'd never have let Gianni hold me, but his embrace was comforting. Or maybe it was just his body heat—I'd take it.

"What is it?"

"Just—everything! This whole night was such a shit show! Nothing about it went right. I had all these high hopes and big plans, and now I'm going to die of

"But it's better than dying alone, right?"

I sniffed. "Is it?"

"Listen, I know tonight didn't go as planned, and I'm sorry about that, but let's look on the bright side." While he talked, he kept stroking my back.

"What bright side?"

"Well, we're not stuck on the side of the road, right? We have shelter for the night. We have some heat. We have snacks and—"

"Wine." I picked up my face from my hands and looked up at Gianni. "We have a few bottles of wine left over from the dinner party. It's in the car."

"Be right back," he said, letting me go and taking his keys from his pocket.

When he opened the door, an icy wind rushed in and I hurried behind him to close it. There was a window right next to the door, and I pushed the plaid curtain aside, watching as Gianni opened the hatch and poked around in the back of his car. The snow was still coming down, and cars on either side of Gianni's were covered. A minute later, he shut the trunk and came hustling back toward the room with a box in his arms.

Quickly, I opened the door and slammed it behind him. "Jesus! The windchill has to be twenty below!"

Gianni set the box on the floor and blew on his cold hands. "Seriously. My fingers are frozen and I was only out there a minute."

Without thinking, I pulled my mittens off and walked over to him. "Here. Mine are warm." I wrapped my hands around his best I could, since his were considerably larger than mine.

"Thanks." He looked down at our handclasp. A moment

I let him go and took a step back.

"Shit. Do we have an opener?" he asked, glancing at the wine. "I could try running back to the gas station, but Milton said he was closing up soon."

"I *always* have a wine opener on me," I said, going over to my bag.

He laughed. "Of course you do."

"Hey, my mom's a pain in my ass, but she did teach me a few useful things." I pulled out my little corkscrew. "I never go anywhere without one of these, a spare pair of panties, and a toothbrush."

"Smart." He pulled off his boots and left them at the door next to mine. "My dad told me never to go anywhere without a condom."

I rolled my eyes as I opened a bottle of pinot noir. "Because everywhere you go, girls want to have sex with you?"

"Hey, I can't help it if I'm too hot to handle. And it's good advice."

"It is." After working the cork free, I took two small glass tumblers from the cabinet above the stove and filled them.

"Want to give me your coat? I'll hang it up for you."

"I might keep it on. I'm still cold."

"Here. You can put this on if you want."

When I turned around, he stood there holding out the black sweater he'd been wearing earlier today. "Don't you want to wear it?"

"I'm fine." He tossed the sweater on the bed. "It's yours if you want it."

"Okay." I set the wine down and gave him my coat. While he hung it next to his, I pulled his sweater over my head. It was huge and thick and warm. "Much better. Thanks."

"What?" I said, unnerved by his stare.

"Nothing. I just never see you with your hair down. It looks nice."

I studied him with suspicion. "You hang up my coat, you give me your sweater, you say something nice . . ."

"I let you get snot on me," he reminded me, gesturing toward where I'd been standing when I burst into tears.

"Yeah, what is this? Who *are* you?"

"Hey, you're the one who held my hand in the kitchenette."

My jaw dropped. "I did not *hold your hand* in the kitchenette! I was merely trying to prevent frostbite."

"Well, I was merely trying to make you feel better after a rough night. Because I'm a *nice guy*." He reached out and flicked my earlobe.

"Stop it." I swatted his hand away. "Just when I think you've changed, you turn into the playground bully again."

He flashed his palms at me. "Hey. How about we call a truce for the night? No fighting."

"Is that even possible when it's just you and me holed up in this knotty pine igloo with no chance of escaping?"

"Yes. Because we are no longer eight-year-olds on the playground or even teenagers at the dunk tank—we are grown-ass adults and co-workers, and we are perfectly capable of surviving this night in peace." He grabbed the plastic bag of snacks from the gas station and dumped them out on the bed—chips, cookies, candy, protein bars. "Plus we have good wine and enough salt and sugar in this bag to get us through winter."

I turned around and picked up my wine. "Okay, then. Truce."

He tapped his glass to mine. "Truce."

I sat on one side of the mattress criss-cross applesauce,

the ankles.

My eyes traveled over him from head to foot. His muscular, six-foot-plus frame was going to take up a lot of space in this bed. We'd be right next to each other, under the covers, in the dark.

All. Night. Long.

I took a hefty gulp of wine.

"So what should we talk about?" Gianni reached for a bag of potato chips and opened it up. "Our goals and dreams? Our biggest fears? Our deepest, darkest secrets?"

"My goal is to make it through the night," I said, taking another sip from my glass. "Maybe get a little drunk."

"Aren't you worried about what I'll do if you get tipsy?"

I eyeballed him with suspicion. "What would you do?"

"I don't know. Sit on you and let drool ooze out of my mouth until it's about to hit your face and then suck it back in?"

"You wouldn't dare. We called a truce, remember?"

"Oh, yeah." He crunched on a chip. "I should have thought that through first."

I set my wine on the table next to the bed and grabbed the package of M&M's. Tearing it open, I popped a couple in my mouth. They were comforting, although I did wish I had a spoon and a jar of peanut butter. I should have looked for one at the gas station. "You know what? Junk food is exactly what I needed."

He watched me shovel in another handful. "Is that your favorite candy or something?"

I nodded. "They melt in your mouth, not in your hand."

"I love things that melt in my mouth," Gianni said, and something about the way his lips wrapped around the words made me feel hot in the cold room.

I took a sip of my wine.

"No."

"Good. Then let's play a drinking game."

Tossing a few more M&M's in my mouth, I narrowed my eyes at him. "Such as?"

"I don't know. Truth or dare."

"No, you'll just dare me to get naked or something."

He looked offended. "I don't have to trick women into taking their clothes off, thank you very much. They volunteer."

"Of course they do. Wait—I have an idea." I got off the bed and dug my phone from my bag. "There's an app called Truth or Drink. We used to play it at parties in college. You get random questions and you have to answer truthfully or drink."

"So it's honor system?"

"Yes." I returned to the bed and looked at the screen. "Winnie called back. Hang on, let me listen to her voicemail." I put the phone to my ear and heard Winnie's voice, frantic with concern.

"Ellie! Oh my God, I can't believe you're out in this storm, it's so bad! Please get off the road and don't worry about anything here. Desmond is all set to cover your eleven o'clock tasting tomorrow, and he can cover the one o'clock too if necessary. But call me when you get this, or text me or something, so I'm not awake all night worrying about you!"

I looked at Gianni. "I should call her back. Do you think we'll make it home by noon tomorrow? I have a one o'clock tasting."

"If it stops snowing and the roads are plowed, yeah. We can leave first thing." He crumpled up the empty bag of chips and picked up a protein bar. "Can I have this?"

I nodded and dialed Winnie's number. She picked up immediately.

"Thank God! You guys okay?"

"We're fine." I watched Gianni unwrap the bar. "We found a motel with a vacancy."

"You mean you're staying in a motel room *together*?" she asked, loud enough for Gianni to overhear.

"Yeah. And there's only one bed."

She laughed. "How's that going?"

"Fine."

"You guys are getting along?"

Gianni made a lewd gesture involving his fist, his tongue, and his inner cheek. I gave him the finger. "As well as you'd expect."

"I can't wait to hear about it."

"We're going to try to get out of here as soon as we can in the morning. I'll let you know when we're on the road."

"Sounds good." She laughed again. "Sleep tight."

"Oh. We will." I eyed the length of the bed. "We have no choice."

After ending the call, I opened the Truth or Drink app on my phone and picked up my wine. "Ready to play?"

"Hit me."

I scrolled through the options. "Do you want to play normal mode, party mode, or dirty mode?"

Gianni looked at me like I was crazy. "Duh."

I sighed and reached for my wine. "Okay, fine. I feel like I'm going to regret this, but dirty it is."

"Can I take my pants off?"

"No. What's your age range for a one-night stand?"

"Hmm." Gianni thought for a moment.

"Please say at least eighteen."

"No teenagers. I'll say twenty to forty-five."

"Forty-five? Really?"

He shrugged. "I think mature women are hot. But I can't

"Right."

"So what about you? Same question."

"I'd have to say . . . thirty to forty."

He looked offended. "Why thirty? You're only twenty-three."

And so was he, which was why I'd said it. "I know, but I think older men are just better in bed." I'd actually never been with anyone over twenty-eight.

"In what way?"

"Just . . . more patient. More knowledgeable. More generous. Guys in their twenties think they're all that just because they have younger bodies, especially if they're—you know—well-endowed. But it's not just the size of the boat. It's definitely the motion of the ocean."

He harrumphed. "You've been in the wrong boats."

"Next." I glanced at the screen. "Describe the perfect foreplay."

"What's foreplay?"

I looked up at him and blinked.

"I'm just kidding," he said, laughing. "God, you should see your face. The perfect foreplay, hmm. I mean, it's different every time. As opposed to whatever twenty-something two-pump chumps you've been with, I think I'm very patient and generous. I try different things and see what she responds to."

"Like what?" The words were out before I could stop them.

His mouth hooked up on one side. "Just . . . different things. With my hands. Or my mouth." He took a sip of his wine. "My tongue."

I couldn't stop staring at his lips on the rim of the glass. Beneath his sweater and my blouse, my skin was damp with heat. I struggled to breathe quietly.

"Now you," he said. "Describe the perfect foreplay."

"Ellie?"

I focused on his eyes again—those deep blue eyes knew what I was thinking, I could tell—and then took another drink. "Pass."

He chuckled, his expression triumphant, like he'd won a round. "Next question."

"If I had a hot sister, would you let her seduce you?"

"Hm. Is your mom an option?"

I glared at him, even as that dream about his hot dad jumped into my head.

"Relax, I'm kidding. Yes, I'd let your hot sister seduce me. But I'm not even asking you about my brothers."

"Why not? How do you know I wouldn't let the twins seduce me? They're twenty-one, right?" I gave him a coy smile. "I might even let them seduce me at the same time."

Gianni's chiseled jaw fell open. "That's not funny. You'd let those assholes seduce you but not me? They're not even in your approved age range."

I shrugged. "They didn't tease me the way you did. And they don't bug me every day at work."

He reached for my phone. "Let *me* have a turn choosing the questions."

"Fine." I opened a bag of barbecue chips and started munching on them. "You know, these chips pair surprisingly well with this wine."

He leaned over and stuck his hand in the bag, shoving a chip in his mouth. "You're right, they do. We should have an event where we pair gas station snacks with good wine. Like, you save on the food, splurge on the wine."

"Yes!" My glass was empty, so I got up and went over to get the bottle from the counter. After pouring myself a generous refill, I brought it over to the bed and refilled Gianni's glass too. Setting the bottle and my glass on the table, I

He looked up from my phone. "Why?"

"Because I want to take my dress pants off. They're not comfortable."

"You said I couldn't take off *my* pants." He pointed at me. "That's a double standard."

"Fine, then take yours off, but turn around and face the other way."

"Works for me." Gianni got off the bed and dug a pair of jeans from his duffel bag. After tossing them on the bed, he faced the bathroom and unbuckled his belt. Then unbuttoned his pants. Then lowered the zipper. Then peeked over his shoulder at me. "Are you going to stand there and watch?"

Embarrassed, I spun around and faced the kitchenette. Hurrying, I removed my dress pants, tossed them aside, and grabbed the red and black plaid blanket off the foot of the bed. Wrapping it around my lower body, I snuck a glance at Gianni as he tugged up his jeans. The hem of his dress shirt covered his butt, so I couldn't even see what kind of underwear he had on—or if he wore underwear at all. What if he was a commando kind of guy?

I quickly faced the kitchenette again and waited, my heart beating fast. After I heard his zipper, I asked, "Are you decent?"

"Yeah. Can I turn around now?"

"Yes."

We faced each other at the same time, and when he saw me wrapped in the blanket, he started to laugh. "Ellie, that sweater covers way more than a bathing suit, which I have seen you in a hundred times."

"Doesn't matter." I got back on the bed and pretzeled my legs again, keeping the blanket tucked around my lap. "Okay. Ask me your question now."

I drank some more wine. "I thought it was overrated."

"You did?" He laughed. "I thought the opposite. I was like, 'how the hell does anyone ever get anything done?' It was all I could think about."

"I think I was expecting it to be like the movies. Or like in a romance novel. You know, a lot of *bursting* and *exploding*," I said dramatically. "*Cries* of *passion. Moans* of *ecstasy*. Instead it was more like . . . grunt, grunt, snap, crackle, pop. I wondered what all the fuss was about."

Gianni snorted with laughter. "I sincerely hope things have gotten better since then."

"They have." I grabbed my wineglass and brought it to my lips. "Mostly."

"Mostly?"

"Never mind."

"Oh, no. You can't just put that out there and walk away. What did you mean?"

I exhaled and took another sip. "I just feel like the guys I've been with are always in a rush. They don't listen or pay attention. I mean, they *act* like they want me to finish, and they *ask* me things like, 'Are you close?' But I never feel like that question is actually about me. And I always feel like I have to say yes, even when the answer is no. I feel pressured, I get nervous. And then I fake it."

Gianni's jaw dropped. "You fake your orgasms?"

"Not all the time," I said quickly. "Just sometimes."

"How often?"

"Maybe like half the time. Or . . . three quarters."

"Damn." He shook his head. "That sucks."

"Tell me about it." I drank again. "Why can't guys just slow down and figure out what I like? It's not that complicated."

"What is it you like?"

drink. "Tell me what you like."

I swirled the wine in my glass. "I would like someone who doesn't treat sex like it's a race."

"Do you *tell* them to slow down if they're moving too fast?"

"I try to, but sometimes it's awkward. I don't want to seem like I'm too demanding."

"Ellie, unless a guy is a total asshole, he wants you to finish. And it's not in our nature to be patient when it comes to sex."

"You said *you're* patient," I pointed out.

"I wasn't always. I had to be taught."

"Who taught you?"

"This woman I saw for a little while when I lived in New York. She was older—maybe like twenty-five—and I was nineteen, literally a fucking bull in a china shop. The first time we were together, she set me straight." He drank again. "Taught me some very valuable lessons."

I couldn't imagine how confident a woman would have to be in order to give sex lessons.

"Anyway," Gianni went on, "next time, tell him to slow down." He sipped his wine. "What else do you like?"

I thought for a moment. "I like it when someone pays attention to unexpected places on my body—I'm not a target with a bullseye."

"Okay, but you have to admit, there *is* sort of a bullseye when it comes to a woman's orgasm."

"Yeah. It's called her brain."

Gianni laughed. "Fair enough."

"Look, I know the body part you're thinking of, and I won't say it's not important—a guy should definitely be able to find it—but you can't just flick it like it's a light switch or go at it like you're trying to scrape ice off your windshield."

"At least to start," I said. "I like sex that *goes* somewhere. It can get fast or rough eventually, but I need a little time to go from zero to sixty. I understand that it's less . . . complicated for a guy, but that's no excuse for flooring it and expecting me to enjoy the whiplash. I want him to show me I'm worth the effort it takes to have some control."

He nodded slowly. "I get that. But haven't you ever just wanted to rip someone's clothes off and go at it?"

My face grew hot. "Not really. So maybe it's me that's the problem. Maybe I'm too uptight. Is that what you're thinking?"

"Not at all. You deserve what you want in bed, Ellie. I was only curious about what that is." His eyes danced with mischief as he took another drink. "After all, we're stuck in this room with one bed all night, and it's like snowmageddon out there. What if we have to have sex to continue the human species? I need to know how to approach it."

I rolled my eyes. "We will not be having any sex tonight."

"So you'd let the human species die out rather than do it with me?"

"Yes."

But every single nerve ending in my body was suddenly alive and humming.

CHAPTER 7
GIANNI

For a moment, I thought maybe I'd gone too far. Ellie had this sort of stunned, uncertain look on her face, like she wasn't sure she could trust me. I was about to apologize when she slammed the rest of the wine in her glass and reached for the bottle.

"So what about you?" she asked, filling her glass again. "What do *you* like?"

"As you said, guys are less complicated. I pretty much like everything." I shrugged. "Slow, fast, rough, gentle, loud, quiet, floor, ceiling, lying down, standing up, morning, night, bedroom, shower, kitchen, blindfold, restraints—"

"Okay, okay. I get it. You can stop." She poured the rest of the bottle into my glass.

I smiled. "Just letting you know I'm up for anything."

"In case I was in the mood to let you tie me to the bedposts or something? Forget it. I'm already feeling restrained in here." She set the empty bottle on the table.

"Have you ever?"

"Have I ever what?"

"Been tied up."

Her face grew pink. "None of your business."

goody? Let's just move on."

"Guess I have my answer." I looked at the screen and laughed. "How much money would a billionaire who likes to watch have to pay you to have sex with me in his velvet blimp?"

"A million dollars." She guzzled some wine.

"That much?"

"More if I have to fake the orgasm."

I smirked. "You wouldn't have to fake it."

Her shoulders rose as she sipped her wine, as if she didn't believe me.

"Just out of curiosity, what would you do with a million dollars?"

"Hmmm." She thought for a second. "Honestly, I'd probably try to buy more land around Abelard. Plant more grapes. Hire more people. Build myself a house on the property."

"Really? You'd stay right where you are?"

"Yes." She made a grand sweeping gesture. "Go ahead and tell me I'm boring."

"I don't think it's boring at all. It's your passion. Yes, my dream is to go wherever life takes me and do big things in far-off places. But your dream is to be true to your roots and do big things at home, and I respect that."

After another sip from her glass, she looked at me. "What about you? What would you do with a million dollars?"

"Well, first of all, I wouldn't make anyone pay me to have sex with you in a velvet blimp. I'd do it for free."

"Very generous of you."

"But if I ever had a million dollars, I'd probably use it to travel around the world and eat and cook and meet people and learn about food in all kinds of places—like Anthony Bourdain in *Parts Unknown*."

"I wouldn't mind the cameras and crew, as long as I had a say in how the show was produced. *Lick My Plate* was fun, but it wasn't really about cooking or food."

She snickered. "And will your new, serious food show be called Gianni Lupo: Too Hot To Handle?"

Sitting up, I reached over and pulled her hair. "Hey. We called a truce, remember?"

"That's right. So I want to stay put and you want to roam the planet. I guess that means our moms' dream that we walk down the aisle together is dead."

"Pretty sure that dream died a long time ago, probably around the time I smashed your umbrella."

"Agreed. Do you even want to get married?"

"Maybe when I'm, like, *seventy* and out of good ideas."

"Because you'd get bored?"

I shrugged. "Yeah. I hate the thought of settling down, being tied to one place or one person. I like being free to make my own decisions, to pack up and leave when I feel like it."

"Then you should definitely not get married."

"I take it you want to get hitched?"

"Yes. I'd like a family." She stared into her wine. "But the thing is, I've never even come close to feeling that thing I'd want to feel if I was going to spend the rest of my life with someone."

"You mean you've never been in love?"

"I don't think so." She looked up at me. "Have you?"

I shook my head. "No. I've been in a few relationships, but they were pretty casual. I move around a lot, and working in restaurants, it's hard to date. You don't have many nights free."

"Yeah." She played with her empty glass. "I don't know, it just seems like such a gamble, falling in love. Winnie was always losing her heart to some guy who didn't deserve it—

"What? Tell me."

"No. You'll think it's dumb, and you'll make fun of me."

"Try me."

She sighed. "I want someone to look at me the way my dad looks at my mom. I mean, you can tell when they're in a room together that she's everything to him. He doesn't even have to say it."

"Yeah," I said, thinking about my parents. "My mom and dad are like that too. But I think it's rare."

"It's almost worse, knowing that kind of love exists, but worrying you'll never find it. Like maybe if I hadn't seen it in real life, I'd think it was only in fairy tales and I'd be willing to settle for less." She shrugged. "But I've seen it. And that's what I want."

"I hope you find it. Ready for the next question?"

"Wait, I have to use the bathroom first, and we need more wine." She got off the bed and tightened the blanket around her.

I tipped up the last few drops in my glass. "Okay, you go to the bathroom and I'll get the wine."

She waddled over to the window like a pig in a blanket at IHOP and elbowed the curtain aside. "Wow. It's still coming down. It's pretty, though."

I walked over to the window. Standing right behind her, I caught the scent of her hair again. It looked so soft and warm, I had the urge to bury my face in it. Or maybe take it in my hands and push it aside so I could press my lips to the back of her neck. I'd done that once before . . . did she remember? The crotch of my jeans started to get tight.

"God, it doesn't even look real, does it?" she whispered in awe.

I forced myself to look out the glass. "No. It doesn't."

"Do you think we'll get out of here by morning?" Ellie asked.

"We'll try." Right now I was more worried about making it through the night next to her in that small bed and keeping my hands to myself.

Letting the curtain close, she spun to face me, her eyes worried. "What if we don't?"

"We'll be okay no matter what."

"But what about work? Desmond could cover for me at the winery, but who's going to—"

"Hush." I put my finger on her lips. "We'll figure it out."

She nodded, but I didn't take my finger off her mouth. Instead, I thought about the way she'd sucked the melted butter off my thumb earlier tonight, and my cock swelled even more. Her lips fell open slightly, but a second later she pushed my hand away. "Move."

I stepped aside and she shuffled past me, still trying to keep that stupid blanket wrapped around her. But no sooner had the door shut than it opened again, and she walked out, tossed the plaid blanket on the bed, and faced me, hands on her hips. "I give up. This is what I look like without pants on."

The hem of my sweater hit her mid-thigh and she still wore her hedgehog socks, so the only bare skin visible was from her shins to just above her knees.

"Is that what you're going to wear in the velvet blimp?" I asked.

"Yes."

"Then I might change my mind and ask for some compensation. Those socks are not sexy."

But as soon as the bathroom door shut behind her, I had to adjust the growing bulge in my pants and take a few deep breaths.

my mouth so I wouldn't smell her. I could face the opposite direction so I wouldn't see her. I could put the pillow over my head so I wouldn't hear her breathe. I could pin my hands between my knees to keep them from wandering over to her side. It might be the greatest test of willpower in all my life, and I'd probably only earn a C, possibly a C-, but I could pass it.

Except then she came out of the bathroom with her blouse balled up in her hands, and when she tossed it onto the table by the window, her black bra flew out and landed on the floor.

"Wait, we're allowed to remove *undergarments*?" I asked in mock surprise. "Does that mean I can ditch my boxer briefs?"

"Only if they have underwire." She quickly scooped up the bra and stuffed it into her shoulder bag.

"They do not."

"Then keep them on." She sat on the bed again and rummaged through the snack pile. "What's our second bottle of wine? I'll find something to pair it with."

But I was frozen in place. It hit me that she was wearing my sweater with nothing underneath it.

That was so hot.

Granted, it was only my sweater and not my hands against her skin, but my body reacted as if it couldn't tell the difference. And the way she was sitting with her knees jutting out gave me a glimpse of her underwear—it was also black, and I stared at it like a middle school boy salivating over a centerfold. Were they cotton? Satin? Lace? What would they feel like beneath my fingertips? Against my lips? Under my tongue?

I swallowed hard, a groan trapped in my throat.

"Gianni?" She looked over at me, and I quickly raised my eyes to her face. "You okay?"

didn't matter what it was—I just needed more alcohol to numb this attraction to her, this *awareness* of her body, so I didn't do anything stupid.

With my back to her, I lifted the wine to my mouth and took a long drink straight from the bottle.

Round Two of Truth or Drink commenced with Ellie relaxed and mellow and me uptight and anxious—a complete reversal of our usual roles.

I started with a non-dirty question on purpose. "What smell takes you back to childhood?"

"Hmm." She thought for a moment. "I have a crazy sensitive nose, so I can think of lots of things, but one smell I always loved was the scent that hits you when you open a fresh box of crayons."

I laughed. "That's so you."

"I can't help it. They're all lined up and perfectly sharpened and the entire box just bursts with possibility . . ." She inhaled, her eyes closing blissfully, as if she had a brand new Crayola box in her hands and not a wineglass. "What about you?"

"Two things—the smell of Bolognese simmering will always remind me of my Great-Grandma Lupo's house. And the smell of Middle Eastern spices always reminds me of my Lebanese grandmother's house."

"So it was always about food, huh?" She ate a few more M&M's.

"A lot of that is my dad's influence. He'd try to get me to

"I love your dad," she said, a little dreamily.

"You do?"

Color stained her cheeks. "I just mean he's nice. Next."

"What do you secretly think I'd be amazing at?"

"Is that really a question? Are you trying to trick me into saying I think you'd be good in bed?"

"No!" I showed her the screen. "It's really a question. But do you think that?"

She sighed and swirled her wine in the glass. "Yes. I can't even believe I'm saying this—I must be drunk. It's only because of what you said about foreplay. And being patient. And asking what I like. It makes me think that you probably aren't as self-centered in bed as I imagined you would be."

I grinned. "So you've imagined it?"

"I didn't say that."

"But have you?"

She looked me right in the eye. "Have *you*?"

"Yes."

Her mouth fell open.

"I've imagined sex with pretty much every hot girl I know."

She rolled her eyes. "God, I walked right into that one. Never mind. Give me the phone."

I handed it over and took a drink, trying desperately to keep my eyes from straying between her legs. Did she have to sit like that? She had to be buzzed from the wine—otherwise there was no way she'd let me see London and France.

She started to giggle. "Would you trust me to pierce your ear?"

"Fuck no."

"Why not? I'd let you pierce mine."

"You would?"

Our eyes met. "That's true."

"Moving on," she said, clearing her throat. "Who's your secret crush?"

"I don't have one."

"Come on," she scoffed. "Everyone has a secret crush."

"I don't. If I like someone, I make it obvious. Why wouldn't I?"

"Because it's inappropriate."

"So who's your secret crush?"

"Your dad, obviously."

She tried to play it off like a joke, but there was something about the way she said it that made me pause—and her cheeks were rapidly turning red. I cocked my head. "Do you have a thing for my *dad*?"

"What?" She looked nervous for a second. "Don't be ridiculous."

"You do, don't you? You have a thing for my dad!" I started to laugh.

"Will you stop it? I do not!" She scrambled off the bed and backed up. "It was a joke!"

"Then why are you blushing?"

"I'm not blushing, I'm just—it's not a *thing*, okay?" She began pacing back and forth at the foot of the bed. "Your dad is objectively a very attractive man."

I grinned at her. "So you're attracted to him?"

"No! I didn't say that, I said *objectively*, he's attractive," she said quickly. "Anybody would find him attractive. It's just biology. I just made a joke. That dream meant nothing."

"What dream?"

"Shit!" She put her hands in her hair and squeezed her eyes shut. "I didn't mean to say that!"

"Well, it's out there now, so you might as well elaborate." I

"Nothing."

"Liar."

Sighing, she faced me and held up her hands. "He kissed me, okay? That's all. It was one kiss, and then I woke up."

"Where were you? In the dream."

Her face turned an even deeper shade of scarlet. "My bed."

"So you'd let my dad *and* my brothers in your bed, but not me?"

"That's not funny. And why is it suddenly so hot in here?" She turned away from me and fanned her face.

"It's not hot in here. I think you're just warm thinking about your crush on my dad."

She spun around, flustered and frantic. "It's not a crush! He was very nice to me when I was little, okay? I remember once when I was at your house in Detroit, before you moved up north, I fell and got a bloody knee and he came outside and carried me in. It's a sweet memory."

"It is a sweet memory. Except that it was *me* who carried you in the house."

"What?" She stuck her hands on her hips. "No way, Gianni. We were like five years old."

"I know. We were at my house, and you were trying to run faster than me down the driveway—which was never going to happen, by the way. You wiped out so hard you bloodied both knees. I felt bad for you and somehow I knew I was gonna get yelled at for it, so I thought I'd try to be nice and help you into the house."

She was staring at me from across the room with her mouth open. Her eyes narrowed. "You're lying."

"I'm not," I said, laughing. "That's what actually happened."

I shrugged. "Maybe this will just be another one of those things we remember differently."

She lifted her chin. "Maybe so."

The silence between us was thicker than the snow drift outside the windows.

"Are we ever going to talk about it?" I asked.

"About what?"

"You know what. Those seven minutes."

"I don't see what there is to talk about. Nothing happened."

"Ellie, come on. It's time to admit it—something happened."

"Fine. What happened was you tricked me."

"What?" I gaped at her. "I didn't trick you!"

"Yes, you did!" Her eyes lit up with fury. "I said I wouldn't kiss you, and you bet me you could change my mind in seven minutes."

"And I *did*." I was annoyed at the accusation that I'd done something shady, but I couldn't help smiling. "I *did* change your mind in seven minutes, and I didn't even break a single one of your rules." I ticked them off on one hand. "I didn't force you, I didn't touch any private parts—I didn't even talk. And before that timer went off, you begged me to kiss you."

Seething, she drew herself up like the Queen of England. "I. Did not. Beg."

I laughed. "Sorry. You *told* me to kiss you. Twice, in fact."

"And you didn't."

"The seven minutes were up," I said with a shrug, although that wasn't exactly true.

She pointed a finger at me. "You had time to kiss me, and you know it. You just wanted to humiliate me. That's all you ever want to do—tonight included!" She grabbed her bag off the floor and stomped off toward the bathroom in a huff.

The bathroom door slammed shut.

Exhaling, I let my head fall back against the headboard and rubbed my face with both hands. I hadn't meant to provoke her, but somehow that was exactly what I'd done. Now instead of tipsy, mellow Ellie to share a bed with, I had angry, resentful Ellie. I probably owed her an apology, especially after the shitty night she'd just had, but I'd give her a minute or so to cool down.

With my eyes closed and my head a little woozy from the wine, I let my mind wander back to that night six years ago in Tanner Ford's basement. I didn't have much talent when it came to memorizing shit for school, but I remembered everything about that night.

Ellie had cleaned up after the dunk tank incident, and she'd been wearing a super short skirt, which was rare for her —maybe she'd even borrowed it from someone. She sat over on one side of the room with a bunch of girls, while I played air hockey with my friends, stealing looks at her legs from the corner of my eye. As always, she refused to even glance in my direction. She was like the one girl at school who wouldn't give me the time of day, and it drove me crazy because she'd grown up to be fucking *gorgeous*.

I probably shouldn't have dunked her fifty times, but the opportunity had been too tempting to resist. And she'd gotten me back with all those pies in the face! We were even.

But it felt like something was unfinished between us. Some tension lingered. Or maybe I was just curious.

So later, when we were playing Seven Minutes in Heaven, I pretended to pull her name from the hat. When she heard me say her name, her eyes met mine, a little defiantly—for a moment, I thought she might refuse.

But she stood up, tugged her skirt down a little, and walked into the large cedar closet without a word. As

heard someone say, "I'll set the timer!"

The door slammed, and we were alone in the dark.

"I don't want you to kiss me," she announced imperiously.

"Why not?"

"I just don't."

"Can I try to change your mind?"

She laughed. "Sure."

"You think I won't be able to?" My eyes were adjusting to the dark, and I took a step closer to her.

"No, but . . . go ahead and try. Just respect my rules."

My heart hammered wildly with the challenge. "What are your rules?"

"Don't touch any private parts, not even over my clothes. Stop if I say no. And don't talk."

"Why can't I talk?"

She folded her arms over her chest. "Because it will all be lies, and I'm not interested, Gianni."

"Okay." I moved closer to her, so close my chest bumped her forearms, and my lips brushed her forehead. "But is it okay to touch your, um, public parts?"

"I—I guess."

I took her by the wrists and put her arms down by her sides, then dropped to my knees in front of her.

She sucked in her breath, and I grinned.

CHAPTER 8
ELLIE

nside the bathroom, I scrubbed my teeth with enough force to wear off the enamel and stared at my face in the mirror—flushed cheeks, bright eyes, lips stained a little from the wine. My chest rose and fell with quick, heavy breaths.

It wasn't fair, how he could still get to me. He didn't play fair.

Not when we were kids. Not tonight. And certainly not in that closet.

I could still smell the cedar.

Scowling, I spit and rinsed out my mouth, wiping my lips with the back of my hand.

Then I closed my eyes, remembering how he'd dropped to his knees in front of me.

My breath caught.

I was scared—not that Gianni would break the rules, but that he wouldn't even have to. The truth was, I *wanted* him to kiss me. I wanted it so badly, I could hardly stand it—and I *hated* myself for it.

Why should I want him to kiss me when he'd done nothing but torment me my entire life? When he'd made a

guy like that be the one I secretly dreamed about? The one I thought about at night? The one I wished more than anything would whisper to me in the dark?

And speaking of dark.

He brushed one hand over the curve of my left hip.

He touched the inside of my right ankle and slowly dragged his fingertips up the inside of my leg. When he passed my knee, I trembled, whether in fear or anticipation I wasn't sure, but his hand stopped short of my inner thigh.

My shirt was slightly cropped, and I could feel his breath on my stomach—and then his lips. He planted a row of three devastatingly soft and gentle kisses across my belly.

Every inch of my skin was tingling. I almost dropped the act, fell to my knees and crushed my mouth to his right then and there.

But I didn't. I didn't.

He rose to his feet and moved behind me, one hand skimming across my stomach where his lips had just been. With the other hand, he moved my hair aside, and kissed the back of my neck.

My entire body shivered—I couldn't help it. I almost expected him to laugh, but he didn't. Keeping one palm on my stomach, his lips moved from the back of my neck to the side of my throat, his tongue warm and soft on my skin. My head tilted to one side without my permission. His arm tightened around my waist. My heart was beating out of control, and my head was spinning. I licked my lips.

Then I turned to face him, breathless, helpless, desperate. "Okay," I whispered. "Kiss me."

His lips were so close. All he had to do was drop his mouth to mine. All I had to do was rise on tiptoe.

"Ten second warning!" came the shout from outside the door.

"Yes." I could feel the tension in his body—he wanted it too. I know he did.

"Six! Five! Four!"

"Gianni," I said, more impatiently. "Kiss me. Hurry up."

But instead of putting his mouth on mine, he let me go and stepped back.

"Three! Two! One!" The door opened, light streaming in.

I raced out of the closet and went straight for the bathroom, where I stared at myself in the mirror, furious about the way I'd given in—given him exactly what he'd wanted. Now he'd probably tell everyone about how he *made* me want to kiss him and then wouldn't do it. They'd all laugh at me.

"Ellie!" Winnie knocked on the door. "Are you okay?"

"I'm fine." My voice sounded surprisingly normal. I took a couple breaths and let her in.

"What the hell happened in there?" She was breathless with excitement.

"What did Gianni say happened?"

"Nothing. He just came out and started playing air hockey again."

"Really?"

She nodded. "So what happened?"

"Nothing." I looked in the mirror and fussed with my hair. Adjusted my skirt. "We argued and then nothing."

She crossed her arms. "Seriously?"

"Seriously."

"He didn't even kiss you?"

I shook my head as mortification at being rejected pulsed through me. I was so embarrassed I couldn't even tell my best friend. "Nope."

And now here I was, alone in the bathroom at the Pineview Motel, reliving it.

The knock on the door made me jump.

"You can't stay in there all night."

"Yes, I can. I'll sleep in the tub."

"I have to use the bathroom."

I swung the door open and swept past him, careful not to let any part of my body touch his. "Fine. I'm going to bed."

He watched as I stuffed all the empty chip bags and candy wrappers into the trash and the uneaten snacks back into the plastic bag.

"Do you want this?" Without looking at him, I held up the toothbrush and toothpaste he'd bought at the gas station.

"Oh. Yeah." He came toward the bed, but instead of risking our hands touching, I dropped the items onto the mattress. Exhaling, he picked them up and went into the bathroom.

As I was plugging my phone into the charger, I saw that Winnie had texted me.

I'm dying. Can you talk?

Dropping onto the bed with my back to the bathroom, I listened carefully for a moment and heard the water running. He was probably brushing his teeth, but I didn't think that gave me time for a call.

Not right now. I'll call you ASAP.

But what is HAPPENING?!

We were doing fine until he brought up the past. Then I got mad because clearly I enjoy hanging on to this grudge with all my might. Pretty sure I need therapy.

Or sex. You could take out all your anger on his body. I bet it would feel good. A blizzard bang. It wouldn't even count.

sexual decisions in order to stay warm and/or alleviate boredom. But *Gianni?*

NO WAY. I HATE HIM.

Boo. Call me when you can and stay safe.

Behind me, the bathroom door opened. With my back to him, I plugged in my phone. Then I folded my arms over my chest, refusing to look at him.

"Ellie, come on. What is it you want me to say? I'm sorry for making you want to kiss me when we were seventeen? Fine. I'm sorry. But you started it."

"Me!" Outraged, I whirled around and faced him. "I didn't start it! You brought up the seven minutes night!"

He moved closer to the bed. "I meant back then. You were always too good for me, you wouldn't even look in my direction. And the first thing you said to me in that closet was, *I don't want you to kiss me.*"

"I didn't!" Because he had the advantage of height, I jumped onto the bed so I could feel bigger than him. "And you want to know why?"

"Because of the dunk tank?"

"No! Because I was scared."

He looked perplexed. "Of what?"

"Liking it too much. Wanting you that way. Being kissed by you because you had no choice, then being laughed at and tossed aside."

"Why would I have done that?"

"To humiliate me! The same reason you refused to kiss me after you did all that stuff to change my mind."

He looked genuinely surprised. "I didn't do it to humiliate you, Ellie. I did it to get back at you."

"For what—the pies?"

was strongly considering both. One of his shoulders rose. "I guess because I wanted you to know how it felt to want something and not get it."

"Ha!" I was bursting with so much shock and indignation, I had to jump up and down on the bed to burn some of it off. "I think you have it backwards, Gianni. You were the one who got away with everything! You were the one who could have anybody—and you did! Because you were the one everybody wanted. You still are—look at what happened tonight!"

"Ellie, stop." He grabbed my arm, but I wrenched it free and kept jumping. "You don't understand what I'm saying."

I couldn't stop. It felt too good to get everything out. "I understand perfectly! The world is Gianni Lupo's playground."

He chuckled at that. "Listen. You are welcome on my playground any time you want. You always were—that's what I'm trying to tell you. Yes, I messed around with a lot of girls in high school, but I thought you were hot as fuck and I *wanted* to kiss you that night. I was scared to let you know how much."

"Bullshit!"

"Oh yeah? Let me tell you something—I didn't even pull your name out of that hat. I pulled someone else's."

I stopped bouncing. "What?"

"You heard me."

"Whose name did you actually pull?"

"Fuck if I know. But not yours. I lied and read your name off so I'd finally get to make out with you. I didn't think I stood a chance otherwise."

I jerked my chin at him, although my heart was pounding. "You didn't."

I shrugged, wishing for the millionth time he wasn't so hot. "For those ten seconds. Yeah, I did. I wondered what all the fuss was about."

"Do you still?"

My heart stopped. "What?"

"Do you still want to know what all the fuss was about?"

"No," I snapped, although my heart had started beating again at a speed that was highly unsafe for these conditions. "You're too late."

He reached for me, but I shrieked and leaped off the opposite side of the bed. Laughing, he vaulted the mattress and came after me, and I ran around the foot of the bed, squealing and panting. He rounded the bed too, and I hopped onto the mattress again, scrambling to the other side once more as he continued to chase me.

He caught me around the waist on the third lap, flipping me onto my back. Breathless and sweaty, I beat my fists against his chest. "Get off me, you scoundrel!"

"No." Somehow he got my wrists in his grip and pinioned them to the mattress above my shoulders. "I want another chance. For years, I've been kicking myself for fucking up in that closet."

"Good."

"I let pride win, when I should have just gone with my gut."

"And what was your gut telling you to do?" My voice was low and breathy now, and my eyes dropped to his mouth.

"The same thing you were telling me to do. This." He crushed his lips to mine.

The kiss was hard and deep and demanding, and sent shock waves reverberating throughout my body. He opened his mouth and slanted his head and let his tongue move between my lips. My hands were still locked in place next to

I kissed him back like I wanted it, like I wasn't ashamed, like I wasn't even afraid—and maybe I wasn't. I was mad about it, but I had no fear.

The realization struck me hard, as hard as the bulge in Gianni's pants that was pressed between my legs. He began to rock rhythmically against me, and a sound escaped my throat, a muffled cry of need and frustration. I wanted him closer. I wanted his hands on my skin. I wanted that mouth on the back of my neck again, that tongue on my throat.

A strangled moan worked itself free from Gianni's mouth too, and he picked up his head. "Fuck," he growled. "This could get out of control really easily."

"I don't care," I panted. "Let it."

"You're sure? You drank a lot of wine kind of fast, and I don't—"

"Gianni." I thumped his ass with my heel. "Don't fuck this up a second time. You're never going to have this chance again."

"You're not drunk? You really want this?"

"I'm not drunk." I lifted my head and stroked his bottom lip with my tongue. "And I really want this."

"Sex can ruin a friendship, you know."

"Then it's a good thing we're not friends."

I only caught the boyish grin on his face for a second before he was kissing me again. A moment later, he stood up and started to unbutton his shirt. "Wait," I said, getting to my knees and placing both hands on his chest. "Do *you* really want this?"

"Are you fucking serious?"

"Yes."

"I've wanted this every single night for six months. Probably farther back than that. You've always been the unattainable girl of my dreams, Ellie."

"Then let me."

Quickly my fingers worked their way down the row of buttons, and I enjoyed the way his chest was expanding and contracting so fast. I pushed the shirt down his arms and it fell to the floor. Beneath it he wore a plain white T-shirt, and I grabbed the hem and yanked it over his head.

When he was shirtless in front of me, I couldn't help myself—I gasped. Then I put my hands on his warm, smooth skin and ran them over his chest, down his shoulders and biceps, up his stomach, his muscular abs rippling beneath my touch. He was beautiful, more beautiful than anybody I'd ever been with, and I had to know what that golden skin would feel like against my lips.

I pressed my mouth to his chest right beneath his collarbone, and just like he'd done years ago in that closet, planted a row of kisses right to left. When I reached his sternum, a light patch of hair tickled my lips. His hands reached beneath the sweater I wore and slid up the outside of my thighs to my hips. His fingers dug into my flesh as my mouth continued to travel across his chest.

Desire was running hot through my veins, and previously unthinkable urges overwhelmed me. I caressed his nipple with my tongue, circling it, licking the taut peak slowly and deliciously. Gratified by the groan of pleasure it elicited from his throat, I did the same thing to the other one, sliding one hand between his legs and rubbing the thick, hard bulge through his jeans.

I kissed my way up to his neck and breathed deeply—the scent that had stirred me up in the car filled my head again, making me dizzy with lust. I reached for the button on his jeans. After slipping it through the hole, I dragged the zipper down and slipped my hand inside, wrapping my fingers around his cock as I stroked his throat with my tongue.

as I worked my fist up and down his shaft. "*Fuck*, that feels good."

I teased the crown with my fingertips, brushing the tip with my thumb, pleased when I felt the droplets of slick wet warmth beneath my touch.

Gianni grunted in frustration and yanked at the sweater. "I want this off."

I raised my arms, and he whipped it over my head, throwing it aside. I wore nothing beneath it, and his eyes popped. His palms immediately covered my breasts. I worked my fingers into his hair, pulling his mouth back to mine, craving his kiss again. His thumbs teased my nipples, and I arched my back as electric pulses hummed along every nerve ending.

He slipped one hand between my thighs, rubbing me slowly but firmly over my black satin panties. My hips rocked over his hand instinctively, my underwear growing damp. I widened my knees slightly, hoping he'd understand the invitation—and he did.

His fingers worked beneath the satin, and my breath caught as he teased me open, gently sliding one of those talented fingers inside me. My hands fisted in his hair as the tension in my body pulled tighter. "Yes," I whispered against his lips. "Yes."

Wrapping one arm around my shoulders and the other circling my knees, he tipped me onto my back and pulled my panties down my legs. After tossing them to the floor, he stood up to remove the rest of his clothes, hopping on one foot when his jeans stubbornly clung to his legs. I laughed when he finally wrested them from his body and pounced on me, covering my body with his and burying his face in my neck.

"No fucking way." He picked up his head and looked down at me. "If I'm never going to have this chance again, I'm not about to fumble around in the dark. I'm going to see every inch of your body so I can live on this memory forever."

I laughed. "Stop it. Don't make jokes."

"I'm serious."

"Then how come you're smiling?"

"Oh come on." His grin was playful. "You can't blame me for that. I've got a former Cherry Princess naked in my bed at the Pineview Motel. Fucking pinch me."

I reached down and pinched his butt. "How's that?"

"It's good," he said, moving his mouth down my chest. "It's so fucking good."

"Can we at least get under the covers? It's still chilly in here."

"I *promise* I will keep you warm tonight," he said, but he worked the sheets and blankets down and slipped in beside me, pulling them to our shoulders.

"I believe you." I rolled to my back and cradled his head in my arms as he lowered his mouth to my breasts, sucking one swollen pink tip and then the other, sending delicious little darts of lust straight between my legs. On his side next to me, he slid one hand up my inner thigh. Anxious to feel his fingers inside me again, I opened my legs wider, but his palm moved up past my hip, across my stomach—making it quiver —and down the other leg.

"Don't tease me," I whispered, lifting my hips.

"I'm just trying to go slow." He circled my nipple with the tip of his tongue. "The way you like it." But he dipped one finger inside me, then slowly stroked my clit with his warm, wet fingertip.

I moaned as the sensations swept through my body, liquid

between my thighs.

And then he moved on top of me, sliding down my body, kissing his way down my belly until his tongue replaced his fingers on my clit. For a moment, I couldn't breathe as he stroked me, gently at first, then building the intensity with soft little flicks and artful swirls and clever tricks that had me clawing at the sheets in delightful agony. Then he slipped his fingers inside me—two this time—and the tension in my body ratcheted up with an intensity that nearly made me scream. Something inside me was closing around his fingers as he nibbled and sucked and pushed in deeper.

"Gianni," I whimpered. At least, I *tried* to say his name. I wanted to. But my mind was a jumble of crisscrossed wires and the signals were flying too fast for me to think straight. My body took over, my hips flexing, my insides tightening, my breath caught, my skin on fire, my vision going black, until everything burst wide open in wondrous pulses of pleasure and light, my core muscles clenching around Gianni's fingers. I cried out with every beat of pleasure.

I felt and heard his moan as he delivered and devoured my orgasm at the same time. His breathing was ragged as he tore his mouth off me and moved up my body. "Did you fake that?"

"Are you kidding?"

He gave me his cocky grin. "Don't move."

I stared at him in disbelief as he got off the bed and went over to his bag. *Move?* I wasn't even sure my legs would hold me up.

He rummaged around in his duffel bag, found what he was looking for, and returned to bed. Kneeling on the mattress, he tore the condom wrapper open with his teeth and rolled it on while I watched, breathless with desire and anticipation. He was so fucking gorgeous—from his messy

The thought had me shaking with the unbelievable thrill of it.

But I barely had time to enjoy the moment because Gianni was back between my thighs in a heartbeat, teasing my clit with the tip of his cock. His eyes glittered with hunger as he watched, his sensual mouth slightly open, his breathing hard and fast.

Then he was easing inside me, and I caught my bottom lip between my teeth as my body stretched and adjusted to his size. He lowered his chest over mine, the weight and warmth of it reassuring. I wrapped my legs around him, closing my eyes as he began to move—deep, slow strokes that told me he'd paid attention during our conversation earlier.

It was totally infuriating.

"I'm so mad right now," I whispered in his ear as my hands slid down his back.

He laughed. "Yeah?"

"Yes." I grabbed his ass like I'd thought about a hundred times before. "How dare you feel so good? How dare you make me come so hard? How dare you be generous and patient when I was convinced all along you'd be selfish and greedy?"

He paused, buried deep, and looked down at me. "I guess you don't know me as well as you thought."

Uncertainty flickered inside me, and I wondered if he was right, especially when he put his lips on mine and kissed away any smart-ass remark I might have made. In fact, he kissed me so deeply and passionately, I started to worry I was losing my grasp on what this was.

"Gianni," I whispered. "I don't want to wake up tomorrow and like you, okay? So maybe you could just be selfish for a minute? Just fuck me like you don't care? Better yet, fuck me like you hate me."

"What?"

"Tell me how you want it."

This time I put some venom into the words. "Fuck me like you hate me."

Inside me, his cock throbbed. "Goddamn it," he growled. "Why is that so fucking hot?"

He began to move again, but it was different than before. Faster. Harder. Rougher. There was a jagged edge to his rhythm—angry thrusts of his hips rather than that undulating motion of his body over mine. His breathing grew raspy and labored. His cock plunged deep, causing a twinge of pain within me.

I gasped, but he didn't slow down.

"Is this what you wanted?" His voice was gruff. "To be right about me after all?"

"Yes," I managed, the pain subsiding, replaced by a wicked sense of pleasure—not just in the friction between our bodies but in the game we were playing. Not only had I found a way to play it on *my* terms, but I'd just scored a point.

"Fine. I'll fuck you like I hate you." He grinned above me. "I'll still make you come."

And he did. That bastard did what no guy before him had ever managed to do—give me a second orgasm.

Hell, most guys couldn't even manage the first!

I don't know if it was the size of the boat or the motion of the ocean—it also could have been the way the boat smelled and tasted and moaned—but I found myself cresting at the top of that wave again in no time at all, and then crashing onto the shore at the same time he did, our bodies in perfect sync.

Afterward, I felt as if I really had just washed up onto the beach. Breathless. Damp. Exhausted. Shipwrecked.

Stranded.

CHAPTER 9
GIANNI

My heart banged hard against my ribs. My skin was stuck to Ellie's. And my dick was still inside her.

Holy shit. I had sex with Ellie Fournier.

And it was amazing.

I picked up my head and looked down. Her expression was something between awestruck and *aw, fuck*.

"Well. That was . . ." I searched for a word that could even come close to describing what had just happened.

"A surprise."

"Uh, yeah."

She pummeled my chest lightly. "Let me up. I need some air."

"Oh. Sorry." I rolled off her and got out of bed. "Be right back."

In the bathroom, I disposed of the condom and cleaned up a little, and when I opened the door, she was standing there naked.

Well, almost naked.

I looked at her from head to foot. "Two things. First, if I didn't make it clear already, you have an amazing body."

"Thank you."

"I guess they're *your* lucky socks too." She tugged on my arm. "I need to use the bathroom."

"Okay." We traded places, and Ellie closed herself into the bathroom while I wandered back toward the bed in a daze, looking at it with a kind of wonder. My brain was on a loop.

Holy shit. I had sex with Ellie Fournier.

And it was good. Like, better than good. It was intense and fun and crazy hot.

What were the chances she'd be up for doing it again while we were stuck in this room together? I tried to calculate the odds, but really didn't see them turning out in my favor. Most likely, that had been a one-time thing, a strangely enjoyable way for the two of us to get back at one another or finally satisfy our curiosity.

At least I'd given her two real orgasms. The thought made me smile with satisfaction.

I pulled the covers back and climbed back into bed. I was lying on my back, hands tucked beneath my head when Ellie shuffled back into the room.

Grabbing the blanket she'd been wearing earlier from the foot of the mattress, she wrapped it around herself and wandered toward the window. After switching off the light, she moved the curtain aside and stood looking out. Her dark hair spilled down her back, and I had the urge to touch it again.

"Still snowing?" I asked.

"Yes. Your car is buried. Everyone's is."

"I'll clear it off tomorrow."

Sighing, she closed the curtain again and went over to her bag. "I wish I would have thought to pack emergency pajamas. I don't really want to sleep in your sweater."

"Sleep naked."

"I can't sleep naked with *you*."

"That's not the point." She faced me and spoke in the know-it-all voice I was used to. "Sleeping naked next to someone is something that people in a relationship do. Not us."

"*I'm* sleeping naked."

"Gianni! Can't you at least put underwear on?"

"No, I'm saving my clean underwear for tomorrow. And I'm perfectly comfortable being naked next to you. It seems ridiculous to get shy about it after what just happened between us."

She sighed. "Then can I have your T-shirt?"

"Sure."

She walked around to my side of the bed and found it on the floor. Scooping it up, she shook it out for some reason before tossing the blanket back onto the bed and pulling the shirt over her head. Then she sniffed the collar. "It smells good."

"Come closer. You can have the real thing." I turned down the covers and moved over, making room for her.

But instead of climbing in, she walked around to her side of the bed. "No. You have to stay over there on your half. I'll stay on mine."

"Ellie, I'm twice as big as you. Half and half isn't fair."

"Well, try not to move around too much, okay?" She lay on her back and pulled the covers up to her chin. "Goodnight."

"Night."

Minutes ticked by in the dark.

There was no way I was going to fall asleep. All I could think about was the fact that she wasn't wearing panties under my T-shirt. I rolled onto my side and propped my head on my elbow. It was so dark I couldn't see if her eyes were open or closed.

"I'm trying to." She shivered. "I'm cold again."

I reached for the plaid blanket she'd tossed at the foot of the bed and spread it over her. "Better?"

"I think so. Thanks."

"You can always move closer to me."

"I don't think that's a good idea."

"Why not?"

"Because it might lead to other things."

"It's fine, I have another condom."

"*No*, Gianni. Goodnight."

"Wait, I have a question." I tapped her on the shoulder.

"What?"

"Was I as good as my dad in your dream?"

She sat up and hit me with her pillow. "You're a jerk! I can't believe I told you that. You have to promise you won't ever tell anyone about it—or about anything that happened here tonight!"

I couldn't stop laughing. "What happens at the Pineview Motel stays at the Pineview Motel."

"Good." She thumped her pillow down and huddled up facing the wall instead of me. "God, I'm going to regret everything about these twenty-four hours with you, aren't I?"

"Oh, come on. We're having a good time. In fact, this truce we have going is even more fun than fighting with you."

"Ha." She was silent for a few minutes but seemed to curl up tighter and tighter into a ball. Then she started to shiver.

"Permission to approach your side in order to share my body heat," I stated robotically. "In a completely non-sexual way, of course."

"Fine." Her voice was small. "But only because I'm so cold."

Smiling, I wrapped an arm around her waist and pulled her toward me so my body curved around hers—my chest

inhaled the summer-day scent of her hair. I closed my eyes and felt seventeen again, bursting with reckless energy and stupid ideas. I recalled walking around at the Cherry Festival with friends and seeing her in that bikini, sash, and crown, posed above that dunk tank. Her legs were crossed at the ankle, her knees side by side, her thighs pressed tightly together.

But she'd opened those thighs for me tonight, hadn't she? And she'd tasted better than a dream.

"Quit it, Gianni."

"What?"

"I can feel you getting hard."

"Sorry. I was thinking about earlier. I'll try to stop."

She was silent a moment. "What were you thinking about, specifically?"

I smiled. "The way you taste."

"Oh."

"Your hair smells good, and something about it reminds me of summer, so I started thinking about the Cherry Festival, and picturing you in your bikini, and remembering how hot you were sitting up there, and how your legs were all pressed together like a good girl's, and then I remembered the way you spread them open for me, and my face was buried between them, and—"

"Jesus. So that's how it happens."

"That's how it happens." I continued to get hard, and I knew she could feel it. "Want me to let you go?"

"I'm—I'm not sure. Now I'm getting all confused." She squirmed a little, which only made things worse. "You are nice and warm. Can't you just make it go down?"

"Maybe, but I'd rather make it go in and out."

She laughed, which surprised me. "Think about something unsexy."

all we get."

"What's a blizzard bang?"

"It's a sort of hall pass you get during really bad weather to make questionable sexual decisions."

I laughed. "But it's a one-time use?"

"Yeah."

"Too bad." I held her closer and started kissing the back of her neck, fully prepared for her to push me away or tell me to stop. When she didn't, I slipped my arm inside the shirt she wore, placing my hand on her bare stomach.

"Oh God," she whispered. "Don't make me want this again."

"Should I stop?" Slowly, my palm slid up her rib cage.

"Yes." But she took my wrist and moved my hand over her breast. "I have so many reasons why this should not happen."

"Such as?" I played with the hard peaks of her nipples.

"We've known each other too long." Her hand snaked back and brushed over my hip.

"Definitely."

"We don't get along." She slipped her hand between us.

"Nope." My eyes closed as her fingers wrapped around my erection, which grew thicker in her grasp.

"We're total opposites."

"Well, you know what they say about opposites." Heat prickled all over my skin as she worked her hand up and down my shaft.

"If I give in to you again, you'll hold it over me for the rest of my life. You'll remind me constantly that I couldn't resist you, and then I'm just like every other girl you've ever been with."

"Ellie, for God's sake." With my palm still covering her breast, I kissed my way down the curve of her neck to her

your resistance."

"No?" Her breath was coming faster.

"No. I want you to give in because it's what you want. Because it will feel good. Because even though we're total opposites and not friends and I love giving you a hard time, you know I will always have your back." I tugged her shoulder, rolling her toward me so we were face to face. "Our history might not be perfect, but it goes back a long way."

"It does," she whispered.

I pushed her hair off her forehead. "And you matter to me."

"Okay. That's enough." She looped her arms around my back and hauled me on top of her.

"Enough what?"

"Convincing. Our hall pass is good for one more blizzard bang, but that's it!"

"Works for me." Kneeling between her legs, I lifted the T-shirt over her head, eager to get on with things before she changed her mind. "Should I go get the condom?"

"Gianni." She sat up and ran her hands up my arms, over my shoulders, and into my hair. "Slow. Down."

I grinned and pulled her onto my lap, my cock trapped between us. "Good girl."

Straddling my thighs, she rocked her hips above me, sliding her warm, wet pussy over my thick, hard cock. She moaned softly, her hands in my hair, her tongue in my mouth, her breasts pressing against my chest. I put my hands on her perfect ass, and held her tight to my hips. It took all my strength not to come as she moved on me.

When I begged her to stop for a second, she laughed and kissed my jaw and throat before whispering in my ear, "What's the matter, Gianni? Too hot to handle?"

Growling, I flipped her onto her back, and she squealed.

over my own stomach." I hopped out of bed. "And then it will be *you* that makes fun of *me* for the rest of our lives."

"Maybe." She giggled, rolling to her side and watching as I blindly felt in my bag for the condom. "Doesn't mean I wouldn't like it."

I looked over at her. "Now you're just talking crazy."

"Hey, you're the one who told me to say what I'd like in bed, and now you're judging me for it."

"I'm not judging you." My fingers closed around the condom and I stood up, tore the wrapper with my teeth and rolled it on. "You just keep surprising me is all."

"In a good way?"

"Definitely." I took a running leap back onto the mattress. "Have I mentioned how glad I am that the rooms at the Pineview Motel only have one bed?"

She laughed. "I can't say I'm sorry either."

"Look at us agreeing on something." Taking her by the arm, I pulled her onto my lap again. "Now where were we?"

"You were there." Ellie straddled my thighs again, taking my cock in her hand and giving it a few tight pumps with her fist before positioning it beneath her. "And I was right about here."

I held my breath as she slowly lowered herself onto me one hot, wet inch at a time, pausing occasionally to move up and down as she eased my hard length inside her. Her fingers clung to my shoulders. Her eyes fluttered closed. Her mouth fell open. When her ass finally rested on my legs, she exhaled slowly and opened her eyes.

My cock throbbed once inside her. Her lips curved into a wicked smile.

"Not. Yet," she whispered as she began to move. "You have to wait for me."

"Oh fuck. I want to," I said, my voice cracking. "I really

even look at you."

She laughed, grinding against me. "Okay, then just close your eyes and let me have my way with you."

But it didn't matter whether my eyes were open or closed, whether my hands were on her skin or fisting the blankets, whether I held my breath or inhaled the intoxicating scent of her hair. I was completely lost to the sensation of being inside her as her hips circled and swiveled, to the idea that she was using me for her own pleasure, to the insane realization that this wasn't a fantasy—she was actually here in this room, in this bed, riding my cock like she'd never felt anything this good.

Asking God to grant me a little more control than I was capable of on my own, I wrapped an arm around her back and buried my face in her breasts, sucking one nipple, taking it between my teeth and flicking its stiff little tip.

She cried out and moved her hips faster, and I felt the telltale rush of heat unfurling at the base of my spine—but at that point, all I could do was pray she was with me. Her voice rose in pitch and my lower body tightened, and then I was coming inside her in hot, feverish bursts while she continued to move above me. I panicked that I'd finished way too soon, but the moment my orgasm subsided, hers began, and I felt her body contracting around me in quick, rhythmic pulses that rendered her silent and slowed the movement of her hips to near stillness.

When she caught her breath, she realized my head was still cradled in her arms and dropped her hands. But I stayed where I was, an arm around her back, my forehead tipped against her chest.

She squirmed. "Let me go."

"Never." I wrapped the other arm around her. "You're mine now. And I'm going to keep you locked in this room to

"Gianni, come on." But she laughed, and the sound made me feel ridiculously happy. "I need to get up and stretch out my legs."

"Fine." I released her, and she carefully lifted herself off me and then headed for the bathroom.

A couple minutes later, she came out and I went in. When I returned to bed, she was bundled up under the covers on her side of the bed, facing the opposite wall. I got in on my side, fully prepared to observe her no-touching rule.

I was lying on my back, eyes closed, just drifting off when she surprised me yet again by rolling over and tucking herself along my side.

"What's this?" I asked, wrapping an arm around her. She'd put my T-shirt back on.

Her cheek rested on my shoulder. "This is staying warm, that's all."

"Okay, so to be clear—we're not cuddling?"

"We are not cuddling. And don't get any more ideas."

"Don't worry. Even my body has limits. I definitely need a break before morning."

She slapped my chest. "You can put that thought right out of your head. This is over. We used both your condoms anyway."

"True." I stroked her back for a moment. "It was fun while it lasted."

"It was." She laughed softly. "I don't even want to tell you this because you'll get smug, but that's the most orgasms I've ever had in a night."

"Fuck yeah, it was." With my free hand, I thumped my chest a couple times, caveman style. "But you know, as much as I would like to take all the credit, you deserve some too."

"Gee, thanks."

"I mean it. You were vocal about what felt good and what

"Maybe." She started to play with my chest hair. "Or you're just talented."

"In the spirit of our truce, let's say both are true."

"Works for me. But tomorrow, the truce is over, okay? We can't start getting along all the time. My entire life would feel like a lie."

"Deal. I'd never be able to stop messing with your head anyway. It's too much fun—maybe not as much fun as the banging, but a close second."

She was silent for a couple minutes, but I knew she wasn't sleeping because her fingers still tickled my sternum.

"Ellie. Can I ask you something?"

"Sure."

"What made you say yes to the second time?"

Her answer didn't come right away. "It was what you said. About having my back."

"Really?"

"Yeah. Something about that made me feel really safe."

"Good." I was weirdly touched that she'd used those particular words, that I'd made her feel safe. Had I ever made anyone feel safe?

"It was the acknowledgment that no matter what things are like on the surface, our history runs deep. I felt like you were being truthful when you said I matter to you."

"I was."

"So that's what pushed me over the edge—the notion that you'd never really do anything to hurt me, and you'd protect me if it came down to it."

I swallowed. "I would."

Except now I was thinking about something—that stupid offer from Fiona Duff. I hadn't told Ellie about it. Was that the same as a lie? Would she see it as a betrayal? Would it hurt her to know that I'd kept that to myself?

I swallowed, then spoke quickly. "Fiona Duff offered me the final spot on the 30 Under 30 List. And—and the cover of that issue of *Tastemaker*."

It took her a second to process it, and then she sat up. *"What? When?"*

"When she gave me the check for tonight. You were already in the car, and she and her daughter ambushed me."

"Why didn't you say something earlier?"

I sat up too. "I don't know. You were so upset already, and it seemed like it would be adding insult to injury. I couldn't bring myself to do it."

"Until you fucked me."

"Ellie, don't," I said forcefully. "You know that's not true."

"I don't know what's true right now." Her voice had grown softer, quieter. Sadder.

"You can scream at me if you want," I told her, half hoping she would.

"What good would that do?"

"I don't know. Make you feel better?"

"It won't. I wish it would, but it won't. The truth is, I wasn't impressive enough to get the gig. You were."

"The circumstances going in weren't equal," I argued. "It wasn't a level playing field."

"It doesn't matter anymore."

"I told Fiona I wouldn't do it."

She shook her head. "Gianni, don't be stupid. Take the spot."

"No."

"It'll be good for you—and for Etoile."

I hesitated. "That's the only reason I'd do it. For Etoile. For Abelard. If you thought it would help."

"I'm sure it would." She sighed. "It'll be great publicity for the summer rush."

Ellie gathered the blankets closer to her chest. "You're leaving? Already?"

Exhaling, I leaned back against the headboard. "I had an offer for another show, and if I take it, I'd have to leave by the end of March."

"Another reality show?"

"Yes."

She was silent a moment. "When did you get this offer?"

"A couple weeks ago."

"You've known for weeks that you're leaving at the end of March and you're just telling me this *now*?"

"I haven't decided whether to accept or not. I'm still thinking, and I want to talk to your parents. I don't want them to think I'm abandoning Etoile."

"Well, that's exactly what they'll think because that's what you're *doing*!"

"Ellie, come on. This is a hard choice for me to make. You know I love Etoile and being in the kitchen."

"I don't know anything for certain right now. A moment ago, I thought I did—and then you started talking, and everything turned upside down."

"I haven't decided anything yet. And I was going to talk to you about it."

"Well, now you have." She thumped a hip into the mattress and turned away from me, gathering the covers at her shoulder and scooting to the farthest edge of the mattress. "Goodnight."

"Can't we talk about this some more?"

"There's nothing to talk about. If you want to do the show, do the show. And you'd be stupid to turn down Fiona's offer."

"I don't want it."

"It's a great opportunity, Gianni." Her tone was insistent.

want."

"And you'll never speak to me again?" At the thought, my chest grew painfully tight. "Is that it?"

"I'll speak to you as long as we're working together. And when you leave, you won't care anyway."

"Yes, I *will*, Ellie. That was my whole point tonight."

She looked over her shoulder. "About having my back?"

"Well . . . yes."

She turned away from me again. "Go to sleep, Gianni."

"I can't. Not if you're mad at me."

"Oh, Jesus. I'm not mad at you. I'm mad at myself. Now will you sleep?"

I wanted to keep talking, but what would be the point? In her eyes, I'd won a prize that she'd coveted, I was abandoning her family, and I'd hidden it all from her until right after we'd had sex—and all of it confirmed the idea she'd had about me from day one. I was kicking myself for confessing it all tonight, although I wasn't sure it would have gone any better if I'd waited. Actually, it might have gone worse.

She was always going to be hurt.

Sighing heavily, I lay down again and stared at the ceiling.

I didn't want that stupid magazine cover. I wasn't sure I wanted to do the show. And I had mixed feelings about leaving Etoile so soon.

But one thing I knew for sure—I hated that tonight had ended this way. If I had more time alone with Ellie, I was sure I could make her understand my side of things. That I hadn't hidden anything from her on purpose. That I was trying to protect her feelings as long as I could. That I wasn't leaving Etoile because I was unhappy or thought it was too small town or something. That tonight had meant something to me beyond just having a good time.

But tomorrow, we'd get up and drive home, and she'd

—she'd likely ignore me entirely. I probably wouldn't be able to get a rise out of her anymore. All the ground we'd gained inside Room 13 at the Pineview Motel would be lost.

Unless we were still stranded here.

There was that possibility—two feet of snow might keep us buried another night.

But I didn't want to leave it to chance.

CHAPTER 10
ELLIE

I lay awake for hours, struggling to make sense of my feelings.

There was the obvious hurt that Gianni had been offered the 30 Under 30 spot and *Tastemaker* cover when I'd had my heart set on it, but after the initial anger and humiliation wore off, I didn't think that's what was bothering me.

I mean, could I blame Fiona Duff for wanting to put him on the cover? He'd sell magazines. He'd get online hits. And *Tastemaker* was a business that had to worry about its bottom line, not just about rewarding good or interesting work.

I wasn't all that stunned by the news that he'd been offered another reality show either. Honestly, I'd figured that was inevitable. It had never made sense to me why he'd come back to Michigan anyway, let alone signed a six-month contract with Abelard to open Etoile. And if he took the offer, I'd be rid of him.

So what was my problem?

After I'd sorted through it all a hundred times, I was left with one thing—I didn't want him to go.

But that was absurd! Why wouldn't I want him to go? It's not like I'd miss him. I'd miss his skill in the kitchen at Etoile

And as for the personal feelings, well . . . there weren't any. At least, there wouldn't be any as soon as the stupid oxytocin wore off. Just because he'd given me a few orgasms and we'd had some laughs tonight didn't diminish what he'd done to me his entire life, which was ruin my nice things for sport.

My sharp crayons. My dolls. My Cherry Princess moment. My pride.

And now he'd gone and ruined sex for me too. How was I supposed to find another guy so patient and yet so sizzling hot? A guy I felt comfortable enough with to boss around? A guy who could rile me up with half a smile? A guy who turned me on and drove me crazy in equal measure?

Then again, maybe it was good he was leaving. The last thing I needed was to develop any kind of weird attachment to Gianni Lupo. He'd been bad news my whole life, and this only proved he was bad news now. In the morning, I'd make sure he knew I wanted him to take the offer, and I wouldn't even be resentful or bitter about it.

Good riddance.

I must have drifted off at that point, because the next thing I knew, the sound of a door slamming yanked me from a deep sleep. I sat up and saw Gianni standing in front of the door, stomping snow off his boots. His wool coat was dusted with snow too.

"Morning, princess."

"Is it *still* coming down?" I asked in disbelief.

"Hard." He brushed off his coat, pulled off his gloves and tossed them aside.

"Is your SUV totally buried?"

"*Dead* and buried."

"What do you mean, *dead*?" I watched as he removed his boots.

"Tried that. Didn't work."

My jaw dropped. "So now what?"

"Now we wait for a tow truck."

"A tow truck?" I got out of bed wearing just Gianni's white T-shirt and ran for the window, throwing open the drapes. Immediately, I was blinded by the brightness. Everything was white except the pale gray sky, and the snow continued to fall. The parking lot hadn't been plowed, and most of the cars from last night were still buried.

"Yeah, but the nearest towing company is backed up all day. We're going to be here a while." He crossed behind me and went over to the closet.

"No!" I faced him. "We can't! We have to work today. I've got tastings, and the restaurant opens at five. We're booked!"

Gianni laughed and shrugged out of his coat. "Ellie, no one is on the road today. The tasting room and Etoile are officially closed, along with every school and most businesses in northern Michigan."

"How do you know?"

"Because I already talked to Des and Kanani."

"What time is it? Is she still at the front desk?" Kanani was the night manager. She normally left by eight each morning.

"It's nine-thirty, and yes she's still there. She said she can stay until Toby or Winnie arrives."

Toby was the daytime manager. He and Winnie could handle anything, but I still felt panicked. "What about Des? Did he make it there?"

"Not yet, but he's doing his best to get there as quickly as he can." Gianni laughed as he hung up his coat. "He says he might snowmobile in."

"What about the guests stuck at Abelard? If the restaurant is closed, how will they eat?" Etoile wasn't open for lunch,

"Relax. Kanani was able to put out a continental breakfast, as always, and together she and Des will manage something for lunch."

"What about dinner?"

"I've got that covered too—Trattoria Lupo is closed today, so my dad will go over to Abelard as soon as he can get there and put something together in Etoile's kitchen."

"Well, what about us? What are we supposed to do?"

Gianni stretched out across the foot of the bed, head propped on his hand. "Don't worry, I planned out our whole day. First, we'll make snow angels for two hours, then we'll go ice skating, and then we'll eat a whole roll of Tollhouse cookie dough as fast as we can, and then—to finish?—we'll *snuggle*." He gave me his most charming grin.

"Gianni!" I stamped my foot. "This is no time to quote Buddy the Elf. That isn't prop snow out there, it's the real thing! And this is a real emergency! We're stranded here, and I want to leave."

"I do too, but we can't go anywhere until my car starts and the roads are clear, and that could be a while, so we might as well make the most of this unexpected opportunity to spend more time together."

I folded my arms across my chest. "If you think I'm going to sleep with you again, you're crazy."

"I don't think that."

"Good." Sighing, I dropped my arms and closed my eyes. "This sucks."

"Come on. It could be worse."

I opened them and stared at him. "How?"

"You could be trapped with someone a lot less fun than me. You could be trapped alone. You could be trapped in a burning building."

"I guess this is preferable to *that*," I muttered. "But I still

"I definitely will."

"In the meantime, I guess I could make some coffee." I glanced at our kitchenette. "What should we do for breakfast? Gas station treats?"

"We could, but I asked Rose in the office what the options were, and she said we could snowshoe up the highway to her sister Mae's diner. It's open."

"We don't have snowshoes!"

"Rose said the motel owns some they rent out, but we can use them for free."

"How come that diner is open but everything else is closed?"

"I asked that too, and she said Mae lives above the diner and has been open every single day for twenty-seven years. Apparently, it's a point of pride."

I nodded. "I wish I had some snow pants. That snow looks deep."

"You don't have to go. If you want, I can go and bring food back."

"So that you can tease me about being such a princess that I can't go out in the snow? Forget it," I snapped, heading for the bathroom. "I can manage."

Thirty minutes later, Gianni and I were trudging up the road with snowshoes and poles borrowed from Rose. The snow was a foot deep at least, and continued to fall in thick, heavy flakes, although the wind wasn't as bad as it had been last night. Still, it was freezing cold, and I could hardly feel my nose, toes, or fingers after just a few minutes. My pants were warm.

Even so, I was happy when we reached our destination—an old, two-story house whose clapboards had been replaced with vinyl siding with an addition off to one side. A wooden sign out front read Mae's Diner, Open 365 Days a Year. Several snowmobiles were parked outside the place, and it occurred to me we hadn't seen a single car or even a plow on the road.

The front walk had been shoveled at least once this morning, so we took off our snowshoes and carried them up the steps onto the porch. Leaving them outside the door along with our poles, we entered the diner. It was a small place—really just one big room—with polished oak floors and furniture. Despite the fact that it was late January, Christmas lights were still strung up, shining in all their multi-colored glory. It was blissfully warm and smelled delicious, like bacon and savory potatoes and something sweet too, maybe donuts. My mouth watered as my toes thawed.

A plump silver-haired lady who looked a lot like Rose came bustling over to us, a coffee pot in her hand. "You must be the two Rose called me about. Come on in and sit wherever you'd like," she said. "Not too busy this morning, so plenty of options."

We thanked her, and I followed Gianni across the room to a booth where I slid in across from him. It was set for two, with upturned mugs on a paper placemat featuring different birds of North America. Mine was a tufted titmouse, which I hoped Gianni wouldn't notice. After removing my hat and gloves, I unbuttoned my coat and pulled my arms out of the sleeves.

"Want me to hang it up?" Gianni offered.

"No, thanks."

Mae came by a minute later with menus and the coffee

ones I ever seen, and I seen a lot. I wasn't even sure Harold—that's my son, he just lives across the street—would make it over to cook this morning, but he did." She chuckled with pride. "Otherwise I'da been cooking *and* serving today. Sign says three-sixty-five, and I mean three-sixty-five. Never been closed a single day in twenty-seven years."

"That's what we heard from Rose," said Gianni. "So what should I have?"

"The farmer's omelette," said Mae without hesitation. "With a side of breakfast sausage and toast. We make our own sausage here, and you don't want to miss it."

"Sounds perfect." He handed her the menu back.

"I'll have scrambled eggs and bacon please," I said. "And a side of breakfast potatoes."

"You got it. Any juice for you?"

Gianni and I both shook our heads, and Mae left to put our order in with Harold.

Alone again, I picked up my thick white coffee mug and took a sip, carefully avoiding Gianni's eyes.

"So are we going to talk?" he asked.

"About what?"

"About what I told you last night."

"I don't see what's to talk about," I said evenly. "You should take the offers—both of them."

"Are you saying that because you want to be rid of me?"

I hesitated. "Partly."

He laughed. "At least you're honest."

"Always. And I think that's what had me so upset last night. I felt like you'd been dishonest."

"Ellie, I just needed time to think the offer through—I was going to tell you. And the *Tastemaker* cover . . ." His eyes pleaded with me to understand his position. "I couldn't tell you right away. I didn't want to hurt your feelings."

"That's true."

"And the next you were like, 'and while I'm here at your back, rubbing my dick on your butt, let me just stick this knife in and twist it a little.'"

He laughed, then quickly straightened his face. "Sorry."

I shrugged. "And maybe it's not really what happened, but that's what it felt like in the moment."

"I get it," he said. "And I really am sorry."

I took another sip of coffee and tried to ignore the way my heartbeat was quickening at his puppy dog eyes. "But let's forget about me for a minute. What do *you* want?"

Gianni lifted his coffee to his lips and thought about it. "I want to wake up and feel alive every day. I never want to dread going to work. I never want to be bored. I want to challenge myself to do new and different things. And most of all, I want to prove Mrs. Peabody wrong."

For a second, I was confused. "Wait. Mrs. Peabody, our fourth-grade teacher?"

"Yeah. She once told me I'd never amount to a damn thing."

My jaw dropped. "She said that to your *face*?"

"Yeah. She said I was lazy and stupid, a waste of her time, and I'd never amount to anything."

"That's horrible."

"I mean, looking back, maybe I can't blame her, since I was always missing assignments, constantly talking and fooling around in class, breaking playground rules."

"But she was an *adult*, and you were a kid."

"Yeah. I never told anyone about it either—not my parents or my brothers or my friends. But I never forgot it." He focused on his coffee again, like it was no big deal, but something struck me.

"She was an adult and authority figure, so you believed her." My heart ached for the nine-year-old kid who must have been devastated to hear his teacher say such mean things. "Gianni, it wasn't true. I mean, maybe you weren't well-behaved, but you weren't stupid."

"I wasn't smart like her favorites though. She preferred the brainy, quiet kids like you. The ones who sat still with a book and actually read it. I couldn't sit there for a *minute* without looking around and trying to think up some other way to pass the time, even if it meant getting in trouble."

"Your talents just weren't obvious to her. I bet she's the one who feels stupid now. Look how far you've come."

He shrugged. "Maybe I should thank her. Sometimes when I feel like giving up on something, I remember what she said."

I smiled. "Think she watched *Lick My Plate*?"

Gianni laughed. "God, I fucking hope so."

"If she came into Etoile, would you poison her dinner?"

"No way. I'd make sure it was the best meal she ever had." He grinned at me over his mug. "And for dessert, I'd make her eat her words."

I chuckled as I set down my coffee. "Always a bitter dish. Anyway, if you're feeling stuck or bored at Etoile, Gianni, you should go."

"That's just it—I'm not feeling stuck or bored. I really love Etoile, and if it weren't for this offer, I wouldn't leave before my contract was up."

"Tell me about the offer."

While we waited for our food and the blizzard continued outside, Gianni explained the idea behind Hot Mess. My side hurt from laughing so much, and I nearly spit coffee, but I could understand why he had a feeling it would take off—especially with him as host.

be really hard to walk away."

"Then don't."

Mae appeared with our food. "Are you ready?" she asked with a grin.

"I sure am." Gianni moved his coffee mug and tapped his bird placemat. "You can put it right here on my nuthatch."

I shook my head as Mae set down two enormous plates of food. Gianni would always be a ten-year-old boy at heart.

Our meals looked delectable, and we eagerly dug in. The last real meal either of us had eaten was nearly twenty-four hours earlier, and we were both ravenous. I wasn't sure if that was the reason the food tasted so delicious, but it did. The eggs were fluffy and perfectly done, the bacon was thick but crispy, and the potatoes had the perfect amount of crunch to each bite. Gianni said his omelette was fantastic, and traded me some house-made breakfast sausage for a piece of bacon and a forkful of potatoes, which he stole off my plate.

"So you say do the show?" he asked thoughtfully.

"Yes. If it takes off—and I bet it will—you can probably write your own ticket after that. Maybe the network would give you that travel show you want."

"Maybe," he said. "The main reason I don't want to do the show is that it involves zero cooking." He ate another bite of his omelette. "What if I'm bored?"

"Think of it as a stepping stone. You said yourself, the money is great. After it's over, you can invest in a passion project."

"That's what my dad said." Gianni smiled. "You two think alike."

My face grew hot. "Hey. You said that secret would stay at the Pineview Motel."

"I did, that's right." He pushed some food around on his plate. "How about I trade you a secret in return?"

He kept his eyes on his fork. "My mom had breast cancer last year."

I gasped and sat up straight, setting my fork down with a loud clank. "What? Gianni! How did I not know that?"

"She didn't want anyone to know about it."

"Well—is she okay?"

He nodded. "She's okay now. It was non-invasive and she had a lumpectomy and six weeks of radiation. She's considered in remission now, because her last scan showed no sign of cancer."

"I can't believe it." I wiped my hands on my napkin. "Does *my* mom know?"

"Yes. Your parents were the only people to know outside my immediate family."

"They never said anything!"

"She didn't tell them right away. I think she was worried your mom would cancel the plans to go to France. She didn't want to be the reason they didn't go."

"But you can't go through something like that alone. You need friends around you!"

"She had my dad. He cut his work hours way down to be with her more, and that's why I took over at Trattoria Lupo last summer. Actually, that's why I came home in the first place."

I nodded slowly. Now it made sense. "I didn't know that."

"I never told anyone." Gianni picked up his fork and started eating again. "After she finished radiation, my dad was able to go back to work. He told me I didn't have to stick around, but I was glad when the offer from your parents came in to open Etoile. Not only because I liked the concept and the setting, but because it gave me a reason to be around home a little longer . . . just in case."

"But everything is okay now?" I asked with concern. I

easygoing and spontaneous, to the point where I often wondered how she and my mother were such good friends.

"Everything is okay now," he said.

I exhaled in relief, putting a hand over my heart. "Poor Aunt Coco. I wish I'd have known."

"Honestly, I wanted to tell you a bunch of times. But I had to respect my mom's wishes."

It struck me how devoted Gianni was as a son, and I admired him for it. "That had to be tough for you—not saying anything. Were you scared?"

"Yeah. My family is everything to me." His tone was fierce and sweet at the same time, and my heart cracked open a little more.

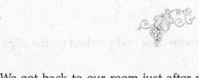

We got back to our room just after noon, stuffed and sleepy. "I'm too tired for snow angels," Gianni said, falling face first onto our bed.

"Same." I sat on my side and pulled out my phone. I had texts from Des and Winnie telling me not to worry about anything and asking me to call them when I could, and I had a voice message from my mom.

"Hi honey, just calling to check on you and see how everything went last night with the tasting. Looks like the weather is awful at home. Call me when you can. Love you."

I knew I should call her back, but I didn't feel like rehashing the evening just yet. Instead I texted: **Everything went fine, Gianni and I ended up not driving all the way home because of the snow, but we're safe at a motel and heading back as soon as the roads are plowed.** I decided not

Then I called Des, and he picked up right away, letting me know he'd made it into Abelard on his snowmobile and would handle tastings all day for guests who were stranded. "It's actually great for the winery," he joked. "What else is there to do here today but taste wine and then buy what you like so you can drink more of it while you wait out the blizzard?"

"Good," I said with a laugh. "Thanks, Des. I'm hoping to be back later tonight, but I'm sure I'll miss anything scheduled today."

"Not a problem. Be safe on the road—it's bad out there."

We hung up and I called Winnie. Glancing down at Gianni next to me—his eyes were closed and his breathing was deep and even—I decided to take my phone into the bathroom so I could actually talk to her.

"Hello?"

"Hey." I shut the bathroom door and perched on the edge of the tub. "It's me."

"Hey! How are you?"

"Fine."

"Why are you whispering?"

"I don't want Gianni to hear me. He's asleep in the bed, so I'm in the bathroom."

Winnie laughed. "This is so insane."

"You have *no idea*."

She gasped. "Did something happen? Something happened."

"Yeah—twice."

"Shut up! Tell me everything!"

"I will, but first, are you at Abelard? What's happening?"

"Yes. Dex managed to get me here about an hour ago, but it was rough. In fact, he stayed with me so he wouldn't have

"Doing what?"

"Right now he's shoveling the front steps, but after that he's going to help Felicity and me serve lunch."

"Felicity is there too?"

"Yes. My dad brought her a little bit ago, and she's been working in the kitchen ever since. She's making soup and sandwiches."

"Please thank her for me." The tension in my shoulders eased. "So you're all good there?"

"Totally. And I think Gianni's dad is heading our way this afternoon to help with dinner."

"Are guests miserable being stuck inside?"

"Not at all! Some people wandered out into the snow for hikes, some people are just lounging in the lobby by the fire, playing cards or board games, lots of people are asking when the tasting room will open."

I laughed. "Should be soon. It's nice of Dex to help out—please tell him thanks."

"I will, now on to the good stuff! What happened with Gianni?"

"Uh, lots of things." My stomach whooshed.

"And? Was it good?"

"Yes," I whispered even softer. "Crazy good. So good I'm mad about it."

She squealed with delight. "I knew it would be."

"I didn't even have to fake the finish!"

"Good. You shouldn't."

"I know, but it's so annoying. How come I have such good chemistry with that asshole?"

"Because this has been simmering for a long time, Ell. All that built-up tension was bound to erupt."

"I guess."

"So what's the scoop? Are you guys a thing now?"

"Because it was just a blizzard bang, okay? It didn't mean anything." A knock on the bathroom door made me jump up. "Shit! I have to go. I'll call you later."

"Okay. Be safe."

I ended the call and pulled the door open. Gianni stood there with his hair matted and mussed from his winter hat and maybe the pillow. "Sorry," he said, running a hand through it. "I drank too much coffee. I need to use the bathroom."

"It's fine. I was just talking to Winnie."

"In there?" He cocked one brow.

"I didn't want to wake you." I slipped past him into the room.

"Everything okay at work?"

"Yes. Have you heard from the towing company again?"

He shook his head. "No. They said they'd call me later this afternoon."

"Okay." I glanced at the window. "Should we try to start it again?"

"No!" he said with such vehemence that it startled me. "I mean, I'll try it again in a minute. I don't want you to have to go outside." He shut the bathroom door.

After one more hopeless look out the window—the snow-pocalypse raged on—I plugged my phone in and flopped into bed. When Gianni came out of the bathroom, he put all his winter gear on again and went outside. A few minutes later, he came back in and shook his head.

"Still dead?" I asked, stifling a yawn.

"Still dead." He took off his stuff again and looked at his phone. "And no call from the towing company. Sorry."

"Whatever." I sighed and plumped up my pillow before falling back and staring up at the ceiling. "I'm giving up on this day. And this week. Maybe this year."

"I know. But nothing is going right so far."

"Stop it." He pushed some hair off my face. "The blizzard is out of your control, and Fiona Duff is just an editor. Who even reads magazines anymore? You can do bigger and better things."

I closed my eyes, folding my hands on my stomach. "It's just embarrassing."

"What is?"

"To swing and miss."

"But better than not swinging at all, right?"

I shrugged. "I'm not sure."

"Ellie, it is." He took my hand. "Trust me. No one hits a home run off every pitch. This wasn't your pitch."

"My mother does."

"Huh?"

I exhaled, annoyed with myself for what I'd just admitted. "My mother does everything right the first time, and everything just comes easy to her. Sometimes I feel like I can't even be related to her, let alone her only daughter. She's perfect."

"Ellie, you are one *hundred* percent your mother's daughter." He linked his fingers with mine. "And no one is perfect —although you're pretty damn close."

"Stop it."

"I'm serious. You're too hard on yourself, but you're beautiful and great at your job. You're smart and professional. You're creative and loyal and you work your ass off. You can talk to anyone, probably in two languages. And in addition to all that, turns out you're an amazing fuck!"

I laughed, even though I didn't want to. "Thanks."

"You are destined to do big things, and Fiona Duff is going to kick herself for not getting you in her magazine when she could."

"I wish I hadn't told my mother about Fiona Duff. She

"It went fucking great! You sold a ton of wine and everyone there raved about the bottles you brought. Your parents are in France because they trust you, as they should, to be the face and voice of Abelard Vineyards while they're away. It's like they left their baby in your hands."

"I guess." I yawned again, suddenly exhausted. "Why am I so tired?"

"We were up all night."

"Oh yeah." A tiny smile tugged at my lips.

He moved a little closer to me and draped an arm over my waist. It felt so good I let him leave it there as I dozed off.

CHAPTER 11
GIANNI

I woke up with my arm still around Ellie, who'd rolled over to face the wall. I was surprised by how nice it felt to hold on to her while we slept. In fact, my first instinct upon waking was to pull her even closer, my body curled tightly behind hers like two spoons in a drawer.

But as soon as I realized what I was doing, I took my arm off her and rolled onto my back. She'd probably get irritated if she woke up to unauthorized cuddling. Besides, being that close to her was giving my dick ideas that I definitely couldn't follow through with. Not only were we out of condoms, but our hall pass had expired. No way was Ellie going to agree to any more sex.

Exhaling, I stared at the knotty pine ceiling of our room and faced the fact that I should probably go pretend the car suddenly started and get her home. She'd forgiven me for last night and told me she understood about leaving Etoile. What more could I ask for?

With one last reluctant glance at the curve of her hip and her dark, wavy hair on the pillow, I got out of bed, grabbed my keys, and shrugged into my coat. Opening the door just enough to slip out, I quietly closed it behind me and slogged

snow blew into the front seat. Cursing, I brushed as much of it out as I could and slid behind the wheel.

But I didn't push start.

Instead, I sat there looking at the door to room thirteen, thinking about the woman on the bed inside, and the night we'd just spent together. There wasn't a thing about it I would change, and my only regret was that it would never happen again.

Unless . . .

I frowned. No, I couldn't. That was too mean, too duplicitous, even for me. If she ever found out I'd kept her here against her will for a whole extra night, she'd never forgive me.

But she would never have to know, said an evil, horny little voice in my head. *And you'd give her lots and lots of delicious orgasms. You could make dinner for her too—just walk over to the gas station and grab a few groceries. She deserves a night that's just about her. You could make her feel so fucking good.*

I caught my eyes in the rearview mirror. No. It was wrong.

Despicable, even. We'd just reached a place that felt like friendship—we'd confided in each other. We'd aired the grievances. We'd made peace with the past and with what happened last night.

Mmm, what happened last night.

Suddenly I had a visceral memory of her naked body beneath me, of her hands in my hair, of the way she moved and kissed and tasted. I recalled how she told me to slow down, how she swiveled her hips over mine, how her orgasm had wrung every last drop from me as her pussy clenched my cock again and again.

Jesus—I opened my eyes and realized I was breathing heavily, and my dick had grown hard. I grimaced and

I looked out the windows. The snowfall hadn't abated, and the roads would still be terrible, making the drive unsafe. I took out my phone and checked the radar—the storm wouldn't let up until early tomorrow morning, and it was three o'clock already.

So really, staying one more night was the responsible thing to do, right? And as long as I could get her back by her first tasting tomorrow, which was usually at eleven, she might not even be mad. In fact, she might *prefer* the safer drive. She'd probably even *thank* me if she knew how protective I was being. She'd liked it when I said I'd always have her back, right? That's what this was. I was keeping her *safe*.

Of course, that was total bullshit, and I just wanted her to myself for one more night, but what she didn't know wouldn't hurt her. Besides, if she ever found out the truth and hated my guts for the rest of our lives, so be it. I had the feeling it would be worth it.

And really, what was my crime—wanting to be alone with her so badly I was willing to lie for it?

With my mind made up, I got out of the car, strapped into my snowshoes, and set off down the road to the gas station.

CHAPTER 12
ELLIE

When I woke up, I was disoriented. The surroundings were unfamiliar—the room didn't smell like home, the bed didn't feel like mine, and the total silence was strange.

I sat up and blinked. The room was gloomy and cold and unfamiliar, but as my eyes wandered left to right—the kitchenette, the knotty pine walls, the buffalo plaid drapes pulled across the window—the memories filled in.

I wasn't home—I was at the Pineview Motel with Gianni. We'd spent the night together. But where was he now? Shivering, I made my way over to the window and peeked out.

His SUV was still buried in the snow, which blanketed everything in sight and continued to fall. The wind whistled at the windowpanes, and the neon motel sign cast an eerie glow through the white.

"Gianni?" I called, walking toward the bathroom. But the door was open, and he wasn't in there. I checked the closet and saw that his coat was gone, as were his boots from the rug by the door. He must have walked somewhere.

Wrapping my arms around myself, I perched on the edge of the bed and listened to the howling wind, hoping Gianni

I grabbed my phone to see if he'd texted, but he hadn't. My mother had called again, and Winnie had sent a message saying lunch had gone great, Mr. Lupo had arrived and was working with Felicity on dinner, and if anything else happened with Gianni I had to text her right away.

I plugged my phone back in and sat there biting my thumbnail. What if it got dark and he wasn't back? What if he got lost? What would I do if he didn't return?

I was still huddled there, my heart drumming with concern, when the door opened and Gianni came in on an icy gust of wind, several white plastic bags in his hands. He slammed the door behind him, but a bunch of snow drifted in anyway.

I jumped to my feet, taking in his red, ruddy face. "Where were you?"

"Hunting and gathering. Acquiring provisions."

"Where?"

"First, I went to the gas station." He traipsed over to the kitchenette and set the bags on the counter, getting snow all over the floor. "Plenty of canned and dry goods, although woefully lacking in fresh organic produce and artisanal cheeses. But I managed to find enough things for dinner."

"Why do we need dinner? What happened to the tow truck?"

He shrugged. "Can't get to us until tomorrow."

"Shit!" I put my hands in my hair. "You mean we're stranded here another night?"

"Looks like it. But the snow is going to slow down after midnight, and the towing guy said he'll get to us first thing in the morning. And don't worry, we have groceries and good wine, and I will prepare and serve a delicious emergency feast for you." He pulled out a box of pasta and a couple cans of tomato sauce from the bags. "When I stopped in the office

them free of charge. You might not dine like a queen tonight, but I'll do my best to make you feel like one."

I folded my arms, watching as he stuck a couple things in the mini-fridge. "Thanks."

"And . . ." He opened another bag and pulled out a sweatshirt. Unfolding it, he held it up against his chest. "Tada. Clean clothes. I bought one for each of us."

I laughed as I took in the logo on the front. "Merch from the Pineview Motel?"

"Exactly. Now we'll have a souvenir of our romantic time here together." He tossed the sweatshirt at me. "Sorry about the size, XL is all they had."

"It's fine. Thank you."

"And." He pulled out a pair of navy blue snow pants. "They're from the motel lost and found, but Rose says they're clean. She washed them."

"Thanks." I took them from him. "Am I supposed to sleep in them?"

"No. But I thought we could take a walk." He balled up the empty plastic bags and stuck them in his duffel. "Unless you'd rather stay in, get naked, and let me do unspeakable things to your body."

"Let's take a walk," I said, stepping into the snow pants. "I could use some fresh air."

"Sounds good to me. Maybe we'll find some truffles in the forest I can use for our dinner."

"Sure," I said, zipping the pants, which actually fit nicely. "Or some sort of wild game you can take down with your bare hands. Venison or pheasant."

"I *am* good with my hands." Gianni scooped up his gloves and tugged them on, his smile turning cocky. "But you know what?"

"What?"

my body as our eyes locked and the memory of last night passed between us. I glanced at the bed, realizing we'd have to spend another night in it together. I cleared my throat. "Come on. Let's go."

We bundled up, strapped into the snowshoes we'd borrowed, and traipsed into the woods behind the motel, following a path between the birches and maples and evergreens.

Snow fell around us, but we were sheltered from the worst of the storm, and it was quiet and peaceful along the trail. Soft gray light filtered through the leafless tree branches and needles of the pines. I took deep breaths of air that smelled like winter—woodsy and sharp with cold, a hint of smoke from a nearby fireplace. A few icy breezes occasionally whispered through the trees, but the loudest sound was from the snow crunching beneath our feet. My muscles grew warm.

Neither Gianni nor I spoke for a while, and I surprised myself when I broke the silence with, "I was worried about you."

He glanced at me. "When?"

"When I woke up and you were gone."

He laughed, his breath creating puffs of white. "Sorry. I guess I should have told you what I was doing. But you were so tired, and I didn't want to wake you up."

"Yeah. I needed that nap."

He was quiet for a few seconds. "Are you feeling better?"

"I guess so."

"Good. Because it was only one thing that didn't happen.

"You're right." I took another lungful of bracing air. "I'll brainstorm some new ideas when we're back."

"I'd be glad to help you."

"Thanks." I snuck a glance at him, and his profile made my body feel hot beneath my clothing. "Look at us getting along. Maybe it *is* the end of the world."

"Does that mean we can have sex again tonight?"

"Nope."

"Why not? Last night was fun, wasn't it?"

"It was," I agreed. "But it happened before we were friends. Now that we have a friendship, we'd better not ruin it."

"I think I liked it better when you hated me. Is there a dunk tank around here? Or some sort of forest pond I can push you into?"

I laughed. "You wouldn't dare."

He stopped walking and looked around. "God. It's so fucking pretty here, isn't it?"

"It is." I'd gone a few steps ahead of him, but I stopped too, looking around. Then I tipped my head back to catch a few snowflakes on my tongue.

He watched me, then slowly caught up. "I know you're going to think this is bullshit, but I have to say it."

I looked at him warily. "What?"

"You're really fucking beautiful."

"Gianni, I already said no more sex."

"I'm not saying it because I want to have sex. I mean—I do, but that's not why I said it. I said it because it's true."

"Stop it. I'm a mess right now." But I could feel my cold cheeks warming. "No makeup, I didn't even brush my hair today let alone take a shower, and my nose is probably bright red."

"It is." He smiled, and for once it was genuine, not arro-

a shower isn't really an issue. By the way, this isn't anything new. I've always thought you were beautiful, but it really struck me just now."

"Oh." Self-conscious, I touched a mitten to my hair. "Well, thanks. Maybe it's good light out here or something."

"It's not the light."

I met his eyes, and my heart performed a few acrobatic tricks. He was close enough that he could have leaned over to kiss me, and I would have let him. God help me, I *wanted* him to. I imagined his tongue on mine, warm where the snowflakes had been cold. I looked at his mouth and let my lips fall open.

But he didn't kiss me.

"Should we go back?" he asked, glancing over his shoulder the way we'd come. "It's going to get dark soon. I don't want to lose our way."

"Sure. Yes. Let's go back." Flustered, I tried to pivot in place, but one of my snowshoes somehow caught the edge of the other, and my left ankle wrenched painfully. Crying out, I tipped over sideways in the snow.

"Fuck! Are you okay?" Gianni tossed his poles aside and reached for me.

"I'm fine," I said, although my ankle was throbbing. "I just twisted my ankle."

"Can you stand up?" He took me by both arms and lifted me to my feet. "Does it hurt?"

"It's not too bad." Gingerly, I put some weight on that foot. It was bad, but not excruciating. "I think I'm okay."

Gianni looked up the trail toward the motel. "It's a ways back. Do you want me to go see if I can get a snowmobile or something?"

"No!" The prospect of being left alone out here as it got dark was terrifying. "Don't leave me."

I handed him my left pole and looped my arm through his, grateful for the support. We took a few tentative steps.

"How's that?" he asked. "Do you need to go slower? Put more weight on me?"

"No, I'm good." The ankle still hurt, but something about leaning against his solid body and knowing he wouldn't let me fall was taking some of the pain away. "Just don't let go."

"I won't. And when we get back, I'll find you some ice."

"Thanks. Sorry I ruined our walk."

"You didn't ruin it. You made it more memorable. We'll never forget it."

I half-groaned, half-laughed. "No, we won't."

Slowly and carefully, we made our way back to the motel. It was dark by the time we reached our door, where Gianni helped me out of my snowshoes, then insisted on carrying me inside, taking off my boots and lowering me onto the bed. Then he pulled off my snow pants and hung up my coat.

"Gianni, I'm okay. This isn't necessary." But my heart rapped with pleasure at his sweet attention.

"Let me see that ankle."

Sighing, I tugged off my sock and hitched up my pant leg, glad I'd shaved my legs yesterday. I also made a mental note to thank my mother for encouraging me to get nice pedicures even in the winter. "See? It's barely swollen. And I can move it." I pointed and flexed my foot gently, but I winced. "A little."

"Stay there. I'm going to find some ice."

"Okay, thank you. Hey, I have some ibuprofen in my purse, could you grab it for me?"

"Definitely." He brought me my purse and a glass of water before heading out the door.

I watched him leave, wishing my pulse wasn't galloping

It was better that he hadn't.

Ten minutes later, Gianni returned with a plastic bag of ice. "Rose is the best," he said, stomping the snow off his boots. "She even gave me an ACE bandage to wrap it."

"Aw, that's so nice."

"But first, let's get some ice on it." Gianni grabbed a kitchen towel, wrapped the bag of ice in it, and placed it on the bed. Then he carefully lifted my leg below the calf and placed my ankle on the ice.

"I can still move my leg," I said, laughing. "You don't have to do that."

"Fuck off and let me take care of you."

"Okay, but your bedside manner could use some work."

He sat on the bed, where he examined my ankle from all sides. "Doesn't look too bad."

"It isn't. Honestly, it's fine."

He touched the top of my foot. "You have very small feet."

"Don't make fun."

"I'm not, I'm just stating a fact. And your toes are cute."

"Thank you." I noticed the way his eyes were moving from my foot to my calf and up my leg and felt warm. "How about some wine?"

He jumped up. "Sure. I'll pour you a glass and then start dinner. I'm getting hungry."

As soon as the door shut behind him, I took a couple big, deep breaths. Inhale. Exhale. Inhale. Exhale.

I couldn't stop thinking about his hands on my skin.

Twenty minutes, 400 milligrams of Motrin, and one glass of wine later, I was able to put some weight on my foot.

"I'm going to take a shower," I said, limping over to my bag and taking out my clean underwear, socks, cosmetics case, and the sweatshirt Gianni had purchased for me.

"Okay," Gianni said from the stove.

"I can help you with dinner when I get out."

"I don't want you on that foot. I've got this." He glanced over his shoulder at me, a grin playing on his lips. "But let me know if you need help in the shower."

Rolling my eyes, I hobbled toward the bathroom. "I'm fine, thanks."

But I wasn't.

As I shut the bathroom door, I leaned back against it and put a hand on my fluttering stomach. While I got undressed, all I could think about was the night ahead. Hour after hour alone in the dark with him, sharing that little bed with the memory of his body on mine fresh in my mind. The memory of his kiss. Of his tongue. Of those orgasms.

God, why couldn't he have been shitty at sex? Clumsy and selfish, with no clue what to do with his hands or his mouth, let alone his dick? Why did he have to know just how to touch me? The right things to say? Exactly how to move? No one had ever made me feel that good—desirable, wanted, sexy.

And he was being so sweet today. I thought I'd seen all his sides, but maybe there was more to him than a big ego and a hot body.

I just wouldn't think about it, that was all. I'd take a nice, long shower and think about other things—special events I could do at Abelard this summer, engaging social media

winemakers in the region about what they were doing.

Distracted by business, I began to feel better. The water at the Pineview Motel didn't get very hot, of course, and I had to keep most of my weight on one leg, but I managed. In my cosmetics case, I'd discovered tiny travel bottles of my shampoo and conditioner, so I even managed to wash my hair.

After I got out, I dried off, wrapped the towel around me, and combed through my wet hair. Since there was no blow dryer, I'd have to let it air dry. I hung up the towel on a hook, and pulled on my clean underwear, socks, and the XL sweatshirt. It was huge, even bigger than Gianni's sweater from last night, so I didn't feel too self-conscious coming out of the bathroom in it.

When I opened the door, I was greeted with an aroma that made my mouth water—tomatoes and garlic and herbs and fresh bread. But how was that even possible?

"What are you making?" I asked, limping up behind Gianni. A pot of pasta was boiling on one burner, and he was stirring sauce on the other. On the counter was olive oil, a few dried herbs and spices, the bottle of white wine, and something wrapped in foil. "Why does it smell so good?"

"Rose gave me a loaf of bread she baked today and I sliced it open, brushed it with melted butter and garlic powder, and warmed it up on the stove. It's wrapped up there." He nodded toward the counter. "And this is going to be our spaghetti pomodoro."

"Wow. I'm impressed."

"Good." He tasted the sauce and added a little more salt. "Rose also offered me a frozen bag of spinach—she said her husband won't touch the stuff—and as soon as the sauce is done, I'll use the pan to sauté it with some white wine."

"Speaking of wine." I poured us each another glass,

"Nothing. I told you, I've got this." He glanced at me and smiled. "You look cute. How's the ankle?"

"Thanks. It's okay." Hating the way my heart beat a little faster at the compliment, I took my wine over to the bed and sat down. "I think I might try to get ahold of Winnie."

"I just talked to my dad." Gianni drained the spaghetti in the sink.

"You did? Is he at Abelard?" Leaning back against the headboard, I extended my legs in front of me.

"Yes. All good. Apparently, he's got Winnie's sister in the kitchen, and he likes her so much he's about ready to offer her a job at Trattoria Lupo. Says she's quick on her feet and a fast learner."

I smiled. "That's Felicity. She's crazy smart. She just moved back from Chicago to start her own catering company."

"Oh yeah? Now which sister is she?" He returned the pasta to the pot. "Aren't there like twenty MacAllister girls running around?"

"No, but there are five," I said, laughing. "Millie is the oldest—she's the event planner at Cloverleigh Farms. Then Felicity—she went to culinary school, and she worked in restaurants for a while but for the last few years she's been a food scientist."

"Really? Like test kitchen stuff?"

"Yes," I said, enjoying the view of Gianni moving capably and confidently at the stove. He still wore his jeans and white shirt from last night. It was a wrinkled mess, but the sleeves were rolled up, exposing his solid forearms, and he looked so good, perfectly at ease in the small kitchenette as he made dinner for us without one word of complaint about the lack of gourmet ingredients or luxury appliances. I recalled undressing him last night, and what his body had looked like

comforting feeling spread from the center of my belly to the tips of my fingers and toes. Realizing I'd stopped speaking, I refocused on what I was saying. "And then after their dad married Frannie Sawyer, they had twin girls, Audrey and Emmeline. They're in high school now."

"Jesus." Gianni shook his head. "That's a lot of girls in one house. I feel bad for their dad. No way could I handle that."

"I take it you don't want kids?"

He added the sauce to the pasta and stirred it. "I don't know. I've never really thought about it in any real way. I'm not ready to grow up myself yet, you know? How the fuck would I manage raising a kid?"

I laughed. "I can't imagine."

"Babies make me nervous."

I set my wineglass on the table next to the bed. "*Babies* make you nervous?"

"Yes! They're so tiny and breakable, and they need so many things. You constantly have to feed them or change them or carry them around. And they're *always* there. You have zero freedom once you have kids." He picked up his wineglass and turned to face me. "My cousin Sam said after his wife had a baby, they pretty much never left the house again. And it's not like they stayed in and had sex all the time —he said they never even did it anymore because they were always too tired or the baby interrupted them."

"Yes, well, babies don't really get the concept of waiting until it's convenient to need things."

"Exactly." Gianni took a drink. "Plus, having a kid with someone is like a major commitment. You basically have to be willing to spend the rest of your life with that *one* person."

"You don't think you could be faithful to one person?" Okay, this was good. Something negative about him.

"I could be *faithful*," he said finally, staring into his glass.

"Why is that?"

His shoulders rose as he met my curious gaze. "I really don't know."

"Come on. There must be a reason."

"When things start to get serious, I just get fidgety or something. I feel like it's time to move on, so I do. I've never felt like *this is it, this is the one I'll want forever.* It's not just with relationships—it's with jobs, apartments, cities. It's like I'm never satisfied with where I am and always need the rush of a new thing."

"But maybe you're not giving the thing or the person you *have* a chance. Maybe the rush would be replaced by something even better."

He thought about that for a minute. "But that's a risk."

I laughed. "Yeah. It is."

"And what if I take it and feel nothing? Or what if I take it and I'm not good at it? Or what if I like the something better, but the other person doesn't?" He shook his head. "My way is better for everyone involved."

"In that case," I said, "keep using those condoms. You should not get married or have kids."

"Told you." He lifted his glass to his lips. "By the way, I bought more at the gas station. Just putting that out there in case you felt like reconsidering the whole no-more-sex rule."

"I won't." But my stomach jumped as I reached for my phone. "Give me a minute to call Winnie."

"Wait, what about you? Do you want kids?"

"Sure. Someday." I shrugged. "I loved growing up at Abelard and think it would be a great place to have a family. I want to teach my kids all the things I've learned about farming the land and family history. I want to take them on trips and cook with them . . ."

"Thanks." I paused. "For what it's worth, I think you'd be good at it too."

"You do?" He seemed genuinely surprised.

"Sure. Look at the way you took care of me when I hurt my foot today."

"Yeah, but you're a grown adult. I mean, you're small like a child, but you're not a baby."

I narrowed my eyes at him. "I'm trying to say something nice about you."

He laughed. "Sorry. I just meant that taking care of you is not the same as being responsible for a baby. When I walked out of here, you were fine."

"It *is* true that you cannot walk out on a baby."

He cocked his head. "But I do sometimes think it would be fun to teach little kids to cook, like my dad taught me. I need some nieces or nephews or something."

"You should do classes," I suggested, "although they'd probably fill up with women hoping you'll cook shirtless."

He grinned. "Is that your way of requesting I get naked right now?"

"No." I hit Winnie's number. "Keep your clothes on, please."

Gianni turned around again, whistling "Fever," and I shook my head. It was actually good to hear him say all this stuff—it confirmed my opinion of him as the kind of guy who was never going to be right for me. I wanted commitment, he wanted freedom. I wanted a family, he wanted independence. I wanted deep roots, he wanted to be a tumbleweed.

When we left here tomorrow—and please, God, let it be tomorrow—he'd accept that TV show offer and tumble on back across the country to Hollywood . . . and from there, who knew? But I probably wouldn't see him much once he was gone, and even if that tugged at my heart in a way I

every day.

When I got Winnie's voicemail, I left her a message. "Hey, Win. We're stuck here another night, but hopefully we'll be on the road early tomorrow. The snow is supposed to slow down after midnight, and the towing company told Gianni they can get to us first thing in the morning. I hope everything is going okay there—call me if you can. Love you, and thanks for everything."

After I set my phone down, I watched Gianni wipe out the sauce pan for a moment, but mere seconds had gone by when I started to feel that heat rising in me again. Suddenly I had the crazy urge to walk up behind him, wrap my arms around his waist, press my cheek to his back.

What would his reaction be? Shock? Laughter? Confusion? Would he give me that cocky grin that said *I knew it*? Or would he be so surprised he wouldn't even have a smart-ass response?

And what if this was my last chance to feel the way I'd felt last night? To experience that rush? To share my body so freely? To be that close to someone so warm and solid and beautiful?

I rose to my feet and walked toward him, unsteady on my one bad ankle, my hands clenched at my stomach, my pulse racing, my breath caught in my lungs.

CHAPTER 13
GIANNI

"Okay," I said, setting the clean sauce pan back on the stove. "I just need a couple minutes to—"

But then I couldn't speak, because Ellie's arms suddenly twined around my waist, her hands slipping beneath my untucked shirt. I went completely still.

Her palms slid over my abs, making them clench. I swallowed, still unable to find words. Was this a dream?

"Gianni," she said, her voice low and breathy.

My cock surged to life at the sound of my name on her lips. I tried to swallow again and couldn't. "Yeah?"

"Remember last night when you asked me if I ever wanted to just rip someone's clothes off and go at it?"

Oh, fuck. "Yeah?"

Her hand moved down over the growing bulge in my jeans. "Now I know the feeling."

I spun around so fast I knocked the pan to the floor, and it banged loudly against the wood. But Ellie was already dragging the shirt over my head and reaching for the button on my jeans. As soon as I yanked her sweatshirt off her body, our mouths came together in a searing hot kiss punctuated by breathless panting and the frantic tearing off of our clothing.

my mouth. Her fist in my hair. I felt possessed by the urge to get inside her, like the clock was ticking down those seven minutes and I was never going to have the chance again. She'd never let me do this again. I'd never be this close to her again. It was all *now, now, now.*

She winced when I moved her backward toward the bed, and I remembered her bad ankle. I lifted her off the ground and she wrapped her legs around me. But instead of placing her on the mattress, I turned toward the wall next to the stove and put her back against it. And without stopping to think, I pushed inside her.

She cried out with every deep, powerful thrust, her nails clawing at my back. I buried my face in her neck and my cock in her body and lost every ounce of control I'd ever had. I knew I should stop, but I didn't. I couldn't. God help me, I didn't want to. The feeling of being inside her with no barrier, nothing between us, was so incredible I actually *didn't even fucking care* what the consequences might be. I just wanted to be that close to her. I wanted to fill her body with mine. I wanted to do something I'd never done before—and I'd never had sex without protection, ever—and share something with her I'd never shared with anyone and fuck, fuck, fuck, it was so good and she was so hot and she wanted me, she wanted me badly enough to give in like this, and move like that, and make those sounds and say those words . . .

"Don't stop," she begged, her breath hot on my lips. "Don't stop, don't stop, don't stop . . ."

I cursed and groaned and fucked her harder, so hard I was afraid I'd hurt her or we'd take out the wall or possibly shake the foundations of the Pineview Motel so violently the whole place would be reduced to rubble and we'd die here.

I did not want to die here.

But I didn't want to stop either.

"Hurry," she panted.

I ran over to my bag and tore open the new box of condoms. As I rolled one on, the touch of my own fingers threatened to push me over the edge, and I prayed she was as close as I was. Vaulting onto the bed from where I stood, I stretched out above her.

She wrapped her arms and legs around me, her lips parting, her breath quick and shallow. I lowered my mouth to hers as I eased inside her again, thinking the condom was probably a good thing—maybe the barrier would take away just enough sensation to grant me an extra minute or two before I lost control.

This time, instead of pounding inside her like a maniac, I went a little slower, reveling in the feel of her skin, the smell of her hair, the taste of her lips. If I never had this with her again, I wanted to remember every little detail.

The way she rocked her hips beneath mine. The way she clung to my shoulders. The way the dark, damp strands of her hair spilled onto the pillow. The soft whispers, the sharp cries, her head falling back, the arch of her spine, the tightening of her body around my driving cock.

And then I couldn't hold back anymore, and the room went silver as I plunged into her again and again, until I was empty and breathless, nothing but hammering heart and shuddering muscles and warm, tingling skin.

"Good idea." Her voice was muffled, and I realized it was because her face was buried under my chest.

I lifted my upper body off her. "This was *your* idea."

"I meant about the condom," she panted.

"Oh. That. Yeah." I still couldn't catch my breath, and I wasn't sure if it was from exertion or from the way her warm brown eyes were looking up at me with actual affection.

"I wasn't thinking."

"It did. I thought you said—"

"I changed my mind."

"What was it, the ice? The sweatshirts? The cooking?"

"It wasn't anything in particular. I just thought it would be fun." She pushed against my chest. "And it was, but let me up now."

"No."

"What? Gianni, I can't breathe."

I rolled onto my back but kept my arms around her, pulling her closer to my side. "There. Now fucking snuggle with me, dammit. I know I haven't showered in thirty-six hours, but deal with it."

She laughed, shaking her head. "You're insane." But she pulled the covers over us and stayed where she was, laying her head on my shoulder. "And you actually still smell good."

I didn't, but I liked that she thought so. "See? Isn't this nice?"

"I suppose it's kind of nice." Then she gasped. "We didn't leave the stove on, did we?"

"No. We knocked a pan over, and I thought we might take out that wall for a minute, but no damage was done."

"Good."

Neither of us spoke for a minute, and I started to think maybe she was right and I was insane, because the thought running through my mind was something like, *I could get used to this.*

It was so jarring that I couldn't breathe for a second. I didn't like getting used to things—that was always the beginning of the end, wasn't it? That meant I'd get restless and want to move on.

But this felt so fucking good, holding her this way, after

For a second, I understood what my dad meant when he said, *I just knew.*

But that was nuts. What the fuck did I know? Sure, this felt good now, but inevitably, we'd grow tired of each other. Wouldn't we? We didn't want the same things at all. She didn't even *like* me that much. She was only here with me now because she couldn't leave—and if she ever found out I'd kept her in this motel room an extra night just for fun, she'd fucking murder me in my sleep. And I was leaving soon.

I began to breathe normally again.

I was leaving soon, and she'd be glad when I was gone. She'd admitted it at breakfast this morning. She wanted me to go.

My stomach broke the silence between us by growling loudly.

Ellie laughed and sat up. "Hungry?"

"Starving. I never go this long without a meal."

"Sorry," she said, a wicked twinkle in her eye. "I distracted you."

"You can distract me like that any time you want."

She started laughing.

"What's funny?"

"Your hair," she said, reaching over to tousle it. "I've never seen it so messy."

Swatting her hand away, I got off the bed and backed toward the bathroom, arms wide, stark naked. "This is the real me, babe," I said, feeling oddly vulnerable and yet completely at ease. "Eat your heart out."

CHAPTER 14
ELLIE

After dinner, which we ate at the tiny wooden table near the window, I told Gianni I'd take care of the dishes.

"You shouldn't be on that foot," he scolded, following me to the kitchenette with his plate.

"It's fine." Standing at the sink, I pushed up my sleeves. "I can stand on it for the ten minutes it's going to take me to wash a couple plates and forks. Go take a shower, you need it."

He wrapped me up in his arms from behind. "I thought you said I smelled nice."

"I'm trying to get rid of you," I said, gently elbowing him in the gut. "Go away."

"Okay, but if it's still puffed up like that tomorrow, you should let me wrap it. And maybe call the doctor when we get back."

"Yes, *Dad*."

Gianni laughed, and a moment later I heard the bathroom door shut and the water come on, the pipes squeaking and shuddering with age and effort.

I washed the couple pans Gianni had used, our plates and

glasses and brought them over to the bedside tables.

Stretching out on the mattress, I took a sip and leaned back against the headboard—and that's when I realized I hadn't stopped smiling for hours. In fact, this was the most fun I'd ever had with a guy. It was almost enough to make me wish I hadn't told him to accept Hot Mess . . . if he stayed, was there hope for us? Or was I crazy?

I set my glass down and picked up my phone, discovering I'd missed a call from Winnie. She'd left a voicemail.

"Hey! Hope you're still doing okay, everything is good here. Dinner was a huge success, and Dex is driving me home now. Felicity stayed to help close up the kitchen, and Gianni's dad is going to take her home. If we need her tomorrow, she said she can be here anytime. Call me if you can, and I hope you're still, um, enjoying yourself." She laughed. "I cannot wait to hear all the details."

The shower was still running, so I decided to give her a quick call.

"Hello?"

"It's me," I said quietly, keeping an eye on the bathroom door. "Are you home?"

"Still on the way."

"How are the roads?"

"Shitty, but the snow has slowed down a lot. I don't think you'll have trouble getting back tomorrow."

"As long as we get a tow truck," I muttered.

"Oh that's right, his car won't start. Is it the battery?"

"No idea. He says he tried to get a jump, but it didn't work." I thought for a moment. "Although I don't know who he asked."

"Are you guys the only ones staying at that motel?"

"No, there are other people here. In fact, only one room was available last night. And there are still some cars in the

was dead, although I couldn't put my finger on it.

"So how are things going? What did you guys do all day long, stay in bed?"

"We have definitely spent some time in bed, but we did other things too." I told her about snowshoeing to the diner and the walk through the woods, including the part where I twisted my ankle.

"Oh, no! Is it bad?"

"It hurts, but I don't think it's a serious sprain."

"How'd you get back to the motel? Did Gianni carry you?"

I smiled. "He probably would have—turns out he's got kind of a chivalrous streak—but I was able to walk back with his help."

"Chivalrous streak?" Winnie laughed.

"Yeah. Who knew?"

"Actually, it doesn't surprise me. I could see that about him, especially with you."

"Why especially with me?"

"I don't know, just the way he looks at you sometimes. Or the way he gets jealous if you mention another guy."

"He does not!" The shower went off, and I lowered my voice. "You're nuts."

"I am not! You've never noticed how he reacts when you bring up a dude you once dated or someone you think is hot?"

"Yeah, he puts them all down and makes fun of my taste. He's been that way since high school."

"Because he was jealous, Ellie. He had no chance with you, and he knew it."

I thought about what he'd said last night. *I lied and read your name off so I'd finally get to make out with you. I didn't think I stood a chance otherwise.*

"What are you talking about?"

"Seven Minutes in Heaven!" I whispered frantically, my eyes on the bathroom door. "He lied and said he'd pulled my name so he'd have a chance to kiss me."

Winnie gasped. Silence. And then. "I *knew* it! What the actual fuck happened in that closet!"

"Listen, it's too much to explain right now, but I'll tell you later."

My bestie groaned, and I could hear Dex laughing. "But what does this *mean*? Are you guys a *thing* now? Is this finally happening?"

"No!" But I bit my lip. "We're having a good time together, that's all. And getting to know each other better. But I still don't trust him—not completely."

"Trust him with what?"

But that was when he opened the bathroom door, and appeared in just a towel. He held it together at one hip, and it dipped low enough that I could see the V lines on his lower abs. His hair was damp and messy. His jawline and upper lip were scruffy. His blue eyes were sapphire bright.

My insides tightened. My heart fluttered. I might have drooled.

"Listen," I said to Winnie. "I have to go. I'll call you tomorrow."

"But—"

"Bye." I ended the call and set my phone aside without taking my eyes off Gianni, who'd stopped moving and stood next to the bed.

"So can I sleep naked?" he asked.

"You're asking my permission tonight?"

He lifted his broad shoulders. "I guess."

My eyes wandered over his body, igniting my desire. "Drop the towel."

you told me to eat my heart out. What if I'm hungry?"

He let go of the towel and it fell to the floor.

God, he was so fucking beautiful. Every inch of him.

But especially those eyes, and the way they were looking at me, like he knew he should have gotten his fill, but had to have more.

I wasn't sure what had taken my inhibitions prisoner, but suddenly I had zero shame about what I wanted. Maybe it was the wine. Maybe it was the end of the world. Maybe it was some sexual confidence in myself that this time with him had shaken loose from its moorings and set adrift.

Whatever it was, it felt good, and I realized that I might never have the opportunity to explore it again—there was a certain freedom in knowing that what happened here wouldn't follow us home.

I got on my knees. I took off my sweatshirt. I watched as his eyes lit up and his cock jumped.

I smiled, getting on my hands and knees, and looked up at him coquettishly. "So what you said last night still applies, right?"

"What did I say?"

"What happens at the Pineview Motel stays at the Pineview Motel."

"Sure." He blinked at me with those thick black lashes. "But is this really happening? Because I've had this fantasy many times."

"It's really happening. But tell me what I do in your fantasy."

"You crawl toward me wearing nothing but that pageant crown and put your mouth on my cock."

"Well, I don't have a crown, but I can make the rest happen." I smiled seductively and licked my lips. "Come here."

"Lie back."

He obeyed, falling to his elbows. "What's gotten into you tonight?"

"I don't know." I leaned over, bracing a hand on either side of his torso, and pressed my lips to his stomach. His skin was thin there, and warm, and the muscles beneath it were hard and firm. My breath made them quiver.

I shook my head slowly, brushing my mouth back and forth over his skin. I heard him inhale, felt his hands in my hair, gathering it at the back of my head. I sensed his eyes on me.

"I like it. Whatever it is." His voice was quiet and held no trace of the usual teasing tone.

I glanced up at him briefly, curious if he was smiling. He wasn't—in fact, he looked so serious, his face was almost unfamiliar. But still gorgeous, and even more intriguing with his eyes on me that way, like he wasn't sure who I was either. "I guess I just want to thank you for dinner."

That made him crack a grin. "Yeah? Gas station spaghetti puts you in the mood, huh?"

"It wasn't the spaghetti." I moved my mouth down one side of his rib cage, toward the erection that was thickening between his legs. Without touching it, I licked my way up one side of the V, from the top of his thigh to his hip.

"Oh, fuck," he breathed as I moved to the other side and did the same thing. "Then was it the snow?"

I laughed before circling his belly button with my tongue. "No."

"You just—really love knotty pine?" He faltered mid-sentence, probably because I began nipping at the tip of his cock with my lips.

"Never been a big fan, actually." I hesitated. "Although I

"Same. I'm gonna get a big fucking hard-on—in my great-grandma's basement—every Christmas." He struggled for words as I took his length in one hand and swirled my tongue around the crown, tasting him for the first time. He groaned, his fingers tightened in my hair. "Christ. You gotta tell me—what I—did."

I paused what I was doing. "You really want to know?"

"Yes." He was breathing hard. "But you can keep it brief."

Giggling again, I took the tip in my mouth and sucked gently. "You told me the truth."

"The truth about what?"

"About not pulling my name from the hat. About why you didn't kiss me. About wanting a chance with me but thinking you'd never get one." With each example, I stroked his cock with my tongue. "About why you came back here. About the offer for the new show." I glanced up at him. "And for calling me the unattainable girl of your dreams."

"It's true," he said seriously. "It's all fucking true."

"Well, it *was*." I lowered my head, taking him in deep, then kept my lips tight around him as I slowly lifted it. "I think you might have to revise that post-blizzard. I believe you have attained me several times."

"I'd like to attain you again before it's over," he said, groaning as I took him to the back of my throat once more.

And then he lost the ability to speak in sentences, but communicated plenty with curse words hissed through a clenched jaw and long, drawn-out moans, his fists in my hair and his abs rippling as his hips flexed. I used both my hands, working them up and down his solid length as I sucked and stroked him.

At one point, he pulled my hair so hard it hurt, and I gasped.

"Good." I went right back to what I was doing, and quickly discovered he hadn't been exaggerating—in less than fifteen seconds, his body went stiff, his breathing stopped, and his cock got even harder before it throbbed rhythmically between my lips, a hot stream pulsing against the back of my throat.

Pleased with myself, I sat back on my heels and wiped my mouth with my wrist.

Gianni's eyes were closed, his mouth open. His arms rested limply at his sides, his chest rose and fell with labored breaths.

"Are you okay?" I teased.

"No." His eyes opened and he lunged for me, and I squealed as he tossed me beneath him sideways across the bed.

"Aren't you tired?" I asked as he buried his face in my neck and kissed my throat.

"Nope." His mouth traveled down my chest and he stroked my nipple with his tongue before sucking it greedily. "I do need a little recovery time, but I have plenty of ideas about how to fill it." He tugged my underwear off and put his head between my thighs.

Turns out, he didn't need that much recovery time, which suited me just fine, because he made me come so fast with his fingers and tongue.

"Let me do it this time," I said when he jumped out of bed to get the condom.

He brought it to me, and I unwrapped it and rolled it on, knowing this was the last time we'd ever do this. Tomorrow, the sun would come up and the snow would melt and we'd leave our little oasis here at the Pineview Motel. We'd go back to our regular lives. Our real lives.

And as he moved inside me and our hands grasped and

one thought I absolutely could not afford to entertain, no matter what.

I don't want this to end.

CHAPTER 15
GIANNI

I hardly slept that night.

The room went from inky black dark to hazy gray as morning light filtered through the curtains.

Beside me, Ellie slept peacefully, facing me. Her thick, gingerbread-brown hair spilled onto the white pillowcase behind her head except for one wayward curl that trailed down her cheek. I brushed it back off her face, and her eyes opened. Outside in the sun, they'd be a light brown with flecks of honey, but here in the faintly violet light, they appeared dark as molasses.

"Hey," she said softly. "Is it time to get up already?"

"You don't have to. I didn't mean to wake you."

"It's okay." She rolled onto her back and stretched, her bare arms rising above the sheets. It was hard to believe that just two nights ago, our first night here, she'd demanded we sleep with clothes on. We'd been naked together in this bed a good portion of the hours since, including right now.

I wanted it to last a little longer.

Reaching for her, I gathered her close to me, and she put an arm over my chest and her head on my shoulder. We

"Remember when we got here and you said there would be no cuddling?" I asked her.

She laughed. "Yeah."

"You were so wrong about that."

"I was wrong about a lot of things."

My heart stumbled across its next few beats. And then I blurted out something *really* fucking dumb.

"My car is fine."

She looked up at me, confused. "Huh?"

Fuck! What was I doing? Why did I keep telling on myself?

But I kept going. "My car. It's fine. It's not dead."

She bolted upright and stared down at me with hard, narrowed eyes. "You said yesterday morning it was dead. You said you tried to jump it, and it still wouldn't run. Now it's been miraculously resurrected?"

"I made it up. It was never dead."

"Oh my God!" Ellie jumped out of bed, wincing at the pain as she hobbled over to the window and peeked out the curtain.

"Be careful on that foot," I said weakly.

"All the cars out there yesterday morning were totally buried—how did I not see it then? The snow would have been disturbed if you'd tried to get a jump." She whirled around to face me. "You asshole! You kept me prisoner here!"

"Ellie, let me explain."

"I trusted you—like you said I could—and you took advantage of it!"

That one hit me like a punch in the stomach. "You *can* trust me."

"No. I can't. I don't know why I thought I could. I must have been crazy." She looked around and spied her sweatshirt

"But I want to talk about this. Please?"

"Not a chance, Gianni." She spoke through clenched teeth. "All you do is lie. It's very clear to me now what this was to you—a game, just like everything else. A big scam to get me in bed."

"You're wrong!" I got out of bed and went over to her, taking her by the arm.

"Am I?" She wrenched her arm free and blinked at me. "Let's see. You hid the truth about Fiona's offer. About your TV show. You faked a dead car to trap me here another night. Jesus, was everything you said to me in here a bunch of bullshit?"

"No! Everything I told you was true."

"And why should I believe that?" She put her hands in her hair. "God, I'm such an idiot!"

"You're not—will you please hear me out?" I followed her around the room as she limped around gathering her clothes and tugging them on—underwear, pants, socks. "I only lied about the car to have one more night alone with you."

"Well, there's something we agree on—you're a liar."

"But it wasn't just to have sex! I honestly wanted you to myself for another night. Being with you was the most fun I've ever had with anyone!"

"Too bad it was all bullshit," she snapped, shoving things in her bag. "Just one more example of Gianni Lupo treating the world like his playground. You probably arranged the blizzard too. Winked and smiled at Mother Nature, and she gave into you like every other girl does."

"Don't be ridiculous. I just sent a text to God. He's a fan of *Lick My Plate.*"

She stopped moving and glared at me with daggers in her eyes.

"Okay, not the right time for a joke. Sorry." I rubbed the

"You can stop talking, Gianni. I'll never believe another word you say." She was eerily calm as she crossed in front of me on her way to the bathroom. "Get dressed. I want to leave in the next five minutes."

Then the bathroom door slammed shut.

I sank onto the bed and dropped my head into my hands. What the actual fuck was I *doing*? Why had I confessed? All I had to do was go outside and pretend the car started this morning. Maybe she'd have been a little suspicious, but she'd probably have been so glad we didn't have to wait for a tow truck, her joy would have overshadowed her doubt.

Now she hated me again.

I fell onto my back and threw an arm over my eyes. This sucked. Usually, I ducked out of relationships before the other person involved really cared, and I was always careful not to mess around with anyone I worked with. It was too awkward seeing them in the kitchen the next day, and that was a space where I wanted a clear head, the respect of the staff, and positive energy. By telling Ellie what I'd done, I'd not only made things awkward between us, I'd ruined our friendship and polluted our working relationship.

Exhaling, I hauled myself to my feet and scrounged through my bag for some clothes to throw on—underwear, jeans, T-shirt, sweater. As I pulled it over my head, I remembered how she'd looked in it, how she'd worn it with nothing underneath, how I'd chased her around the room and pinned her beneath me and eventually tore the sweater right off her.

I pulled the collar over my nose and mouth, hoping it still smelled like her, but it didn't.

Slowly, I pulled on my coat, boots, hat and gloves, grabbed the keys from my pocket, and went outside to dig my undead car from its snowy grave.

The ride back to Abelard was long, tense, and silent. The storm was over now. The sky was blue and the sun was shining, although the temperature was close to zero, with a wind-chill of eighteen below.

But that was nothing compared to the arctic air in the front seat of my car, where Ellie sat bundled up in the passenger seat with her knees pressed together, her arms folded over her chest, and her face turned toward the window.

A few times, I tried talking to her. Results varied.

"Ellie. Can we talk about it?"

Stone cold silence.

"I'm really sorry about everything. I shouldn't have done what I did."

She harrumphed, and that was it.

"I confessed and apologized, didn't I? Shouldn't that count for something? You never would have known if I hadn't said anything."

"Because I'm a fool, right?"

Shit, that came out wrong. "No! That's not what I meant. I'm just trying to show you that I told the truth voluntarily. I didn't get caught."

"Good for you. But I'm fresh out of gold stars."

"Tell me what I can say or do to make it up to you," I begged.

"You can stop talking."

Exhaling, I gave it a couple minutes and tried again. "I didn't think you'd be so mad."

That earned me a sharp look. "I guess you don't know me very well."

"Yes, I do, Ellie! I know you better now than I ever have."

"Ha!"

know how disappointed you were with the way things turned out. I know you put your heart and soul into everything you do at Abelard because you love it and you never want to leave it. I know you feel like you'll never be as perfect as your mother expects you to be—which you're wrong about, but I'll just shut up about that—and I know what you look like naked, what your skin feels like against mine, how you like to be touched, and what sounds you make when you have an orgasm, so don't tell me I don't know you very well!" I'd managed all of that in nearly one breath and felt my heart beating hard inside my chest.

In response, Ellie reached over and turned up the radio.

I turned it down. "At least say you hate me or something."

"I hate you. Feel better?"

"No," I admitted.

She stared straight ahead and sighed. "You know what? I don't hate you. I feel nothing, which is even better."

I glanced at her. Her profile was set hard.

A minute later, when she turned up the radio again, I didn't touch it.

When we pulled up at Abelard, it was just after ten. Someone had been there with a plow already, and most of the lot was cleared, a huge mountain of snow over on one side. I pulled up close to the kitchen and turned off the engine.

Immediately, Ellie reached for the door handle and I reached over, placing a hand on her leg.

"Don't," she said, pushing my hand off her.

"Only until you leave, and the sooner the better."

"Even if I take that show offer, I won't go until April."

She closed her eyes and exhaled. "Fine. I can be professional until you go. But that's it. We're not friends."

The pit in my stomach widened. "Why can't we be friends?"

"We're too different, Gianni." Her voice had lost its edge. "What happened at the motel was a mistake."

For some reason, hearing her say that gutted me a little. "So you regret it?"

She took a second to think, which made her answer even worse. "Yes. I do."

I took my hand off her leg and let her go.

Ellie and I unloaded the car without speaking another word to each other. When it was empty, she carried the storage cases of dirty wineglasses down to the tasting room, and I brought the heavy box of unopened bottles. The silence was painful, but I knew nothing good would come of trying to soften her up today—she was still boiling mad. I needed to give her anger time to reduce to a slow simmer. Then maybe we could talk more reasonably.

It wasn't that I needed her to love me or anything, but I hated the thought that she regretted everything that had happened between us. That she'd look at me with resentment for the next couple months. That she thought I'd taken advantage of her. That it was all a joke to me. A game.

In the middle of unpacking the bottles, I looked over at her. She was pulling glasses from the storage case with her

before. I took a breath, ready to say her name, kneel at her feet, and beg forgiveness—but it was someone else's voice that broke the silence.

"Ellie!" Winnie came rushing into the tasting room. "You're back!"

Ellie turned and hugged her friend. "I'm back."

"Are you okay?"

"I'm fine."

Winnie studied her friend's face for a moment, and some kind of communication passed back and forth between them. Then she turned to me with a friendly smile. "Hey, Gianni."

"Hi, Winnie."

"You guys look beat."

"Yeah." I threw a quick glance at Ellie, who met my eyes and then looked away. "It was quite an adventure."

Ellie made a noise, something between a snort of disgust and a bitter laugh. "I need a shower."

Winnie looked at her. "You've got time. Des was already planning to cover your eleven o'clock tasting."

"Is he here yet?"

"Just got here."

Ellie nodded. "Okay. I'll check in with him and then go grab a quick shower."

Winnie turned to me. "My sister Felicity is also here again today if you want to run home and clean up, Gianni. She can handle dinner prep, no problem."

"I'll talk to her," I said. "I really appreciate her pitching in last night. My dad said she was great."

"She had fun, I think," Winnie said with a laugh. "It's been a while since she's worked in a restaurant kitchen, and she said she'd forgotten how exciting the chaos can be."

"I'm grateful she was there." My phone vibrated in my

"Just leave the bottles," Ellie said with no emotion. "I'll unpack them."

Nodding, I left the tasting room and answered my dad's call. "Hello?"

"You back?"

"Yeah." I climbed the steps and headed through Abelard's lobby toward Etoile's small dining room, which looked out over the vineyard.

"How was the drive?"

"Fine."

"You okay?"

"Yeah."

My dad paused. "Tired?" He must have sensed from my tone something was off with me.

"Yeah." I walked over toward the dining room windows. At night, Etoile was almost entirely lit by candles and wall sconces to keep the atmosphere warm and intimate, but right now, bright natural light flooded the space. "Thanks again for filling in last night."

"Of course. If you're short-handed today, Felicity said she could come back."

"I think she's here already."

"Is she?" He laughed. "Dammit. If you said you didn't need her, I was gonna see if she'd come work for me. I just lost a station chef last week."

"I might not need her. Depends on who's able to get here today."

"Okay, let me know. She might not want a full-time position anyway. We were talking last night, and she's interested in starting a vegetarian catering company."

I made a face. "I don't understand people who don't eat meat."

He laughed. "Yeah. It's a whole other way of life. But

"Good for her." It came out a little grumpier than I intended.

"You sure you're okay?"

"Yeah." I closed my eyes for a second. "Listen, I gotta go. I'm going to talk to Felicity and see if she can cover while I run home and clean up."

"Okay. Hey, Mom wants to talk. She was worried about you."

I grimaced. I didn't really have time for a worried mom thing right now, but I couldn't say no. "Okay."

"Gianni?" My mom's voice was high-pitched with concern. "You're back?"

"I'm back."

"Thank God. I'm so glad you got off the road when you did."

"Yeah."

"So what was wrong with your car?"

"Uh, nothing. It started without any problem this morning."

"Huh." Silence. "That's weird."

It was probably my imagination—or maybe my guilty conscience—but I detected a note of suspicion. "Yes. But lucky. We made it back in time for work today."

"How's Ellie? She survive the trauma of being stuck in a motel with you for two days?"

"Barely."

My mom laughed. "Well, I'm glad you two were together. It would have been terrible if she'd been alone. Tell her to get in touch with her mom, please. Mia is worried about her and says she hasn't returned her calls."

That was about the *last* thing I wanted to do, but I said okay. "I'll tell her. How are you feeling?"

"I'm fine, Mom. But listen, I gotta go."

"Okay, honey. Love you."

"I love you too."

In the kitchen, I found Felicity chopping celery and carrots. I forced a smile. "Hey, you. Stop being so good at this job. They're going to fire me."

She looked up and laughed. "Not a chance." Setting down her knife, she wiped her hands and came toward me with one extended. "Hi. I'm Felicity MacAllister."

I shook it. "Gianni Lupo. I can't thank you enough for the help."

"My pleasure." She looked around. "You've got a beautiful kitchen here. And the whole trial by fire thing was probably good for me. Saved me from being nervous—I had no time."

"From what I hear, your nerves are unnecessary. My dad is ready to make you a sous chef in his main restaurant—he wouldn't even let *me* be a sous chef. I had to bus tables and make pizzas for three years. Then he let me move up to salads."

Felicity laughed. She didn't resemble her younger sister much—Winnie was blond and blue-eyed like a California girl, and Felicity had brown eyes and hair so dark it was nearly black. "He runs a tight ship, I can tell."

"He yells a lot, you mean?"

She shrugged as she chuckled. "There may have been some yelling. But it was good—he was dealing with an unfamiliar team in an unfamiliar space, and I think we all needed someone to take charge."

"Well, I really appreciate you being here."

She gestured toward the vegetables she'd been chopping. "I know it's not on your usual dinner menu, but I soaked some cannellini beans overnight for a smoky tomato and

"It's a good day for hot soup, and that sounds delicious. What's the smoke from?"

"Harissa paste."

I nodded. "Great. Please make it, and I'll add it to the dinner menu tonight. If you're okay here, I'll just run home for a shower."

"No problem. Is there any other prep work I can do for you?"

"Probably. Let me take a look at what I was planning for tonight's menu and see what I'm dealing with. Was there a meat and fish delivery yesterday?"

"Yes."

"Good." I rubbed my eyes with a thumb and forefinger. "Fuck. I'm tired."

"Why don't you grab a nap while you're home?" she suggested. "Honestly, if you just go over the menu and prep work with me before you leave, I'll get it done."

"That would be fucking amazing. I might need to crash for twenty minutes, if that's okay. I didn't sleep much last night."

She smiled sympathetically. "I think you might need more than twenty minutes."

Felicity was right—the minute I got to my apartment, I fell face first into my pillow and slept for two hours. I woke up in a panic and jumped into the shower, but I had to admit, I did feel a little better.

Except my stomach was still in knots over how I'd left things with Ellie. Every time I thought about the things she'd

Ellie was special to me. She wasn't just a friend. She was part of my history, close to my family, a piece of home. She was someone I respected and admired. Someone I had fun with—okay, often at her expense, but she could give as good as she got. I loved that about her. Had I taken her for granted?

On the drive back to Abelard, I tried to think of something I could do to convince her I wasn't the evil villain she thought I was. I tried to think about what my dad would do, about what he'd done in the past when my mom was really mad at him. But he always seemed to be able to soften her up with just a look. A hand on her back. If I tried to touch Ellie, she'd probably kick me in the balls.

Flowers? Candy? A hedgehog?

Spying a grocery store, I pulled into the lot and ran inside. Their bouquets weren't terribly impressive, but they were better than nothing. In line, I also grabbed a bag of M&M's from the candy rack.

I arrived back at Abelard around three and instead of heading for the kitchen, I went down to the tasting room and peeked in. She stood behind the long counter pouring small glasses of wine for about eight people seated at the bar. Her blouse was pink today, and it reminded me of the color in her cheeks on our walk in the woods. Then she laughed, and the sound made my chest hurt. But when she looked up and saw me standing there, her smile faded. "Excuse me," she said. "I'll be right back."

She came to the arched entrance where I stood, her back straight and her face impassive. Her hair was down, which surprised me. She looked beautiful, but I couldn't help thinking she was even more stunning first thing in the morning, no makeup, her hair a mess, her skin warm and soft against mine.

"Your hair looks pretty."

"Thank you," she said stiffly.

I held out the flowers and candy. "I brought you some roses and M&M's."

She eyeballed them like they might explode or squirt water in her face. "Why?"

"Because I'm sorry. Because I want to be friends again. Because they didn't have hedgehogs at Meijer."

"Friendship cannot be bought, Gianni."

"I don't want you to hate me."

She sighed, shaking her head. "I told you—I don't hate you."

"Okay, well, I don't want you to feel *nothing* for me."

She tilted her head, her eyes penetrating mine. "What is it you'd like me to feel?"

"I don't know. Something," I said pathetically. "I don't want you to walk away regretting everything."

"Don't you?"

"No! That was the most fun I've ever had with anyone. I didn't want it to end—that's why I lied."

For a moment she said nothing, then she took a breath. "I had fun with you too, Gianni. I just don't like being misled. I feel like you batted me around like a toy because you were bored."

"That's not it at all," I insisted. "I just wanted you to myself a little longer, and I knew once we left that place, whatever we had would end. It was a dick move, and I'm sorry. I don't even know why I told you the truth, I should have just left it alone."

"I know why you told me the truth," she said. Like it was obvious.

"You do?"

"Yes. To ruin things."

ber? You ruin things on purpose."

"But that's about *relationships*," I said defensively. "That's not about—about what we have."

She raised her hands. "Look, I don't want to argue. Let's just leave what happened between us where it belongs, back in room thirteen at the Pineview Motel."

Exhaling, I dropped my eyes to the floor and noticed she wore flats instead of heels. "How's your ankle?"

"A little sore."

"You shouldn't stand all day. Can you sit behind the counter?"

"Maybe. But I should get back in there. Are we done?"

"I guess. I came here to make things better, but I'm only making them worse." I searched her eyes. "Will you accept my apology?"

"Yes. On one condition."

"Name it."

"We go back to being co-workers, nothing more. And nothing like that ever happens again—you keep your hands to yourself."

"Fine."

"I'm not done. I want you to be professional around here. Stop giving me a hard time. No more coming in here just to fuck with me—this is *my space*. You stay out of it."

"I can do that. Scout's honor."

She raised her eyebrows. "You were a Boy Scout?"

"For about ten minutes. Until the snacks ran out."

She rolled her eyes. "Of course. I have one more condition."

"Name it."

"You accept the offer to do Hot Mess."

I cocked my head. "You really want to get rid of me, don't you?"

did what you had to do—opened Etoile. Started the fire. Now that it's burning, you're free to go. There's no reason to stay, right?" Her tone was defiant, almost like she was daring me to argue with her.

"I guess not."

"So go."

I nodded, even though something about this felt off. "Okay. I'll go."

"Good. Then I'll accept your apology." She glanced over her shoulder. "I have to get back in there. I'll be up in time for the first seating."

"Okay."

Then she surprised me by taking the roses and M&M's from my hands.

"I thought friendship couldn't be bought," I said.

She hugged them to her chest. "We're not friends." Then she turned and walked away, leaving me with a smile on my face.

And an ache in my chest.

CHAPTER 16
ELLIE

Later that night, after I was finished at Etoile, I met up with Winnie in the kitchen—my family's personal kitchen, not the one at the restaurant, where Gianni was still closing up. I was exhausted, but I'd promised Winnie we could have a glass of wine so I could give her the full scoop on the last two days.

I opened a bottle of wine, poured two glasses, and put some light snacks on a platter for us—cheese, crackers, nuts, dried fruit, olives. It reminded me of sitting on the bed with Gianni, a pile of gas station snacks between us. Definitely less sophisticated, but no less tasty in the moment. I remembered his idea about a tasting with good wine and inexpensive snacks—I still liked it. Maybe I'd add it to the summer lineup of events.

As I was setting the platter on the marble kitchen island, I heard a knock on the back door, which I'd left unlocked for Winnie. Then it opened. "You here?" she called out.

"I'm here. Come on in." I brought the two glasses of wine to the island, sat on one of the counter stools, and ditched my flats. "How were the roads?"

"Not too bad. Dex actually let me drive myself." She took

changed into jeans and a blue cowl-necked sweater that brought out the color of her eyes. It was a shade that would have looked nice on Gianni too, although his eyes were a deeper blue than Winnie's. "But I have to text him when I'm leaving, even though he's already asleep."

"He's working tomorrow?" Dex was a firefighter and worked twenty-four-hour shifts, starting at seven in the morning.

"Yes. So I'm not in a rush to get back tonight, since he's gone to bed already." Her eyes gleamed over the rim of her glass as she took a sip. "Tell me *everything*. The *long* version."

I started with the disastrous dinner at Fiona Duff's house —how everyone had paid so much attention to Gianni, the way I'd struggled to hold anyone's attention, the offer he'd gotten from Fiona at the end of the night.

Winnie paused with an olive halfway to her mouth. "No way. She offered the spot to him?"

"Not just the spot, but the *cover*." I shoved a dried apricot in my mouth. "I was in the car already, so I didn't hear it or I'd probably have died on the spot."

"So he told you about it when he came out?"

"No. He waited until we'd already had sex, of course. He must have felt guilty or something."

"Okay, back up." Winnie reached for another olive. "I need to know how the sex got started. When you two left here on Monday, you swore you wouldn't sleep with him if he was the last guy on earth."

"And I meant it." I frowned. "It must have been the blizzard. I think I lost my mind."

Her eyes grew big as I told her about pulling off the road, finding the Pineview Motel, and discovering our room only had one bed.

"I was not pleased," I said, able to laugh about it now. "The two of us stood there staring at it, and there wasn't even a couch or anything for one of us to sleep on. We *had* to share the bed."

"So then what?"

"Then there was some crying, some wine, some junk food."

"Crying?"

"I was upset about the evening—and mind you, I didn't even know about the offer he'd gotten yet. I was just disappointed in myself and embarrassed that I'd let such a great opportunity slip through my fingers somehow."

"I'm positive that had nothing to do with you and everything to do with *Lick My Plate* and Fiona Duff's bottom line."

"Maybe. Anyway, we just hung out—sat on the bed and drank wine and ate shit and played Truth or Drink on my phone."

Winnie laughed. "Did you learn anything interesting about him?"

"Not really." I munched on a cracker. "He's pretty much exactly who you think he is—a twenty-three-year-old guy who loves food and sex and never wants to sit still or grow up. Al*though*," I went on coyly, "he did surprise me in one way."

"Which was?"

"He's very good in bed," I admitted. "Generous. Patient. Attentive."

"Stop skipping ahead!" Winnie grabbed her wineglass. "How did it *happen*?"

I tried to recall exactly how we'd ended up naked between the sheets. "We had a big fight about something, and he ended up chasing me around the room."

"What was the fight about?"

closet." I explained what had actually gone down that night, and Winnie's jaw nearly hit the marble counter.

"Shut up! So after all that, you *asked* him to kiss you and he didn't? After lying to get you in there and then going through all that trouble to get you to say yes?"

I nodded. "It was infuriating. And humiliating. Anyway, he sort of roped me into giving him a second chance at that kiss, and then things went on from there."

"So was it just the one time?" Winnie asked.

I popped an olive into my mouth. "Nope. It was so good we did it again like an hour later, and *I* initiated it. And there was no faking. Not once."

She laughed and tapped her glass to mine. "I'm very proud of you."

"We had a good time." I sighed and took a sip of wine. "It wasn't until afterward that things went south. That's when he admitted that Fiona had offered him the *Tastemaker* cover, and in addition"—I hesitated here, because I wasn't sure if I was betraying a confidence by telling Winnie about Hot Mess, but Gianni hadn't said it was a secret, had he? And I trusted her. "He's leaving Etoile."

She gasped. "Seriously? Already?"

"April," I said. "He has another reality show offer. But don't say anything about it. It's not really public yet."

"I won't say a word. What's the show about?"

I gave her the gist of it, and she laughed.

"Sounds perfect for him. But kind of a bummer he's leaving Etoile."

"No, it isn't. Good riddance, if you ask me." I tried to sound like my old self, the one who couldn't stand Gianni Lupo, the one who resented him for being so hot and successful, the one who didn't know how he kissed or touched or tasted. The one who'd be glad to see him go, not

Winnie spread brie on a cracker. "I thought everything was better with you guys."

"It *was*. In fact we spent all of yesterday and last night having a really good time. And then this morning, he dropped another bomb on me."

Winnie's eyes went wide as she took a bite.

"That whole thing about his SUV being dead? It was a lie. He made it up."

"*Why*?"

"So he could have me to himself for one more night at the motel."

Winnie started to choke and had to get up and get herself a glass of water. After grabbing a glass from a cupboard, she filled it at the sink and guzzled it. Then she turned to face me. "Are you serious?"

"Yeah." Gratified by her reaction, I went on. "That asshole kept me prisoner a whole other day and night, like I was his toy."

"Wow," said Winnie. "What a jerk." Then her expression changed. "But it's kind of sweet too."

I gaped at her. "No, it isn't, Winnie! He *lied* to me. To suit his own selfish purposes. He was only thinking about himself."

She sighed. "Yeah. You're right—it was shitty of him. But it's *kind* of cute that he wanted to be alone with you that badly. And that he confessed. He must have felt bad."

"I didn't see it that way. I saw it as just one more way he messed with me. I was furious, especially since—" I stopped myself.

"Since what?"

I played with the stem of my wineglass. "I don't even want to say it out loud."

"Do it anyway."

"Maybe just one feeling." I took a breath as the memory of being skin to skin with him washed over me. "But it was a nice one."

Winnie took it in slowly as she walked back around the island to take her seat again. "Are you sure it's gone?"

"Yes. It was snuffed out like a candle as soon as he told me about the lie. Because that's when I knew he hadn't changed —he's still that same kid who tortured me all through school, and dunked me fifty times just for the hell of it, and made me want to kiss him in a closet then refused to do it. He's a game player and always will be. He's gorgeous," I went on grudgingly, "and we have some good chemistry, but he's too immature and self-centered for me. He doesn't even *want* to grow up. He just wants to run around and set things on fire. And I'd be stupid as hell to waste my time hoping he'll change."

Winnie said nothing for a minute. "Well, I guess now you know."

"Now I know," I said with finality. "And I can move on."

And I did.

At least, I tried.

It was hard with Gianni right there all the time. He accepted the offer to do Hot Mess, but production wasn't starting until April, and in the meantime, we still had to work together.

But just when I was positive he couldn't change his ways, he kept his word not to bother me anymore.

He stopped coming to the tasting room to antagonize me. He didn't tease me in the kitchen at Etoile. When we had

flirty references to anything that had happened between us. It was just like he promised.

I was totally baffled.

Worse? I missed the attention—not that I'd admit it to him.

Then one morning, about two weeks after the blizzard, he came to the tasting room to tell me he'd turned down Fiona Duff's offer.

"I hope you didn't turn it down because of me," I said, even though part of me was desperately hoping that was exactly why he'd turned it down.

"There were several reasons. You were one of them." He shrugged. "It didn't feel right."

"Oh."

"Anyway, I just wanted you to know." He gave me an impersonal smile and started to walk away.

"Gianni!" I blurted, because I didn't want him to leave.

He faced me again. "Yeah?"

I wanted to tell him how much I appreciated the gesture and give him a hug and feel the warm strength of his body against mine again. I wanted to confess that I thought about him way more than I should. I wanted to say the words—*I miss you. I pushed you away because I was scared.*

But I couldn't bring myself to do it.

"Um, thank you. For telling me."

"You're welcome."

As he walked away, I felt like crying.

Days passed.

might come in, but he never did. Every time, my breath would catch and I'd hope for something from him, some sign that he was thinking of me too, that he couldn't stay away, couldn't keep his promise.

But he kept it.

At night, I'd lie in bed and remember his kiss, his touch, his hot, hard body over mine. Sounds he made and words he'd growled. Secrets he'd shared and those I'd given up. The intensity of our connection. The pulse of his orgasm inside me. The soft, quiet moments afterward, lying in his arms. The final morning I'd woken up and thought, *maybe . . . maybe.*

But it had only been a dream. Or worse—a game of make-believe. Whatever I'd imagined between us was clearly one-sided. And if I gave into the temptation to be with him again, I'd only be handing him the chance to break my heart for real. I hadn't lasted all this time—*years* of resisting the pull of him —to fall apart now. I just needed to stay strong and wait out this agonizing interim where he was *here*, but not *with me.*

Weeks went by this way.

A month.

The snow melted, Abelard and Etoile were swamped over Valentine's Day, and an early thaw meant spring tourism would pick up even sooner than usual. I kept my nose to the grindstone and focused on my job—there was plenty to do between pruning and planting in the vineyard and working the floor at Etoile at night. I was beyond exhausted when my head finally hit the pillow. Winnie and I also planned summer events for guests, and every day I saw the glow on her face grow more radiant when she spoke about her hopes for the future with Dex.

In the meantime, I grew more grouchy and sullen. My complexion, always pale in winter, grew sallow and greenish. I didn't feel right in my skin, and all I wanted to do was nap all the time, nothing could lift me out of it—not *Friends*, not peanut butter and M&M's, not even wine, which didn't even appeal to me these days. I figured it was my body's way of telling me I'd been consuming too much sugar, alcohol, and salt, so I cut them from my diet and tried to get more exercise and more sleep. But March arrived, and I still felt bloated and exhausted all the time. Then one day I went to get dressed for work and popped the button off my pants trying to get them on.

At first, I just rolled my eyes at the annoyance—I was already running late and didn't have time to sew a button. I was rifling through the hangers in my closet, hunting for another pair of pants that would fit my bloated belly when something occurred to me.

I froze.

How long had it been since I'd gotten my period?

I couldn't remember.

Okay, don't panic, I told myself, calmly walking over to my bathroom. I looked under my sink and took out a box of tampons—it was unopened. Had I emptied a previous box and forgotten about it? I stared at my wretched face in the mirror and tried to think. I'd had one period in early January for sure . . . but after that, I couldn't recall one.

My heart began to pound. Was it possible I was *pregnant*?

With *Gianni Lupo's baby*?

I dropped the box of tampons and put both palms to my hot cheeks. No. No way. Gianni had worn a condom every time.

Except for those five minutes against the wall...

No.

I hurried out of the bathroom, refusing to believe it. There was no way those five minutes could have such catastrophic consequences.

my eleven o'clock tasting. I'd have to cancel coffee with Winnie downstairs, but I'd make up an excuse like a headache or something. She knew I hadn't been well.

And I was scared if I said *the thing* out loud, I might manifest it.

Trading my work blouse for a sweatshirt, I threw on a pair of jeans, shoved my pudgy feet into sneakers, and headed out.

Less than one hour later, I was back in my bathroom, staring at a big fat plus sign and trying not to be sick.

Two plus signs, actually, because I'd been sure the first test in the box had given me an erroneous reading. But I'd taken the second one and gotten the same result.

The test was positive.

I was pregnant.

My vision blurred and swam. Squeezing my eyes shut, I grabbed onto the sink and took a few deep breaths. When I opened them again, I stared at my reflection in the mirror. My face was gray. My eyes were bloodshot.

I was *pregnant*.

Dropping to my knees, I vomited into the toilet until my stomach was empty, my entire body shook, and tears streamed down my face.

I curled into a ball on my bathroom floor and lay there sobbing, pounding a fist against the tile floor. This was so *unfair*! It was just a blizzard bang! It wasn't supposed to have permanent consequences! I was only twenty-three and *totally* unprepared for motherhood! And what about Gianni? Jesus

What were we going to do?

At some point, I realized I couldn't stay on my bathroom floor all day—I had responsibilities at work. Guests were waiting for me. My family was counting on me.

I dragged myself off the floor and did the best I could to clean up my face, avoiding the sight of those pregnancy tests. In my closet, I found a pair of pants that fit and a top that I didn't have to tuck in. I pulled my hair back, covered my splotchy face with makeup, disguised my puffy red eyes with liner and shadow, and applied the brightest red lipstick I had, hoping it would distract people's eyes from anything else on my face.

Pausing for a couple deep breaths, I told myself all I had to do was handle a few hours of work. Then I could come back up to my room and fall apart again. Of course, I was scheduled to work at Etoile tonight, which meant coming face to face with Gianni, but I wouldn't think about that yet.

One thing at a time.

Somehow, I made it through the day.

After my last tasting, I closed up the room and went upstairs to find Winnie. I had to tell someone or I was going to go crazy.

I found her in my mom's office, which was just off the lobby. The door was open, but I knocked on it. "Hey."

She looked up, and at first she smiled, but it quickly faded. "What's wrong?"

"Got a minute?"

"Of course. Come in."

going on?" she asked, coming to sit in the chair next to me.

I pressed my knees together and looked down at them. Took a deep breath. "It's bad."

"How bad?"

I met her worried eyes. "Bad," I said, my voice cracking, my eyes filling. "And I'm so alone."

She leaned forward and took my hand. "You are not alone. You will *never* be alone. Tell me what's going on."

I closed my eyes, tears spilling over. "I'm pregnant."

She gasped, then immediately popped out of her seat to hug me. I rose to my feet and clung to her, sobbing on her shoulder. I'd held it in all day, and it felt so good to finally let everything out. Winnie held me and rubbed my back, saying nothing, just being there, which was what I needed.

After a few minutes, I calmed down enough to let her go and grab a tissue. "Sorry," I said before blowing my nose. "I just made a mess of your shirt."

"Forget my shirt," she said. "Ell, are you sure? About the —the—" She gestured vaguely at my stomach.

"Baby," I said, grabbing a second tissue. "And there's no use avoiding the word, because I'm as sure as two positive pregnancy tests can be."

"What if it was a false positive?"

"Twice?" I blew my nose again. "No. Plus, it explains a lot of other symptoms. I have not felt right in a month. And this morning, I popped a fucking button off my pants."

For a second, I thought Winnie was going to laugh, but she just pressed her lips together. "Is it . . . from the time with Gianni?"

I nodded. "Yeah."

"You guys didn't use protection?"

"We did," I protested. "Every time! Except—except for those five minutes."

were a few minutes we didn't use a condom. But I guess that's all it took. Or else the condoms failed."

Winnie sighed. "It doesn't really matter, does it?"

"Nope. It sure doesn't." I closed my eyes, fighting off more tears. "God, Winnie. What am I going to do?"

"What do you want to do?"

"I want to go back in time and tell him to get off me!"

She couldn't quite hide her smile. "I bet."

"It was just a blizzard bang!" I started pacing. "It wasn't supposed to count! You even said it wouldn't count!"

"Yeah, I guess I didn't exactly think it through *this far*."

"Clearly we didn't either." I stopped moving and buried my face in my hands. "Oh, God. I have to tell him, don't I?"

"Yes, Ellie. You do."

"Jesus, I have to tell my parents too."

"Well, yes. I mean, they'd probably notice the belly eventually."

I sank into the chair again. "My dad will be so disappointed. And my mother . . . I cannot even imagine what my mother will say."

Winnie knelt at my feet, placing a hand on my arm. "She'll be supportive, Ellie. They both will. I mean, maybe they'll even be happy."

"I'm about to make Mia a *grandmother*, Winnie. Does that strike you as something she'll be happy about?"

"Umm . . ." Winnie looked to the left.

"God." I dropped my face into my hands. "This is such a nightmare. I don't know what to do. I'm too young for this. And Gianni is worse."

"You could give the baby up for adoption," Winnie suggested. "My aunt April did that when she got pregnant at eighteen. She said she couldn't give the baby the kind of life he would deserve, and it was the hardest thing she's ever

"I thought about Chip today," I said quietly. "But I just don't think I could give a baby up. I'm not a teenager. I'm done with school, and I have a good job and a beautiful home. I could give a child a good life, I'm just . . . scared."

"Don't be." She squeezed my hand. "You'll be a great mom, even if you have to do it on your own."

"Oh, I'll definitely have to do it on my own. Gianni is on his way out of here in one month."

"But he doesn't know about the baby," Winnie argued.

"Doesn't matter." I shook my head, every ounce of my body alive with stubborn refusal. "Gianni and I talked about this, and he does *not* want to stay here. He said he wasn't sure he *ever* wanted a family, let alone right now, and I'm not about to tie him down with one."

"Maybe he'll change his mind once he—"

"No." I dug in my heels. "I will *not* be the reason he doesn't chase his dreams, or the person he blames for being stuck in a dead-end life."

"Ellie, I know you're mad at him, but I've known Gianni a long time, and I don't think he'd ever do that."

"Fine, but I'm going to make it clear that I don't expect anything from him. I don't want to be his *obligation*. I can take care of myself. And this baby." I put a hand over my stomach, and a shiver moved through me. It was the first time I'd thought of the little being in my belly in any concrete way. Suddenly I found myself wondering whether it was a boy or girl. What color eyes he'd have. What color her hair might be.

God . . . this was *real*.

"When will you tell him?" Winnie asked gently.

"I don't know." I fought tears again. "I need some time to get used to it. It's my body, and I'm the one who'll have to carry it and explain it and give birth to it."

"You're not alone, Ellie." Winnie's voice was firm and

you've always wanted kids."

I nodded, my throat closing up. I wondered what Gianni's parents would say about this . . . Would his mom cry? Would his dad be angry? Jesus, this would make them grandparents too. It was *so much* all at once. "Yeah. It's just not *how* I wanted kids. Or when. Or with who."

"I know."

The tears came again, and I slashed at them with both hands. "Fuck. I can't fall apart. I have to work."

"Can't you take a night off?"

"No. We're totally booked, and there's no one to cover me."

"I can pour wine. And I've certainly heard you talk enough about the wine list to be somewhat helpful. Let me fill in for you."

"Okay," I said, grateful for her. I needed to go upstairs and cry this out, and I didn't want to break down in front of Gianni, which was sure to happen the moment I saw him. "If you're sure."

"I'm sure. I'll just call Dex in a minute and let him know."

I swallowed hard. "Winnie, I have to tell you something else."

"Lay it on me."

"You know how I said I'd developed a *feeling* for Gianni but then it was snuffed out when I discovered his lie about the car?"

"Yeah?"

"I lied." I dabbed at the corners of my eyes with a tissue. "It's not snuffed out. It's still there, refusing to die no matter how much I try to smother it."

"Are you sure he doesn't have a feeling about you too?"

"Yes, I'm sure! He barely even speaks to me."

"But you told him not to."

want them. And he won't want this baby either."

Winnie sighed. "Why don't you take some time for yourself before you tell him, okay? Think. Breathe. And sleep—you look exhausted."

"I am exhausted," I said, taking a shuddery breath. "Okay. If you don't mind, I'll take the night off."

"Good." She stood up and looked at her clothing. "Am I dressed okay?"

I nodded as I rose to my feet. "Yeah. Thanks, Win. I owe you one."

She smiled. "I think I'd make a good godmother, if you're taking names."

Bursting into tears again, I threw my arms around her.

CHAPTER 17
GIANNI

"Night, Gianni!"

I glanced up and waved at Malik, one of Etoile's two servers, as he passed by the office on his way out for the night. "Later, Malik. See you Tuesday."

It was Sunday night, and Malik was the last to leave. The kitchen was quiet. I looked down at the ingredients list I was making and discovered I'd only written down two things, even though I'd been sitting there for fifteen minutes. Lately, I'd been doing that, getting distracted and staring off into space, losing chunks of time to nothing but daydreams and memories.

And they were all about one person—Ellie Fournier.

Every day, I expected to wake up and discover she was out from under my skin, but it never happened. I was consumed by thoughts of her, and not just about her naked body or the fantastic sex or the unbelievable blowjob, but by conversations we'd had, ways she'd made me laugh, things I'd felt comfortable saying to her I'd never said to anyone. Every memory had me sinking deeper, and frankly, I was tired of it.

It was fucking terrible! How could anyone *like* this feeling?

And why wasn't it going away? Since our two days together at the motel, I'd done exactly what I'd said I would, which was leave her alone. I avoided the tasting room, because it was her space. In the kitchen, I was polite and respectful. If we ran into each other anywhere at work, I kept things friendly but formal. I never brought up our ancient history, I certainly never mentioned our recent history, and I kept my eyes where they belonged. Actually, I tried not to look at her too much at all, because looking at her made me think about touching her, and I'd sworn to keep my hands to myself.

It wasn't easy.

I glanced at the calendar on the desk. It was mid-March, which meant I had just over two weeks left here. Would I make it without losing my mind?

What the fuck did you have to do to evict someone from your head?

I'd tried to distract myself with work—specifically, with training Felicity MacAllister, who would remain in charge of the kitchen at Etoile until the Fourniers found the right chef to replace me. They'd been disappointed when I asked to get out of my contract early, but they said they understood and wanted me to be happy. Every day, Felicity came in early to learn my routines, and every night, she worked alongside me. She was smart and creative, a quick study, asked excellent questions, had amazing recall and no ego. I had total confidence in her.

Which meant that work wasn't a good enough distraction.

And I had to see Ellie there every night! Not that she paid me any mind. She did her job with a smile on her face, but the moment she came from the dining room into the kitchen, that smile would fade. She'd look at me for just a second, and

Was she still intent on punishing me? It had been over a month already!

No. This cold silence between us was ridiculous. *She* was supposed to be the mature one, and she was acting like a child! I said I was sorry, and she said she forgave me, so why did we have to go around pretending like we were strangers? We'd had fun together, dammit! I fucking *liked* her.

Putting my pen down, I pushed my chair back and marched out of the office with my jaw clenched, determined to find her and end this nonsense.

She wasn't in the dining room or tasting room, which was locked up and dark. In the lobby, I asked Kanani if she'd already gone home.

"I think she might be in the kitchen—the family kitchen," she clarified, gesturing to a door that led to the private part of Abelard, where the Fournier family lived.

"Thanks," I said, ignoring the sign on the door that said PRIVATE. I pushed it open and headed down the hall toward the kitchen, where the lights were still on.

When I burst in, I saw her sitting at the island, eating something that looked like a janky cake pop. "There you are! I've been looking for you."

She glanced over her shoulder at me for half a second. "Why?"

I opened my mouth to go off on her, but got distracted by the thing in her hand. "Is that . . ." I squinted at it. "A *spoon*?"

"Yeah. Dipped in peanut butter and M&M's."

Then I noticed the jar of peanut butter and giant bag of M&M's on the counter. "Interesting."

She took a bite off it. "Did you come here to judge me?"

"No. I came to tell you something." Mad all over again, I strode across the room and stood next to her, chest puffed up. "Stop avoiding me. I want to be friends again."

was wrong, and I apologized. I've been good. I've kept my hands to myself, even though it's been difficult. Because the thing is, Ellie, you're hot, and I fucking like you. Okay? There it is. I like you, and I can't just *stop* liking you—believe me, I have tried. So what do you say? Can we be friends again?" I tried the old grin. "Maybe even friends with benefits?"

She kept eating that stuff on the spoon.

"Okay, bad joke. Sorry—unless you *want* the benefits, in which case they are definitely available—but I'm just saying that this silence is ridiculous. We might not get along perfectly, but you have to admit we had a good fucking time at that motel, and I don't see—"

"I'm pregnant, Gianni."

"—any reason why we can't . . ." Slowly, her words sank in. But they were out of place, not part of the script. "Wait, what did you say?"

She took another bite. "I'm pregnant."

"Pregnant?" I repeated, like I wasn't sure what the word meant.

"Yes." She looked at me over her shoulder. "Pregnant. With your baby."

"That can't be right." My vision started to go gray at the edges. "We used a condom every time."

"Almost every time."

"No, we did! I remember! I put one on every single time!"

"If you recall, there were a few minutes where we were a little irresponsible." She lifted her eyebrows, and in a heartbeat I had her back against that wall.

"But—but that was nothing! It was a moment of insanity! It was *before the finish*!"

"It was close enough." She slid off the stool and walked around the other side of the island.

"I took two. And I saw the doctor." She licked the spoon clean. "It's right."

"You saw the doctor already? How long have you known?"

"About ten days."

"You've known for *ten days* and you're just telling me *now*?" I had to grab on to the back of the stool with both hands.

"I needed some time to process it. Decide what I was going to do. And I wanted to see the doctor to be certain—which I did, last Thursday."

I shook my head. "This can't be right."

"Stop *saying* that!" Her eyes glared brightly. "I am pregnant, Gianni. And you know what? It doesn't matter if it's right or not, it's real. And it's all your fault."

"My fault!" I gaped at her. "If I recall correctly, that time on the wall was your idea. *You* were the one who seduced me in the kitchenette!"

She sucked in her breath. "*Seduced* you!"

"Yes!"

She flung the spoon at my head, and I ducked. "All I did was come up behind you and give you a hug! An innocent little hug to thank you for making dinner!"

"You said you wanted to rip my clothes off!"

She reached into the bag of M&M's and hurled a handful of them at me. "Did not!"

"Did so!" I yelled back as the little multi-colored chocolates bounced off me and clattered to the floor.

"Well, you were the one who got so carried away you shoved your junk in me without wrapping it up first!"

I went around the island and got in her face. "And you were the one who kept telling me not to stop! I was going to!"

"It's true!" I shouted, although she was right, that was total bullshit.

"Nothing you say is true! You're a liar." Her eyes were on fire, and she was breathing hard. She swayed closer to me, her voice dropping to a whisper. "You're a fucking liar. And I despise you."

I inhaled, and her scent filled my head. I'd never wanted anyone as badly as I wanted her right then.

We went at each other like wolves.

Our mouths crashed together, tongues slashing, hands groping.

I hiked up her skirt. She yanked off my belt. I tore off her underwear. She shoved down my pants.

Fuck me like you hate me.

Inside a minute, I had her up on the island, driving my cock into her again and again, savagely, furiously, like I wanted to punish her for the way she consumed my every waking moment. For the way she'd pushed me away. For making me doubt everything I knew to be true about myself. And she seemed just as eager to take her rage out on me. She turned her face away when I tried to kiss her, she hissed in my ear, she pulled my hair, she slid her hands beneath my shirt and clawed my back, she *sank her teeth* into my shoulder as her body tightened and convulsed.

But Jesus Christ, I'd never come so hard in my life—my knees buckled as my body spasmed, and I had to let go of her and brace myself on the marble.

When it was over, she shoved me back and slid off the counter. I backed into the sink and dropped my head into my hands. "Fuck. *Fuck.*"

Facing away from me, she picked her underwear up off the floor and pulled it on, tugging her skirt down. Then she was still.

around her from behind—she clearly didn't want that.

"Are you okay?" I asked.

"I'm fine."

"I'm sorry. I lost control."

"I'm not blaming you, Gianni. I lost control too. But we can't do that. We can't . . . use each other like that. As punching bags."

I wasn't entirely sure that's what we'd done, but her assessment seemed safer than admitting it could be anything else.

"Ellie. Look at me."

It took her a couple breaths, but then she turned around and faced me, shoulders back. Chin up. Lower lip trembling.

My chest was caving in. "Did I hurt you?"

"No."

"And the . . . ." I swallowed with difficulty, glancing at her stomach. "Baby?"

"The baby is fine too. It's barely the size of a kidney bean."

For some odd reason, learning its size made me want to fucking cry. I felt suddenly and stupidly protective of that little kidney bean. My knees felt weak, so I went around the island and sat down, on the stool again, burying my head in my arms.

"Are *you* okay?" she asked quietly.

"Yes. And no."

"I'm going to have it." Her tone was slightly defiant, as if she expected me to argue.

But I nodded slowly, realizing I was glad she'd made that decision, even if it meant my life had just drastically veered off course.

"I have an ultrasound scheduled for next week. You can come if you want."

"What's that?"

inside your stomach?"

She almost smiled. "Kind of. Yes."

"Who else knows about—about this?"

"Just Winnie. I haven't told my parents yet."

That surprised me. "You haven't?"

"No. I wanted to tell you first. I only told Winnie because I'd just found out and I was desperate and scared."

"Why didn't you come to me right away?"

She looked down at her feet. "I just couldn't."

I was hurt that she felt that way, but some gut instinct told me to set my feelings aside. There were other things on the counter she might chuck at my head. The knife block was barely an arm's reach away.

Something occurred to me. "The night Winnie filled in for you, when you didn't feel good. This is why?"

Ellie nodded. "That was the day I found out."

"That must have been . . . a shock."

She laughed, a bitter sound. "Yeah."

I leaned back in the chair. "When should we tell our parents?"

"I'm going to call mine tomorrow." She looked down at the marble. "I'm—I'm a little nervous about what my mother will say."

"You think she'll be upset?"

"Yeah. Disappointed."

I felt sweaty and slightly sick. "God, Ellie. I'm . . . I'm fucking lost. Tell me what to do, and I'll do it."

She shook her head. "You don't have to do anything."

"But I'm the father. I feel like I should take some kind of responsibility." Propping my elbows on the counter, I threaded my hands into my hair. "Should we get married or something?"

Her jaw fell open. "Is that a *joke*? No, we should not get

want a shotgun wedding. And you're leaving for L.A. anyway."

"Oh, fuck." I palmed my forehead. "I forgot about Hot Mess. I'll try to get out of it."

"No! You can still do it."

"But I'll be gone for months, Ellie. The shoot is ten weeks long."

"I know," she said. "But the baby isn't due until early October. And—and even then . . . you don't have to do anything drastic. I understand the career path you want. I'll be fine as a single mom."

I frowned. "This is my child too."

"I know it is, but I also know *you*, Gianni. I know what you want in life, and it isn't this baby, it isn't me, and it isn't being stuck here." Her eyes were shining, her lower lip trembled. "You like being free, remember?"

I was about to tell her she had no idea what I wanted when I remembered that wasn't exactly true—we'd talked about this at the motel.

"I know what I said," I began carefully, "but you have to give me a chance to adjust to this new"—I glanced at her belly—"development."

"You told me the Hot Mess money was too good to pass up."

"It is good money," I conceded.

"And good exposure. A stepping stone."

"But—"

"Look, this pregnancy was a mistake," she said, fighting for control. "An unintended consequence of too much time together, too much snow, one small bed, and years of pent-up tension between us. I'm not suffering any delusions that we're suddenly in love. And I'm not about to spend the next eighteen years of my life feeling like you gave up what you

I swallowed hard. "And tonight? What was that about?"

"Tonight was about anger. It was a temper tantrum, that's all."

I exhaled. Was she right?

"Go to L.A., Gianni." She spoke softly now, all the anger gone. "When you get back, we can figure things out."

I watched as the tears she'd tried to battle slipped down her face and felt like I was being torn in half. Part of me wanted to thank my lucky stars she was being so undemanding, run out the back door, and keep going until I hit California. But another part of me knew that would feel all wrong.

I remembered her telling me what *she* wanted in life—not just marriage and family, but the kind of love that filled a room. To know she was someone's everything just by the way he looked at her.

This was . . . not that.

But my chest ached at the thought of a little Lupo boy, a troublemaker like his dad and uncles, or a sweet girl with huge brown eyes that melted my heart.

Just like Ellie's were doing right now.

God, this was so fucking unfair. And as hard as it was for me, it was worse for her. She'd have to carry this baby for nine months and deal with everyone's questions and judgment. Did she really want to do that alone?

Neither of us moved for a minute, and then I got up off the stool. She remained behind the marble island like it was a protective barrier, and maybe it was. But I wanted to be close to her. Put my arms around her. Hold her. Say the words out loud—*everything is going to be okay*.

But what came out was something else.

"Ellie, I'm—I'm sorry. It's my fault."

"You can stop apologizing. It's not your fault, and I shouldn't have said that."

"Well, like you said. We had a good fucking time at that motel."

"It was more than that," I said quietly.

"Don't." Her voice trembled. "Please don't."

My hands were clenched into fists at my side. At that moment, I nearly said to hell with it and vaulted that island so I could get my arms around her, but told myself to respect her body and her wish. I'd done enough damage, hadn't I?

Forcing myself to turn around, I pushed the kitchen door open and walked away.

I barely slept that night, and when I woke up feeling like a zombie, I remembered why in an instant.

A baby. Ellie was pregnant with my baby.

And I was terrified.

I wasn't prepared to be a father. I was only twenty-three! I still felt like a kid myself! And speaking of babies, I'd never changed a diaper. Or fed an infant a bottle. Or helped a kid get dressed or cross the street or read a story.

Babies were so fragile! You had to hold them a certain way or their heads would fall right off their necks. I didn't know how to hold a baby!

I didn't know *anything*.

Plus, I'd been a fucking *hellion* as a kid—a smart-ass, rule-breaking, back-talking, brother-punching, umbrella-smashing little asshole. What business did I have trying to raise a child?

I was immature and vain and egotistical. Food and sex were my two favorite things. I had a hot temper. I liked to sleep in. I threw darks and whites into the washing machine

bed, take vitamins, or drink enough water.

I rolled over and buried my face in my pillow. Ellie would probably be amazing at all the baby stuff. She probably knew everything—what they ate and how to hold them and why they cried all the time. She'd been the perfect child, hadn't she? She'd listened to her parents and teachers. She would know instinctively how to bring up a child to be smart and kind and well-behaved. I'd know how to teach it to cook, that was all. And I couldn't even do that until it was older. Kids weren't supposed to be around stoves, right?

Maybe I'd only be in the way. Maybe Ellie really didn't need me. Maybe she didn't even *like* me. She probably figured she could do a lot better, and maybe she could.

I mean, not in the bedroom or kitchen, but maybe in other rooms of the house.

But she didn't seem to want me around. Was she just letting me off the hook by telling me to go do Hot Mess? Or did she really want me gone? I couldn't fucking tell.

Maybe I should just go do it. Give her space.

Besides, we'd need the money, wouldn't we? Having a kid was probably even more expensive than opening a restaurant. If a restaurant failed, you could close it, but a kid was your responsibility for at least eighteen years. Better to have some cushion going into it.

It was settled. I'd do the show.

I got out of bed and headed for the shower, my mind made up.

Except five minutes later, it still wasn't sitting right with me, leaving her so quickly. It felt like running away. And what were things going to be like when I returned?

I knew fatherhood was forever, and I intended to be a father to my child, but what was I going to be to Ellie? What did she want me to be? What did *I* want us to be?

Yesterday morning seemed very far away.

On the drive to Abelard, I decided I needed to tell my parents immediately. It didn't feel right keeping this from them, even though I was worried they were going to blame me for everything. But first, I'd make sure telling them was okay with Ellie.

Even though Monday was her day off too, I figured I'd find her in the tasting room as usual, but she wasn't there. I checked the restaurant, the Fournier kitchen and family room, and the front desk, but she wasn't in any of those places. Toby, busy at reception, said he hadn't seen her.

Worried, I texted her.

> **Hey. Are you working today?**

I'm not sure. Feeling a little out of it.

Even more concerned, I typed three different questions and deleted them all before sending.

What's wrong?

Duh.

Are you okay?

No, dickhead.

Can I do anything?

Yeah, fuck off.

Frowning, I typed something and hit send before I could talk myself out of it.

> **Are you hungry?**

No thanks.

While I was trying to think of something else to say, Winnie passed by me. "Morning, Gianni."

"Morning." I barely looked up from my phone, but then I thought of something and took off after her. "Winnie," I said, following her into her office. "I want to bring Ellie something to eat. What's something she likes in the morning?"

"Easy." She smiled. "She adores these blueberry scones my mom makes. You'd have to go to her bakery downtown—it's called Plum & Honey—but I promise, Ellie can't resist them."

"Thanks."

Happy to have a mission, I raced out of Abelard, drove back into town, and picked up the scones. The woman behind the counter looked familiar and greeted me by name, so I figured it was Winnie's mom.

"How are things at Etoile?" she asked as she rang me up.

"Good."

"I'm Winnie's mom, Frannie. Mack and I loved our dinner there. We keep meaning to come again, but it's so hard to get in."

"Nice to see you. And just let Winnie know when you'd like to come again. We'll get you in."

"Great." She beamed as she handed me the bag of scones. "Are these for Ellie?"

"Yes. I heard she likes them."

"They're her favorite," Frannie confirmed. "Say hello for me."

"I will, thanks."

When I pulled up behind Abelard, I texted Ellie that I had something for her and asked if she wanted me to bring it to her room.

She replied right away saying she was in the kitchen, but

joggers and the Pineview Motel sweatshirt I'd bought for her.

"Hi," I said, unable to keep a grin off my face. "Nice shirt. Brings back memories."

"It's the biggest thing I own. I'll be wearing it a lot."

"Can I come in?"

"Suit yourself." She shut the door behind me and we went into the kitchen, where I set the bag from Plum & Honey on the table.

"I went to the bakery. Thought maybe you'd like some scones."

Ellie looked at the bag with suspicion. "How'd you know?"

"Winnie," I confessed. "I ran into her in the lobby earlier."

Ellie sat down at the table and opened the bag. "Thanks."

I watched as she took out a scone and nibbled it, swallowing cautiously, like she wasn't sure her stomach was going to accept the offering. "So how are you feeling?" I asked, taking a chair across from her.

She shrugged. "Mornings are the worst."

"Can I get you something to drink?"

"No, thanks."

"Uh, I was thinking about telling my parents today. If that's okay with you."

She chewed and swallowed. "Do you want me to be there?"

"I hadn't thought about it," I said, surprised by the offer. "Sure, if you want to."

"Are you nervous to tell them?"

"No. I mean, maybe. A little." I closed my eyes. "Yes."

She laughed softly—another surprise. "I'll go with you."

"Thanks." I opened my eyes, my body warming with gratitude and affection. "I think it will be good coming from both of us."

shortly to go over deliveries and inventory, so maybe around one?"

"Okay." She looked down at the scone in her hands. "I haven't told my mom and dad yet. Will your parents keep it to themselves until I work up my nerve?"

"I'm sure they will." I stared at the antique tabletop, running my thumb over a nick in the wood. "Ellie, I was awake all night."

"Me too."

I looked up at her. "Is it because you didn't mean what you said about me going to California? Because I can try to get out of the contract."

She shook her head. "No. I meant what I said. I think the ten weeks apart will be a good chance for us both to process this. And figure out what life will look like moving forward."

"But—"

"Gianni. Can you look me in the eye *right now*, and honestly tell me you don't want to do the show?"

"No," I conceded.

"That's what I thought."

"You should come with me." The words came out of nowhere.

Ellie looked alarmed. "What? No."

"Why not? We could get a—"

"Why on earth would I come with you?"

"Because you're pregnant. And I . . . feel bad leaving."

It took her a minute to answer, but when she did, her voice was firm. "I'm not going with you, Gianni. My job is here. My family is here. My life is here." Her eyes filled with tears. "It's better that way. You'll see."

"Okay," I said quickly, hating that I'd made her cry. "If that's what you want, I'll go alone. But I'll come back when the show is done."

Her choice of words confused me. "What will be fine?"

"Never mind." She stood up. "I'll text you when I'm ready to go."

I watched her hurry out of the kitchen, feeling like I'd failed her.

The water continued to swirl over my head.

CHAPTER 18
ELLIE

I went straight to Winnie's office and shut the door behind me. The moment she looked up from her desk, I burst into tears.

"Oh, honey," she said, coming over and giving me a hug. "What is it?"

"I'm pregnant!" I wailed.

She laughed a little, rubbing my back. "I know, babe. I know."

"I told Gianni last night."

"*Oh.* I saw him this morning, but he didn't say anything. He did seem a little distracted though. How did it go?"

"It was rough." I went for the box of tissues on her desk. "We argued about whose fault it was."

"Of course you did."

"I got angry because he kept saying 'This can't be right.' Like he wasn't listening or didn't believe me." I blew my nose. "So I picked a fight. I threw things at him."

"Did it make you feel better?"

"No. It just reminded me how we bring out the worst in each other."

Winnie sat on the edge of her desk. "So then what?"

"You heard me. We had hot, angry sex on the kitchen counter." I closed my eyes. "I'm so stupid. I thought it would get him out of my system, give me closure or something."

"Did it?"

"No! It made everything worse!"

Winnie dropped into her chair. "I've got whiplash trying to keep up here. So are you . . . together? Friends? Enemies?"

"I don't know what we are. Not together. Not enemies. Maybe friends." I shrugged. "He's trying to be nice. He proposed."

Her eyes popped. "Wait. He *proposed*?"

"No, actually, he didn't. He just said something like, 'Should we get married?' And the look on his face told me exactly how he felt about that possibility—sick to his stomach."

"Okay, but he had to be in a serious state of shock."

"He also offered to try to get out of the Hot Mess contract."

"He did?" She smiled tentatively. "That's a good sign."

"I told him to go do the show," I said. "I *want* him to go. He *has* to go."

Winnie stared at me. "Why?"

"Because I need to get over him, Winnie." As I confessed the truth, the tears started up again, and I yanked another tissue from the box. "I need him to go away so these feelings can fade. I'm sure it's just pregnancy hormones on top of the memory of those orgasms, but in ten weeks, I'll feel like myself again. Poof."

"Poof?" Winnie shook her head. "I'm not sure that's how hormones *or* feelings work, Ell."

"But you know what they say—out of sight, out of mind."

"They also say absence makes the heart grow fonder."

"No," Winnie said with a shudder, "although that was horrific."

"You're supposed to be on my side."

She jumped out of her chair, came around the desk and shook me gently by the shoulders. "I am, Ellie. You're my best friend in the entire world, and I love you like crazy. I just think you might be wrong about him."

"I'm not! You know what he did just now in the kitchen? He asked me to go with him."

Winnie's eyes went wide, and she dropped her arms. "To California?"

"Yes. But when I asked him *why* he wanted me to come with him, he said, 'Because you're pregnant. And I feel bad leaving.' Not 'Because I want to be with you.'"

"Okay, but men don't always know the exact right answer," she said carefully. "Maybe he *does* want to be with you, but he was scared to say it. Or he doesn't know how to say it."

"No." I shook my head. "What he *wants* is to do the right thing, because he feels guilty, and I get it. But I don't need his pity proposal or his charity outing to California. I'd rather be alone."

"Are you sure?" Winnie pressed gently.

"I'm one hundred percent sure."

Winnie sighed. "God, you are so strong. I'd have been like 'Yes! Take me with you! Ride me off into your Hollywood sunset!'"

"I've done enough riding." I blew my nose again. "At this point, I need to keep my feet on the ground. And my knees *closed*!"

Someone knocked on Winnie's office door, and I met her eyes with alarm. I didn't want anyone to see me like this.

"Yes?" she called out. "Who is it?"

in!" she called.

Felicity pushed the door open, talking excitedly. "Hey! Guess who texted me this morning!" She stopped when she saw me. "Oh, sorry! I didn't mean to interrupt."

"It's okay," I said, grabbing another tissue.

"Is—is everything all right?" Felicity looked back and forth between her sister and me with concern.

"Yes," Winnie said, her tone overly bright, her cheeks turning pink. The poor thing was an awful liar. "Everything is fine. Totally fine."

"It's okay, Win." I looked at Felicity. "Please keep this between us, but I'm pregnant."

Felicity's brown eyes grew huge behind her glasses. "Oh my God. Wow."

"It's very early, and I haven't told my parents yet."

"I won't say a word. Are you okay?"

"Yes and no." I managed a smile. "I'm still getting used to the idea. I just told the father last night."

She bit her lip. "I hope this isn't out of line to ask, but is it Gianni?"

Winnie and I exchanged a surprised glance. "Yes, but how did you know?" I asked.

"Just a hunch." Her shoulders rose. "He's been training me, and he's an excellent teacher, but he seems distracted a lot. And I've noticed him sneaking looks at you from across the kitchen. I wondered if something was going on with you guys." She smiled. "A secret love affair?"

"No secret love affair," I told her. "Just a baby."

"Really?" She looked genuinely surprised.

"Really. We, um, passed the time during the blizzard by accidentally procreating. It was just a one-time thing . . . or so we thought."

I laughed in spite of everything, tossing my hands up. "I guess?"

"Then congratulations." She came forward and gave me a hug. "If it helps, I think you're going to be a great mom. And if the relationship Gianni has with his father is any indication, he'll be a great dad."

"We'll see," I said. "But I appreciate the well wishes. So who texted you this morning?"

"What? Oh!" She shook her head and laughed. "Your news is much more exciting than mine, but it was Hutton French."

Winnie gasped and fanned her face. "Ooooh, the old flame still burns!"

Felicity rolled her eyes. "Please. There was no flame. There wasn't even a spark. And even if there was, neither of us would have known what to do with it back then."

"Wait, how do I know the name Hutton French?" I racked my brain. "Is he an actor?"

"No, he's a billionaire," Winnie said. "He's one of those cryptocurrency guys."

"I don't even know what that means," I confessed.

"Does anyone?" Felicity laughed as she tightened her ponytail. "I once asked him, and less than ten seconds into the explanation, it was like he was speaking another language."

"How do you know him?" I asked.

"We were best friends in high school. We co-captained the Mathletes Team and co-founded the Chemistry Club. We also tutored together at the middle school."

"Clearly, they went to all the cool parties," Winnie joked.

"We did not go to many parties," Felicity said with a laugh. "Hutton had pretty bad social anxiety back then. But we did go to the senior prom together—just as friends."

young to have made so much money already?"

"He's twenty-eight," said Felicity. "We graduated together, but I was a year younger because I'd skipped a grade."

"Stop bragging about that already." Winnie poked her sister's shoulder and grinned. "We all know you're the smart sister."

Felicity slapped Winnie's hand away. "Anyway, he's home visiting his parents and reached out to me. I wondered if there was any way we could get him into Etoile? He's here all week."

"I'm sure we can. Let me check the reservations for this week and get back to you." I thought for a moment. "Tomorrow night might be the best bet."

"When was the last time you saw him, Lissy?" Winnie asked.

"Gosh, maybe five years ago? He lives on the West Coast, but he came through Chicago on business and we met up for dinner." She laughed. "Which was particularly memorable because I got one of my bloody noses at the table, and we spent the second half of the evening in the emergency room."

"Oh no," Winnie moaned, but she was laughing too. "Your bloody noses are the worst."

"It was pretty horrible," Felicity confirmed. "The white tablecloth looked like a crime scene."

"Would you like the night off so you can eat with him?" I asked her. "I'm sure Gianni can manage without you."

"No, that's okay." She shook her head and laughed ruefully. "He probably has PTSD from our last dinner. He never asked me to meet up again."

"Let me know if you change your mind," I said. "Etoile's dining room is very romantic."

"Thanks, but I'm sure Hutton has his pick of models, actresses, and lady billionaires," said Felicity. "I've seen the

"That's what I thought about Gianni too," I said with a sigh. "Then there was a blizzard. And now there's a baby."

She laughed. "I'll remember that."

CHAPTER 19
GIANNI

"So, we've got something to tell you."

I was seated next to Ellie on one end of the L-shaped couch at my parents' house. Not close enough that our legs were touching or anything, but I could see how my mother was eyeballing the strange sight of us side by side. There was something like hope in her gaze, which I was probably about to pulverize.

"What's up?" My dad, sitting next to my mom on the other end of the couch, leaned back and crossed an ankle over one knee. His thick dark hair was graying at the temples, and his forehead had a couple lines, which were furrowed slightly deeper at the moment, like he knew something bad was coming.

I glanced at Ellie, who sat beside me in jeans and a sweater, her expression serious. On the ride over here, we'd agreed that I would do the talking, but I hadn't exactly settled on the words I'd use, and now I found my tongue tied in knots. "It's—well, it might be a little bit of a shock. Just to warn you."

"Gianni, what is it?" My mother leaned forward, her blue

"Yeah." I looked at Ellie again, but her eyes had dropped to her hands, which were pressed between her knees.

"Oh my God." My mother gasped. "I knew it! Didn't I say that being stranded would bring them together?" She hit my dad's leg and looked at him. "I was right!"

"Is that it?" my dad asked, his dark eyes clouded with confusion. "You two are dating or something?"

"No," I said quickly. "We're not dating. We're just, uh . . . we're only—"

"We're having a baby," Ellie said. "I'm pregnant." She looked over at me. "Sorry, Gianni, but you were taking too long."

"You're *what*?" My mother's face had gone white.

"I'm pregnant." Ellie played with the hem of her sweater. "About ten weeks along. Due in October."

My dad's jaw had fallen open, and he was staring at me without blinking. The silence was excruciating.

I cleared my throat. "We know this is unexpected."

My mother made a noise. It might have been a laugh. Or a scream.

"But everything is going to be fine." I hoped I sounded more confident than I felt.

"Oh, my God. Does Mia know?" My mother, recovering her voice, looked at Ellie.

"Not yet." Ellie's cheeks turned a little pink. "But I'm going to tell her tonight. I've just been a little nervous about what she'll say."

"Oh, honey." My mother came over to Ellie and sat beside her, taking her hand. "It's okay. It's going to be okay."

Then Ellie shocked me by bursting into tears and throwing her arms around my mom, who hugged her and rubbed her back, making calm shushing noises.

"So . . ." he began, sitting up straighter. "So, a baby."

"Yeah." I scratched the back of my neck. "It's definitely, um, a baby."

He gave me a look that could possibly be described as murderous, then focused on Ellie. "Sweetheart, how are you feeling?"

"Fine," she blubbered. "I'm fine. I don't know why I'm so emotional right now. I'm really fine."

"This *is* emotional," said my mom, who had also started crying. "I can't believe it. I'm going to be a grandmother."

"Oh, fuck." My dad's expression was now one of alarm. "That's right. I'll be a grandfather." He ran a hand over his hair, like he wanted to make sure it was all still there.

"We know this is a big shock. But we have a plan." I have no idea what possessed me to say that, since we didn't.

"What's the plan?" my dad asked, leaning forward with his elbows on his knees. "Are you guys getting married?"

"No," Ellie and I said at the same time. She let go of my mom, and we exchanged a look. "We're not."

"But you're not still going back to California to do that show," my mother said.

"Actually, yes. I am." As I said it, I squirmed a little.

"Gianni Lupo." My dad's eyes were hard and his voice had a warning note to it—for a second I was transported back to childhood, sitting on the couch waiting to be yelled at.

"What?" I got up from the couch and grabbed a box of tissues for Ellie from a side table. "It's only for ten weeks," I said, handing her the box.

Ellie plucked a few tissues from the box. "I want him to go. He left it up to me."

"He did?" my mother asked, obviously confused.

"Yes," Ellie said, dabbing at her eyes. "We talked about it, and I told him to go. He'd already signed the contract, it's

nity because of—because of—" She looked at me, and I knew she was thinking about those five insane minutes against the wall.

"A blizzard," I finished.

"Right. A blizzard." Ellie took a breath. "And I'll be fine."

My dad didn't look happy or convinced, but he didn't argue with her.

"What will you do, honey?" my mother asked Ellie, playing with her hair. "Where will you live?"

Ellie shrugged. "I'll probably stay at Abelard. I haven't really thought that far ahead yet."

"This is a lot to take in." My mom brought her hands to her cheeks. "I've thought abstractly about grandchildren before, but I didn't know it would be so soon."

"Believe me, I know." Ellie blew her nose and laughed a little. "This isn't exactly the way I planned to start a family, but it's the hand I was dealt."

"I don't understand why the dealer wasn't more careful." My dad was still giving me threatening looks.

"The dealer *was* careful," I said defensively. "Mostly."

"Nick, stop it." My mother glared at my dad. "That's not helping. And this isn't a catastrophe—it's a baby." She smiled at Ellie, her eyes welling again. "A baby. Mia and I are having a baby! This is incredible!"

"I'm sorry, Ellie." My dad got off the couch, came over and kissed her cheek. "I'm happy too. It's just a shock."

"I get it," she said, blushing a little, which made me feel sort of sorry for myself. My mom was allowed to hug her, my dad could kiss her cheek, but I could hardly get close to her without her flinching. Why didn't she like me?

Fucking everybody liked me!

Except, apparently, my father.

"It's not like I'm leaving her with nothing and never coming back," I said, squaring my shoulders. "I'll support her too."

"What *are* you going to do when you get back, Gianni?" My dad looked at me. "What's the plan? Where will you work? Where will you live?"

"I don't know yet," I admitted. "I just found out she was pregnant last night, Dad. Give me a minute."

"It's going to be fine, no matter what," my mother said. She put an arm around Ellie and pulled her close again. "Better than fine. It will be wonderful. You're going to have all the help you need. This baby is wanted and loved."

"Thank you." Ellie sniffed, leaning against my mom. "I appreciate it."

When we stood up to leave, my dad took my arm. "Can I talk to you alone please?"

Fuck.

"Okay." I looked at Ellie. "Give me a sec?"

"Sure," she said. "I have to use the bathroom real quick anyway."

I followed my dad through the kitchen and into the garage, where he snapped on the light. It was cold in there—cold enough to see our breath—and I buttoned up my coat.

My father stood in a plain black T-shirt with his feet apart, his inked-up arms folded. Somewhere on his chest was my mom's name in a heart, tattooed when he was like twenty or something, the writing blurry and the ink faded now, but the sentiment behind it the same.

"You got anything to say for yourself?" he barked.

I shrugged. "Like what?"

"Like what? I don't know whether to hug you or take off my belt and whip your ass for the first time in twenty-three years."

"For what, Dad? It was an accident."

He shook his head. "Accidents happen. That's not why I'm mad."

"Then what are you mad at? Even Ellie isn't this mad, and she's the one having the baby."

"She's a sweet girl."

"I know." I ran a hand over my hair. "I'm going to support her. It's not like I'm abandoning them."

He cocked his head. "So running off to do some TV show and leaving her behind to deal with everything is supportive?"

"She told me to go, Dad. You heard her." I fidgeted, shifting my weight. "I even offered to marry her. She said no."

"You *offered* to marry her? Or you asked her to marry you?"

"What's the difference?"

My dad rubbed his face with both hands, noisily inhaling and exhaling.

"I also offered to take her with me to California, and she said no to that too. She's very independent, okay? And I'm the last guy on earth she'd want to spend the rest of her life with. She thinks I'm a liar and a game player."

"Why does she think that?"

I cringed. "If I tell you the truth, you can't be more mad."

"I'll bet I can."

Knowing I'd regret this—or maybe that I deserved any shit he'd give me—I took a breath and confessed the truth.

pretty sure is the night she got pregnant."

His stare got even more mean.

"I know, it's shitty. I told her the truth the very next day, I felt so bad."

"Was she upset?"

I nodded. "Yeah. Basically it confirmed everything she thought about me before."

"Jesus. No wonder she doesn't want you around."

"Look, I made a mistake, okay?" I raised my voice to my dad, which I knew was a bad idea. "But I apologized and I'm trying to do the right thing. She's *telling* me to leave."

"Is that what *you* want to do? Leave?"

"Yes," I snapped, although at that point, I didn't know what the fuck I wanted. Mostly I just wanted to get out of this damn garage.

My father gave me a look of disappointment that hurt worse than any belt. "I thought I raised you to be a different kind of man, but maybe I was wrong."

"You raised me to work hard and go after what I want," I argued. "And I never wanted this!"

"This isn't just about you anymore!" He poked my chest. "And I raised you to put *family* first, not yourself!"

I lowered my voice. "She doesn't want me, Dad. Not like that."

"I don't blame her." Shouldering past me, he went into the house.

Which was just as well, since I had no argument.

I didn't blame her either.

Gianni was silent on the way back to Abelard. When we pulled behind the house, he put the car in park but left the engine running. "Do you want me to come in?"

"For what?"

"I don't know." He paused. "To talk?"

"I don't know what there is to talk about."

He stared straight ahead, both hands on the wheel. "My dad . . . gave me some shit."

"Yeah?"

"I'm surprised you didn't hear him yelling."

"I did," I admitted. "And your mom was so nice—she kept trying to talk over it, reassure me that everything was going to be fine. But it was obvious your dad was upset."

"He's not upset about the baby," Gianni said quickly. "He's just mad at me. He thinks I'm running away from my responsibility. I thought he was gonna punch me in the face."

For a moment, I imagined Uncle Nick beating up Gianni for me, and I felt a little better.

"You don't think that, do you?" Gianni turned to me. "That I'm running away?"

whose opinions matter."

He rubbed the back of his neck. "It just felt shitty, hearing him say I'm not the man he thought he raised."

"Ouch. That had to hurt."

"It did."

"But we can't control how other people feel."

"I can't even control how *I* feel," he said. "I've never been this . . . fucked up over anything. I feel like I don't know myself at all."

"That's why you need to go do the show," I urged. "Once you're on the set, entertaining people, having a good time, you'll remember who you are."

He frowned. "But is that me?"

"It's always been you before."

He looked at my stomach. "What will I miss while I'm gone?"

"Me getting bigger. Some doctor appointments. Hearing me complain about shit like heartburn and nausea and having to pee all the time."

"But you'll tell me how you're feeling, right?" he pressed. "And everything the doctor says?"

"Sure. But you don't have to be here for that." I shook my head. "You're not abandoning me, Gianni. If that's what you're worried about. You're just . . . being honest about what you really want."

He didn't reply right away. Then he looked at me intently. "Are you being honest about what *you* really want?"

Panicked that he'd see the emotion in my eyes, I lowered my gaze to my lap. "I'm trying."

He put his fingers beneath my chin, forcing me to look at him. When he spoke, his voice was soft. "You really want me to leave?"

"Why, Ellie?" He slipped his hand to the back of my neck and pulled me toward him. His forehead rested against mine. I felt his breath on my lips. "Are you so sure we shouldn't do this together? All of it?"

"What do you mean?"

But instead of answering, he kissed me, and it was all I wanted—to be swept away by the stroke of his tongue, and the insistence of his mouth, and the grip of his hand on the back of my neck that said *mine*.

He broke the kiss, breathing hard. "I mean, what about us?"

"But there is no us, Gianni." It broke my heart to say it. "There was never an us."

"There could be."

"No! Be realistic. This baby wasn't conceived out of love—it was conceived because we were *bored*! But you don't need to be punished for it, and that's what staying here with me would feel like to you—a jail sentence."

"You don't know how it would feel to me," he said irritably. "Don't put words in my mouth."

"That's not what I'm doing!"

"Because my feelings are all over the place, and my dad made me feel like a terrible person."

"That's not a good reason to be with me, Gianni. Jesus Christ." Tears spilled over and I wiped at them angrily. "I never know where I stand with you. I never know when something is just about your ego or if it's real. And I don't trust you to *really* stay. I'm sorry, but I don't. Because I'll never believe that I'm what you want."

"God." He rubbed his face with both hands. "Everything I say is wrong. I've never been good with words. I should have read more books."

Even at a time like this, he could make me laugh, but that

person I wanted to hold close. "But that's it, okay? Let's not pretend we're anything more."

He exhaled, defeated. "If that's what you want. But don't . . . shut me out, okay? I want to be part of this." Hesitantly, he reached out and touched my stomach, and it was so sweet I nearly broke down and begged him to love me.

Instead, I opened the door and ran into the house.

Once the kitchen door was shut behind me, I leaned back against it and sobbed, furious with myself for letting him get to me, with his dad for making him feel bad, with Gianni for being sweet when I really just needed him to be his old self— an unapologetic man-child only out for a good time.

Because he didn't really want me. He wasn't saying that. He was just ashamed that his father had scolded him. His feelings hadn't changed just because I was pregnant with his child. Even if he thought he wanted to play dad for a while, he'd get tired of it. He'd leave me behind and move on. Deep down, he wanted fame, fortune, and the rush of the next new thing.

I wanted love. Home. The security of family and belonging.

And if I wasn't careful, I'd end up wanting it all with him.

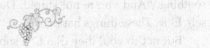

Upstairs in my bedroom, I curled up in my bed and made the call I'd been dreading.

"Hello?"

"Hi, Mom."

"Ellie! I was just thinking about you! At the pastry shop today, I bought a *tartelette au citron* because it reminded me of

you ate the pastry."

I nodded as I started to cry again, the sound of her voice taking me back to childhood. She'd been such a good mom—always there when I needed her, with a hug or a word of advice or a smile. It wasn't her fault she was perfect and I'd never live up. And of course she'd had high expectations for me—wouldn't I have the same for my child? Now I had to disappoint her when she didn't deserve it.

"Your dad reminded me of—honey? What's wrong?"

"Can you come home, Mom?"

"Ellie, what is it?"

"I need you," I wept. "I need you and I'm sorry."

"Why are you sorry, love? Of course I can come home if you need me. But tell me what's wrong—are you okay?"

"I'm okay—but I'm—I'm pregnant." The words came out between sobs.

She gasped. "Oh. *Oh*."

"I'm sorry," I said again. "I'm so sorry."

"Ellie, honey," she said gently, a catch in her voice. "You don't have to be sorry. Everything will be okay."

"But I feel so stupid," I moaned. "I ruined my life and I'm ruining your trip and everything is awful."

"Shhh. You didn't ruin anything." My mother's voice was soothing. "And you're not stupid. Don't be so hard on yourself, Ellie. These things happen."

"But not to you, they don't," I sobbed. "You would never have been so careless. You would never have made such a big fat mistake."

"Ellie, I've made plenty of mistakes in my life. And I've definitely been careless. No one is perfect."

"I don't know how to be a mom," I cried.

"I'll help you, sweetheart. You're not alone." She paused. "But are you—is the father . . . in the picture?"

the first time, she actually seemed rattled. "That's a surprise."

"Yeah. For us too."

"Are you two . . . *together*?"

"No," I said. "It happened during the blizzard."

"Ah." Her laughter was gentle and shaded with regret. "For a moment I was hopeful you two were in love."

"No," I blubbered. "We were just stupid. And cold."

"Well, it's probably not the first baby conceived during a polar vortex."

"No." I laughed and cried at the same time. "Probably not."

"Does Gianni know?"

"Yes. And we told his parents today."

"I'm sure they were surprised too."

"Yes." I took a shaky breath. "But supportive, although they were upset that he's still leaving to do that TV show."

"He is?" My mother sounded shocked once more.

"Yes, and that's how I want it," I said emphatically. "I don't want to hold him back."

"What does *he* want?"

"He still wants to go," I said quickly, although I wasn't one hundred percent sure that was the case. "He's offered to stay, but what's the point? I don't need him over the next three months."

"Are you sure? Pregnancy isn't easy. It's nice to have a partner."

"He's not my partner," I said firmly. "And I've got other people I can depend on."

"Of course you do." Her voice grew stronger. "Everything is going to be all right, honey. I promise. And I'll get on a plane first thing tomorrow. Dad too."

I squeezed my eyes shut. "I guess you have to tell Dad, huh?"

"It's life, Ellie. It's just life. And sometimes, no matter how perfectly we plan things, they just don't go the way we want them to. Or the way we thought they would."

"Not at all," I said, surprised at how easy she was taking this news.

"But you know what? Sometimes they end up being exactly right. Life has a funny way of turning out fine, just when you least expect it."

"You really think that?"

"I really do. Remind me to tell you a story sometime."

"About what?"

"About the asshole I nearly married who jilted me the week before our wedding."

I gasped. "What? Did that really happen?"

"Absolutely. And I was devastated. I had my life all planned out with that dipshit." She laughed. "After he dumped me, I went on our Paris honeymoon alone, with the worst possible attitude you can imagine. I was convinced I'd never be happy."

"And that's when you met Dad?"

"That's when I met Dad."

"I want to hear more about the dipshit," I said, feeling better already. "I can't believe I didn't know this."

My mother laughed. "It's not a piece of my past I'm particularly fond of, but I'll tell you the whole story."

"Okay. Hurry home."

"I'm on my way, love. We'll see you tomorrow."

"Okay." I managed a wan smile. "How are you?"

"Fine." She set a bakery bag on the counter. "From my mom."

"Thanks. Gianni brought me a few yesterday and they're gone already. They're like the one thing that isn't turning my stomach." I peeked into the bag. "Did you tell her about the baby?"

Winnie nodded. "I hope that's okay. She won't say anything to anyone."

"It's okay." I pulled a scone from the bag and took a bite. "We told the Lupos yesterday. And I called my mom last night."

Her eyes went wide. "And? How did everyone take the news?"

"Everyone was pretty shocked. Gianni's mom cried, but not like she was sad. They were supportive."

"Good." She paused. "How about *your* mom?"

"She was great, just like you said she would be."

Winnie was visibly relieved. "See?"

"She's coming home today."

"Wow. For good?" She laughed a little. "Am I out of a job?"

I smiled. "No. It's temporary—just a visit. I asked her to come. You know how she always has the perfect plan for everything? I feel like I could use some of that kind of energy."

"I'm glad." She rubbed my shoulder. "It's okay to still need your mom sometimes, even when you're grown."

"I was worried she would make me feel bad without even trying, but she didn't. In fact, she said something that made me feel better."

"What?"

Winnie smiled. "I definitely think that's true."

"And, she told me that before she met my dad she was engaged to some douchebag who jilted her a week before their wedding." I had to talk around the scone in my mouth because I was so impatient to get the story out.

"No way!"

"Yes. And she said"—I paused for a second to swallow—"she was in Paris on their honeymoon alone when she met my dad."

Winnie gasped. "Seriously?"

"Yes. Can you imagine if she'd married that other guy and never met my dad?"

"You wouldn't even exist," she said, wide-eyed. Then she laughed. "And maybe we wouldn't have found that box of sex toys under their bed."

I frowned at her. "Please. I'm already nauseated."

"Sorry. I wonder who that other guy was."

"I don't know. She said she'd tell me the full story when she got home." I took another bite. "At least it will be a good distraction from my misery."

"You seem a little better today," she said hopefully. "Maybe it's sinking in."

"Yeah. I think telling the Lupos yesterday helped." But then I thought about the kiss in the car afterward and suddenly my eyes went blurry. "God, these stupid pregnancy hormones are awful. I laugh one minute and cry the next."

"I remember my mom being that way when she was pregnant with the twins." She looked around. "Can I get you a tissue?"

"No, I'm fine. It'll pass." I sniffed and popped the rest of the scone in my mouth. "I just need to stop dwelling on things I can't change."

"You mean being pregnant?"

"He wants to be all . . . *involved* in the pregnancy."

Winnie feigned outrage. "Rude."

"I can't handle it, Win. I just can't." My eyes filled with tears again. "He has to stop being sweet. He's only doing it because he feels bad. And because his dad gave him shit. But I don't trust myself not to fall for him, especially in this state."

"Are you *sure* that's the only reason he's doing it?"

"No. I bet he's also doing it because he wants to have sex again and we wouldn't have to use a condom. I know how his mind works."

She laughed sympathetically. "But what if he's changing his ways? Maybe impending fatherhood has him rethinking his priorities."

"We've been over this, Winnie. Guys like Gianni don't change."

Winnie sighed. "You know, it's too bad. You guys could be good together, if only—"

I shook my head. "Don't. That's the trap, Win. The *if only*. I get caught in it every night when I'm trying to fall asleep, because part of my stupid, stubborn heart wants that happily ever after." I grabbed a cocktail napkin for my eyes, helpless against the torrent of tears and the tide of feelings that kept rising in me. "But we can't always have what we want."

My parents arrived home later that night, and the moment I saw them walk into Etoile's kitchen, I ran at them at full speed. I'm sure everyone in there thought I was nuts, but I threw myself into my mother's arms, and then my dad's.

My dad held me tight and rubbed my back and told me

could handle it and promised to come up and talk to them as soon as I could. I saw Gianni glance over his shoulder, his expression suitably anxious, but my parents left without saying anything to him. Later, when the dining room was empty and the servers were finishing up their side work, I found him in the office, sitting at the desk but staring into space. My heart beat faster at the sight of his handsome profile.

"Gianni?"

He looked over at me and stood up quickly. "Hey."

"Hey." I joined my hands at my waist, locking my fingers together. "I'm going to talk to my parents. Do you want to come?"

He went pale. "Do you want me to?"

"It's up to you. Since we faced your parents together, I wasn't sure if you wanted to face mine that way too."

His Adam's apple bobbed. "Do they know yet?"

"Yes. I told my mom on the phone last night."

He exhaled, rubbing the back of his neck. "I wondered if that's why they came back."

"I don't think they're back to stay forever—not right now, anyway. They're just here to make sure I'm okay."

"Do they hate me?"

"No. Don't be ridiculous." I paused. "Have you talked to your dad today?"

"No."

He looked so sad, I felt sorry for him. "Well, you don't have to come with me to talk to Mia and Lucas. I just didn't want to shut you out if you wanted to be there. It's . . . it's your baby too."

"Thanks. But I think I'll just—" He stopped mid-sentence, like he was reconsidering. "Actually, you know what? I will come with you."

more sure of himself and even stood taller. "I want to be there. If your dad wants to throw a punch at me, I'll take it."

That made me laugh. "My dad is not going to punch you, Gianni. I can't imagine my dad punching anyone. Now *your* dad, on the other hand . . ."

Gianni grinned, and I realized how long it had been since I'd seen him do it. It warmed me all the way through.

We found my parents seated on the couch in the family room in the private part of the house. My mother was sipping a cup of tea, and my dad had a glass of something that looked like scotch. They stood up when they saw us enter the room together.

"Gianni," my mother said in surprise, coming forward to give him a hug. "I just got off the phone with your mom."

"Aunt Mia. Uncle Lucas." Gianni faced my dad, who held out his hand. There was visible relief on Gianni's face as he shook it.

"Can I get you anything?" my dad asked. "Beer? Glass of wine? Whiskey?"

Gianni shook his head. "I'm good, thanks."

"Ellie, darling, would you like tea?" my mom asked.

"No, thanks. I'm sure you guys are tired and want to go to bed." I sat down in one of two chairs opposite the couch, and Gianni sat in the other. He looked even more uncomfortable than he did when we told *his* parents, and I didn't blame him, although my parents were handling this entire situation with a surprising amount of calm and grace—especially my mom.

My dad sat next to her and covered her lap with a soft pink throw blanket. "How are you feeling, Ell?"

"I'm okay." I glanced at Gianni, who was nervously rubbing his hands on the tops of his legs. "I'm definitely tired, but we wanted to—"

Gianni suddenly stood up. "I'm going to take care of them," he blurted. "I'm going to be there."

"Of course you are." My mother's tone was soothing.

He glanced at me. "I just didn't want anyone to think that I wasn't taking this seriously. I am. I wish I hadn't signed that contract."

"Could you get out of it?" my mom asked.

"No. Gianni and I have discussed this," I said firmly. "He's going to do the show and come back when it's finished."

"What would happen if you broke the contract?" my dad asked.

"He's not going to break it, Dad. I don't want him to, and there's no need." I made eye contact with Gianni. "You can sit down now."

He did, but he still looked uneasy.

"Your mom mentioned that your dad was a little rough on you," my mom said to him.

"Uh, yeah."

"Give him some time," my dad said. "Nick's temper runs a little hot, but he'll come around."

"I agree," said my mom. "So tell us how things are going at Etoile and what we can do to help."

"Things are going great," I said with pride. "In fact, we had a billionaire in our dining room tonight."

"We did?" Gianni looked at me curiously. "Who?"

"The guy by himself at the early seating. Table by the window."

"I don't know." Gianni shrugged. "A suit and tie? A closer shave? That guy looked kind of scruffy. He's a *billionaire*?"

"Who was it, Ellie?" my dad asked.

"Hutton French," I said. "Apparently, he's an old friend of Felicity MacAllister's. He's one of those cryptocurrency guys."

"Really." My dad sipped his scotch. "Huh."

"That sounds made up," Gianni said. "What's cryptocurrency anyway?"

My mom laughed. "I don't know either. That's always confused me. Did he enjoy his meal, Ellie?"

"Yes," I said. "He's not a huge talker—he seems a little shy —but I chatted a little bit with him before he left. He loved the butternut squash and mushroom Wellington."

"That was Felicity's idea," Gianni said generously. "She's really good at vegetarian recipes, but she can do anything. And she's willing to stay on while you search for another full-time chef de cuisine."

"If you're returning in ten weeks, Gianni, could she just serve as a short-term substitute?" my dad asked. "We'd be glad to hold the position for you."

Gianni glanced at me, as if he was looking for my approval, and I smiled. "That's really generous, Uncle Lucas," he said, "and I do love Etoile. But I don't want to ask that kind of favor. You guys have already been so understanding."

"Nonsense. You're family," said my mother with a smile. "We'd love to have you back after the show is done filming. And I'll speak with Felicity and make sure she's okay with that."

"I bet she'll be fine with it," I said. "She wants to start her own catering business and food blog. That's why she moved back." I tried to stifle a yawn and couldn't. "Sorry, guys. I'm about to drop. Can we talk more tomorrow?"

"I'll walk you out," I said, rising to my feet.

"No need. I know the way, and you're tired. Get some rest." He hesitated, then hugged me.

At first, I was so surprised I didn't know how to react—it was the first time he'd ever hugged me goodbye. But after an awkward second or two, I put my arms around him. He smelled good—a combination of herbs from the kitchen and hair product. I was even more shocked when he kissed my cheek before letting me go.

"Goodnight," he said, nodding at my parents. "See you tomorrow."

"Goodnight," I echoed.

My heart raced as I watched him leave.

Upstairs, I changed into my pajamas and washed my face. Someone knocked on my bedroom door while I was brushing my teeth. "Come in," I called.

My mom entered the room and leaned on the bathroom doorway. "Just checking on you. You okay?"

I spit out my toothpaste and rinsed the sink. "I'm okay enough. Is Dad okay? He was pretty quiet."

"He's fine. It's been a long day."

"Yeah." I switched off the bathroom light and crawled into bed.

My mom turned off my lamp and brought the covers to my shoulders. "You know you can stay here as long as you want. And Dad and I will move back before summer is over."

"Okay."

"None."

She bit her lip. "So there's no chance you two could work things out?"

"There's nothing to work out, Mom. It's not like we were together and then broke up. We weren't a couple. Gianni doesn't do relationships."

She sat on the edge of the mattress and brushed my hair back from my face. "Finding out you were pregnant must have been quite a shock."

"Yeah."

"But it's not the end of the world, Ellie. And I think Gianni will be a good dad."

"You do?"

"Sure." She continued stroking my hair. "He's young, but he's dependable, compassionate, loyal . . ."

"Are we talking about the same Gianni Lupo who tormented me all those years? I'm pretty sure he beheaded at least one doll."

My mom laughed. "I know he was a bit of a stinker growing up, but he was raised right, he works hard, and he has a good heart."

"I guess."

"And he's always been sweetly protective of you."

"Mom, stop."

"He has, Ellie! Remember that time you fell in the driveway at their house and he carried you inside with two bloody knees? You two couldn't have been more than five years old."

I sat up and stared at her in the dark. "Wait a minute. Is that *true*?"

"Yes."

"I always thought the person who carried me inside was Uncle Nick, but Gianni says it was him."

annoying."

My mother laughed before leaning over and kissing my forehead. "Give him a chance, Ellie. I have a feeling you see the boy he was when you look at him, not the man he could be."

"Because he hasn't *shown* me the man he could be, Mom. Only the boy."

"Keep watching him," she said gently. "Goodnight, sweetheart."

"Night."

She pulled the door shut behind her and left me alone in the dark, wondering if there was a chance I was wrong about Gianni Lupo after all.

CHAPTER 21
GIANNI

Every morning that week, I brought her breakfast.

I'd stop at the bakery on my way into work and then bring them to the tasting room on my way to the kitchen—of course, it wasn't really on the way, but it gave me the chance to see her before work and ask how she was feeling.

"The same," she'd say. "Tired, but okay."

On the Monday morning after we'd told my parents, she wasn't in the tasting room. For a moment, I panicked that something was wrong, and I pulled out my phone to text her. While I was typing a frantic message, she breezed in behind me.

"Morning," she said.

"Morning." I looked at her with concern, but she looked perfectly beautiful—glowing and rested, much better than last week. "Are you okay?"

"I'm fine. I slept in a little."

"Oh." The tension in my shoulders eased. "I was worried. You're usually down here by ten o'clock."

She smiled. "I'm okay."

I set the bakery bag on the counter. "Hungry?"

"I like feeding you." I shrugged. "It's kind of my thing."

She opened the bag and eagerly bit into a pastry. "Mmm. Actually, I'm glad you're here. My ultrasound appointment is tomorrow. Do you still want to go?"

"Yes. What time?"

She swallowed the bite in her mouth. "Nine forty-five a.m. The office is in town, so I can just meet you there."

"No, I'll pick you up," I said.

"Gianni, that's silly. It's out of your way."

"I don't mind. I'll be here at nine. Is that early enough?"

She sighed. "That's fine. Come to the kitchen door."

"Okay." I left the tasting room with a stupid grin on my face. I wasn't even sure what an ultrasound was, but knowing Ellie wanted me there, or at least that she didn't mind my being there, felt like a win.

Of course, once I was sitting in the waiting room at the doctor's office, I felt like it was the last place I belonged.

There were no other guys there, and the walls were covered with all this women's stuff about breastfeeding and hormones and birth control. I absentmindedly picked up a pamphlet with a young girl on the front from the table next to me, and when I opened it up, there was this horrifyingly life-like drawing of female anatomy staring me right in the face. At the top it said GET TO KNOW YOUR VAGINA. I slammed it shut and put it down.

In the chair next to me, Ellie snickered. "Um, you've been up close and personal with those bits and pieces."

"I know," I said, squirming in my seat. "I just never

She laughed again. "Relax. You won't have to see anything today. I'll be under a sheet."

I wanted to tell her I wouldn't mind seeing her bits and pieces—or being up close and personal with them—but it didn't seem like the right time.

I chose a safer topic. "Hey, did you tell your brothers about the baby?"

"My mom did." She shrugged. "I don't think they cared much. Did you tell your siblings?"

"I texted them. My sister was really excited. One brother replied with *dude*, and the other with *fuck* in all caps. Several U's."

"Sounds about right."

I glanced down at her feet. "How's your ankle?"

She laughed. "Swollen, but I can't blame the fall. Just the baby."

"It doesn't hurt anymore?"

"No." She was quiet a moment. "Have you talked to your dad yet?"

I shook my head. "He's not interested in listening to me."

"Gianni, try again." She put her hand on my arm. "You won't feel right leaving town without making peace with him."

"He was mean to me," I said grumpily.

"He was just in shock. And he doesn't understand our choices."

I looked at her hand still on my arm. "I'm not sure I understand our choices either."

She took her hand away.

"Ellie?" The nurse smiled at us from the doorway to the hall. "We're ready for you."

Ellie quickly got to her feet and followed the nurse down the hall, and I trailed behind. We were put into a room, and

can."

Ellie sighed. "I guess not. Too late now to worry about getting undressed with you in the room."

I tried to give her some privacy, but it was hard in such a small room. I turned around, looking for something to distract me, but all I saw was a 3D model of a woman's reproductive system and magazines with babies and moms on the front. Where the hell were the dads?

"Okay, you can turn around." Ellie sounded amused.

I spun around and saw her lying back with a blue paper sheet covering her naked lower half—only her hedgehog socks were still on. "Hey, it's your lucky socks."

"Yeah." She wiggled her toes. "I thought we could use some luck."

"Are you nervous?" I took one foot in my hand and squeezed.

"A little." She glanced at the screen to her right. "I just want everything to be okay."

"It will be. I promise." But suddenly I was nervous too.

A moment later, a woman in scrubs came in and greeted us. "Hi there, Ellie. Ready to peek at your baby?"

"Yes," Ellie said. "This is the baby's father, Gianni."

"I'm Beth, the sonographer." She smiled at me. "Big day, huh?"

"Yeah." I stepped out of the way, hoping she couldn't tell how bad I was sweating. "I've never seen one of these before."

"Don't worry." Beth took a seat between Ellie and the screen and did some things I tried not to watch too closely. A moment later, strange, ghostly images appeared on the monitor. "There we go. First things first, it looks like just one critter in there."

"You mean there was a chance there was *more* than one?" I

The images shifted and swirled on the screen. "Okay, I can see some knees right here, and some feet."

Instinctively I moved to look closer and took Ellie's hand. This was unbelievable.

The image shifted again, and something that looked vaguely like the shape of a baby lying on its back appeared. "So there's the head," said Beth, "and there's the bum. And see that flickering? That's the heart."

"That's the heart beating? We can see that already?" My throat was so tight I could hardly talk.

"Yes. Want to hear it?"

"Can we?" Ellie asked.

"Sure." Beth clicked something, and the room was filled with a scratchy, rhythmic sound. The lump in my throat ballooned, and the screen grew blurry.

"It's so fast," Ellie said.

Beth was reassuring. "That's normal for first trimester."

Ellie looked at me, and her eyes were wet too. I wanted to say something and couldn't. I squeezed her hand.

"Can I take a video?" My voice sounded odd to me, weak and raw, like I had a sore throat.

"Of course," said Beth.

I pulled out my phone and took a video of the screen, capturing the sound of the heartbeat and the graph at the bottom.

Ellie sniffed and looked at the screen again. "Does everything look okay?"

"Everything looks fine." Beth went on about spine development, organ functioning, length, and weight. But I was mesmerized by the little creature on the screen, by the sound of its heart, and by the rush of feelings it inspired.

"Can you tell if it's a boy or girl?"

"Not yet. That will be at your next ultrasound appoint-

surprised."

"We've had enough surprises," said Ellie. "I definitely want to know."

A few minutes later, the scan was finished and Beth told Ellie she could get dressed.

"Excuse me," I said. "I'm just going to use the restroom. Is there a dad's bathroom or anything?"

Beth laughed. "You can use the one down the hall on the left."

I told Ellie I'd be right back and left the room. Inside the bathroom, I splashed cold water on my face and looked at myself in the small mirror over the sink. I hardly recognized myself.

But I knew three things.

I was going to be a father.

I was going to be a *good* father.

I was going to do everything in my power to make things right between Ellie and me.

I'd always trusted my gut instincts, which usually told me when it was time to move on to the next place, take the next risk, chase the next thrill. But today when I'd heard that little heartbeat and saw those tiny feet and looked into Ellie's brown eyes, my gut hadn't told me to run.

It told me to stay.

I didn't sleep that night. I just lay there in the dark, the sound of the baby's heart on a loop in my head, each tiny little beat reaffirming what I needed to do.

But how could I convince Ellie to let me try?

"Hey, Gianni." She checked her phone. "Sure. I have a wedding couple coming in at ten, but I have a few minutes. Sit down."

I took a seat opposite her. "I just brought Ellie some scones from your mom."

Winnie laughed. "Between the two of us, we're going to bury her in those things."

"She says it's one of the only foods that tastes good to her, so I don't mind stopping on the way in."

"That's nice of you. I'll stop bringing them, so she associates all the good feelings with you."

"Thanks." I hesitated. "That's actually what I came to ask you about."

"Oh?"

My leg was bouncing up and down, an old habit. "Ellie hates me," I blurted. "Is there any way to change that?"

"I don't think she hates you, Gianni," Winnie said hesitantly. "I think her feelings are more complicated than that."

"Yesterday was the ultrasound, and it just . . ." I tried to put into words what it had done to me. "It hit me really hard."

"Ellie said everything went well."

"It did go well. The baby is fine." I couldn't help smiling. "We got to hear the heartbeat."

"That's amazing."

"Yeah. It really was. It made me feel so close to Ellie, and she even let me hold her hand, but the moment it was over, she was so distant again. She said nothing on the ride home." Closing my eyes, I exhaled. "I know I've given her a lot of reasons to doubt I can be good for her, but I really want to try." I opened my eyes and looked at Winnie with desperation. "You know her better than anybody. Can you give me some tips to make her like me?"

meant a lot to her."

"It did? Did she say that?"

"She did," Winnie said carefully. "But she's nervous, Gianni. That's probably why she doesn't say much."

"About what?"

Winnie glanced at the door, then got up and closed it. "Okay, if I talk to you about this, it has to stay between us."

"I swear."

"I mean it, Gianni. I will never forgive you if you betray this confidence or use it to hurt her."

I held up my palms. "You have my word. *Please*, talk to me. And if you say that she'll be better off without me and I should just leave her be, I will."

Winnie sat down again and studied me, like she still wasn't sure she could trust me. "I don't think she'd be better off without you, but she's scared of being hurt."

"By me?"

"Yes." Her voice softened. "She has feelings for you, Gianni."

"But I have feelings for her too! Ever since those days at the motel, I can't stop thinking about her. I *want* to be with her, but she keeps pushing me away." Too restless to sit still, I jumped to my feet. "Tell me what to say to convince her to let me in."

"At this point, I don't know that she'd believe *words*," Winnie said. "I think you have to be patient and *show* her you really want to be with her, and not just because she's pregnant."

"I want to do that," I said. "But she won't let me. I offered to get out of doing that show so I don't have to leave for ten weeks, and she's insisting that I go."

"Because she thinks if you're gone, she'll get over you."

Winnie nodded solemnly. "And if she ever found out I told you that, she would stab me with a thousand sharp knives. But for some reason, I have this feeling you're telling me the truth, and you really do care for her."

"I do," I moaned. "Swear to God, Winnie, I've *never* spent so many sleepless nights thinking about how to make a girl want me. I had no idea it could be this hard."

Winnie smiled. "Ellie's a tough cookie. She's stubborn and she's proud. She's got it in her head that she could never be what you really want, and she won't settle for being anything less."

I slumped into the chair again. "That's my fault. I said a bunch of stupid stuff to her at the motel about never wanting to be tied down to one place or one person. But it was mostly just me showing off how immature and unattached I was. It seemed like a badge of honor to be so free."

"Have you changed your mind?"

Exhaling, I looked at my hands in my lap. "Yes. I don't care about that freedom anymore. I want to be with her. And I'd give up anything to have another chance."

"Then prove it," Winnie said.

"But *how*? She hardly lets me near her."

"I can't tell you that, Gianni. You're going to have to figure that out for yourself." She paused. "But it should be big."

I went straight to the kitchen office and called my agent. When he didn't pick up, I left a voicemail.

"Hey Spencer, it's Gianni. Listen, I'm sorry to do this, but I need to get out of my contract for Hot Mess. I can't leave

I ended the call and set my phone down, then rubbed my sweaty palms on my jeans. Next, I jumped online and canceled my flight out of town, as well as the small house in L.A. I'd rented for the duration of the shoot. Finally, I called the manager of my Traverse City apartment complex to see if I could extend my lease, but unfortunately, that unit had already been rented starting April 15th.

"But I've got a two-bedroom, two-bath available," she offered. "Rent is higher, obviously, but it's available right now. Would you like to come see it?"

"Yes," I said, "but I can't come today. Tomorrow okay?"

"Sure," she said. "I'm here nine to five."

"I'll be there at nine. Thanks." I hung up with her, took a deep breath, and made the final call.

"Hello?"

"Hey, Pop. It's me."

Silence. "Everything okay?"

"Yes, but can we talk?"

"Have you come to your senses?"

I smiled. "Yeah. And I could use some advice on how to make a girl fall in love with me, even though I'm not good enough for her. I figure you're an expert in that."

He laughed. "Come by the house. I've got some experience there."

My dad was waiting for me at the kitchen table with a cup of coffee. My mother was there too. "Hi, honey," she said, her expression concerned. "Are you okay? You look terrible."

"I haven't been sleeping well."

from my dad and sat down while my mom went over to the coffee maker. "So I dropped out of the show."

His brows went up. "You did?"

"Yes."

"Why?"

"Because you were right. I was making the wrong choice. You guys raised me to put my family first, not my career. And even though this isn't what I had planned, I'm realizing that it could turn out to be what I want."

"Or what you need," my mom said, setting a cup of black coffee in front of me.

"What changed your mind?" my dad asked.

"Honestly, I was never fully convinced doing the show was right for me. And once I found out about the baby, I was even less convinced. But there was one thing that pushed me over the edge." I pulled out my phone and brought up the video of the ultrasound. "This."

They both leaned forward and watched, astonishment on their faces. "*Oh*." My mom's eyes welled with tears, and she put a hand over her heart. "That sound brings back so many memories."

The video ended, and my dad cleared his throat. "Play it again."

Smiling, I played it again for them, enjoying their reaction —my dad's slow, amazed grin, my mom's emotional tears, the look they exchanged.

"Can you send that to me?" my mom asked.

"Me too," said my dad.

"Sure." I messaged it to both of them, set my phone down, and picked up my coffee. "Now tell me how to win over this baby's mom."

My dad sipped his coffee too. "Have you told her you're not doing the show?"

"Because she thinks you don't *want* to stay here," my mom said. "She doesn't want to be the reason you don't get to do what you want, and she thinks by insisting that you go, she's doing you a favor."

"It shows she cares," my dad said with a shrug. "She's just going about it the wrong way."

"Like someone else I know." My mom elbowed my dad. "Anything about this seem familiar to you?"

My dad's face turned a little red. "Uh. Maybe."

"Is there something I'm missing here?" I asked.

My mother sighed. "Back in college I had an opportunity to go to Paris for a year like my mother and grandmother had done. It was a family tradition."

"And she wasn't going to go, because of me," my dad said. "So I did what I thought was best so she wouldn't throw away the opportunity and hate me for it later."

"You convinced her to go?" I asked.

"I broke up with her so she'd go. But it was a mistake." My dad took my mom's hand and kissed the back of it. "And it took me years to win her back."

"*Years*?" I gaped at them. "I don't have years to win Ellie."

"It won't take years," my mother assured me. "I think Ellie wants you to stay, but she's too afraid to admit it."

"I think so too," my dad said. "Because I saw the way she looked at you that day you guys told us. She might not trust you, but she definitely has feelings for you."

"If that were true," I said, thinking about what Winnie had told me, "what could I do to change her mind? To make her trust me?"

"Why doesn't she trust you?" my mother asked.

My dad and I exchanged a look, and I knew right away he hadn't told her what I'd done at the motel. I felt a rush of gratitude for him—he was the kind of dad I'd be someday.

terrible, but if I could go back, I'd do things differently. But mostly I think she's scared because of something I said to her."

"What did you say?" My mother was clearly nervous.

"I said I never wanted to stay in one place or settle down. I said I wasn't sure I ever wanted a family, and that being stuck with one person for the rest of my life sounded boring."

"Gee, can't imagine why she panicked when she realized she was pregnant," muttered my mom, picking up her coffee cup.

"Look, I know!" I jumped up and started pacing. "It was just a bunch of immature bullshit I said because I didn't know then what would happen or how I'd feel about her. When we got back from the motel, I couldn't stop thinking about her, but I didn't know how to handle it. Then all of a sudden she was pregnant, and any time I tried to tell her how I felt, she just accused me of pitying her." I stopped moving. "Also, I'm not the best at saying how I feel so I'm not sure things came out right."

"Safe to say they didn't," my dad remarked.

I started pacing again. "Anyway, I finally came right out and said, 'What about us?' And you know what she said?" I turned to look at them. "She said, 'There is no us. There's never been an us.'"

"Okay," my mom said, tapping her lips with one finger. "So you need to show her two things. One, that you didn't mean what you said about never wanting to stay in one place and have a family—or that you've changed your mind. And two, that *she* matters to you, baby or not."

"But the baby matters too," I insisted. "I want to show her I'll be a good father."

"Be a good man first," said my dad. "The rest will follow."

"I agree," my mom said. "You'll need to work a little harder to show her that it's not just about obligation. And it might take some time, Gianni. Maybe not years, but you have to be patient while you earn her trust."

"I will," I promised.

She sighed. "You know what I was looking at the other day? The photo album from that first summer we moved up here. You were what, like five?"

I stared at her. "You have photos from back then? Of Ellie and me?"

"Of course." She got up and went into the family room, returning with several albums. "I've got a ton of them."

I opened one up and started leafing through, smiling at old pictures of family vacations and holidays and birthdays. Mostly the photos were of my siblings and me, but there were plenty with the Fournier kids too, since we were together so much.

Sledding in winter. Running through the sprinkler during the summer. Standing side by side—and not looking too happy about it—on the first day of school. As the years went by, our appearances changed—I grew taller, Ellie's hair grew longer—but in picture after picture, there we were, side by side, growing up together.

The final photo I found of us had been taken at our high school graduation. We're wearing our navy blue gowns, and I'm standing behind Ellie with both arms around her neck like I might choke her. The grin on my face is a mile wide, and she's tugging on my forearms like she wants to escape—but she's laughing, her face radiantly beautiful and her eyes bright.

Was that only five years ago? We'd come such a long way together.

It gave me an idea.

CHAPTER 22
ELLIE

It had been a week since the ultrasound.

A week since Gianni and I had held hands and listened to our baby's heartbeat together. A week since I'd foolishly let my hopes rise once more.

He'd seemed so moved by the experience, and I'd felt so close to him. I thought for sure he'd say something on the ride home, or want to talk when we got there. But he'd said nothing, so I'd said nothing, and I was left wondering if I'd imagined the connection in the doctor's office.

But every morning, he continued to bring me breakfast from Plum & Honey, sometimes scones, sometimes a cinnamon bun, sometimes an apple crumble muffin—all things Winnie's mom knew I loved. Sometimes I was too queasy to eat them, but I always appreciated the gesture. He'd stay long enough to ask how I was feeling, how things were going for me, and for the first time, I felt like he *listened* to my answers. He often followed up on things I'd said the day before, which made me feel like he'd been thinking about me. One afternoon I came back from lunch to find a jar of peanut butter, a bag of M&M's, and a spoon on my desk, and it made me laugh.

an *us*.

And he was leaving tomorrow.

Not only leaving, but he'd asked *me* to drive him to the airport. I'd actually have to watch him walk away from me.

It should have made me happy that he was going—I'd be rid of him and this horrible ache in my heart, this ridiculous fantasy that he'd suddenly choose me over his career or his freedom. I should have been relieved that he hadn't broken his contract. I needed time apart, days and nights where I didn't have to see his concern for me or hear him laugh at something I said or watch him across the kitchen at work and be reminded so viscerally of the way he'd made me feel. I should have been happy about all of it.

But I wasn't happy. I was miserable. Lonely. Scared.

But there was nothing I could do about it.

After his final night at Etoile, he came over to where I was putting wineglasses away. "Hey," he said. "Still good to give me a ride tomorrow?"

"Yes." I focused on the glass I was putting on the shelf.

"Everything okay?"

"Fine."

"You don't seem fine."

"I'm tired. And hungry."

"Let me make you something to eat."

"That's not necessary." I placed another glass on the shelf.

"Come on, I want to." He poked my shoulder. "I'll even make you a fancy grilled cheese. Aren't those your favorite?"

"Yes," I admitted. "Did I tell you that?"

I smiled ruefully. "I guess you did."

"Give me fifteen minutes. You go sit in the dining room and relax."

Etoile's dining room was dark and silent. I chose a spot over by the window and lit the candle on the table. While I waited, I took deep breaths and told myself that everything would be easier once he was gone. I just had to get through the next twelve hours.

My parents had gone back to France, but they'd be back at the end of May, even before Gianni returned. My mom was going to help me turn one of the bedrooms in the house into a nursery, and she and Aunt Coco were already talking about plans for a baby shower this summer. Winnie was too. I had plenty of love and support, I had a beautiful home, and I had family. I was luckier than most.

But when Gianni came from the kitchen carrying a plate and glass of water for me, my heart nearly burst with longing. I was glad the room was dark and hoped he couldn't see the emotion in my face.

"Bacon, pear, and fig with cheddar," he said, setting the plate and glass in front of me. "I hope it's okay for your stomach."

"It looks delicious." My mouth watered at the crispy golden bread, the cheese oozing from the center, the scent of the bacon. "My stomach will happily devour this."

"Good." He took the chair across from me. "Bon appétit."

After setting my napkin across my lap, I picked up one half and sank my teeth into it.

"Well?" he prompted, but all I could do was moan. He grinned and nodded with satisfaction. "I'll take that as a compliment."

I devoured the sandwich in about three minutes flat.

"Wow," he said. "I'm impressed."

whole sickness part of pregnancy is over."

"That takes about fourteen weeks, right?"

"Yeah." I tilted my head. "How do you know that?"

"I've been doing some reading."

I raised my eyebrows. "Oh?"

"I bought a book at Target, okay?"

"Now *I'm* impressed."

"It's called *From Dude to Dad*."

I laughed. "That's perfect."

"It's very informative. Did you know that our kidney bean has already grown into a small lime?"

"I did. And next week, a plum."

He shook his head. "They grow so fast. It's amazing."

"We'll probably be saying that the rest of our lives."

"Probably." Our eyes met as it sank in deeper—this baby would link us for the rest of our lives. That connection to him I'd felt in the doctor's office gripped me again, but was it real?

I took another drink of water. "Thank you very much for the sandwich."

"You're welcome."

"I should go up to bed." I pushed my chair back, but when I went to stand up, my vision swam and I swayed sideways, grabbing the tabletop with both hands.

"Ellie!" A moment later, his arms were around me. "Are you okay?"

"I'm fine," I said, as the gray clouds faded and I could see again. "I just got up too fast."

"Sit down."

"No, really. I'm fine. The dizzy spell passed. I'll just go up to bed."

"I'm walking you up the stairs," he said firmly.

"Gianni, don't be silly."

up the staircase. "Do you know how terrible I'd feel if you slipped and fell on these steps and no one was here to help you?"

"I'm really fine," I said as we reached the second floor. And physically, maybe I was. But my emotions were a mess, and his strong, protective arm around me wasn't helping.

He glanced around. "I don't think I've ever been up here before. Which bedroom is yours?"

"End of the hallway."

He walked me all the way to the door. "You're sure you're okay?"

"Yes." I faced him and stared at his chest because I didn't trust myself to look him in the eye.

"Because I worry about you."

"I know."

He took my face in his hands and pressed his lips to my forehead. "I'll see you tomorrow morning. Goodnight."

I watched him walk down the hall, telling myself to let him go—this was good practice for tomorrow. Things were settled, we were friends again, and I didn't need to mess with that.

But I heard myself call out. "Gianni?"

He faced me again. "Yeah?"

My throat was so dry. I swallowed hard. "Um, what time tomorrow?"

"Ten should be good. I'll text you my address."

"Okay."

He turned and walked away again, and this time, I let him go.

Then I went into my bedroom and cried myself to sleep.

I woke up to a text from him.

Good morning. How are you feeling?

Fighting off the nausea that always hit me first thing, I typed a reply.

Ok.

Still good to drive me to the airport?

It was the last thing I wanted to do, but I'd given my word.

Yes. I'll be there at 10.

Great. I'll send you my address.
Text me when you get here.

A moment later, his address popped onto my screen, and I tossed my phone aside. Laying back on my pillow, I closed my eyes and willed the tears to stop coming. Willed the sob threatening to escape my chest to stay put. Willed the sick feeling to pass.

But it wasn't just the pregnancy making me ill.

Somehow I'd fallen for him.

And I wasn't sure ten weeks apart was going to cure me.

CHAPTER 23
GIANNI

checked my phone again, but she hadn't sent the text yet saying she'd arrived. When she did, I was going to pretend my flight was delayed and ask her to come in.

She'd be aggravated, but hopefully she'd do it. I wondered when it would hit her that she wasn't walking up to my old apartment, the one she'd been to the night of the blizzard.

I looked around, making sure for the millionth time that everything was in place. Winnie had said to go big, and I hoped this was big enough.

It had been torture keeping the plan to myself for the last six days, especially knowing how Ellie felt and seeing her desperately try to hide it, but that's how long it had taken me to arrange it all—extract myself from the Hot Mess contract, reach out to Fiona Duff again, rent the bigger apartment, move in, and decorate.

That was key. The décor.

From the moment I'd left my parents' house last week, I'd known what I was going to do. I hadn't told anyone what I was planning except my parents and Felicity MacAllister, since I wasn't actually leaving Etoile after all. She'd been

was notoriously bad at lying. No one in their family ever trusted her with anything meant to be a surprise.

I was a little worried that Ellie might inadvertently see something online about me being replaced as the host of Hot Mess, but I'd gotten lucky there.

Now if that luck would just hold out—if I could remember all the things I wanted to say, if I could convince her that she meant more to me than any career move, if I could persuade her to give me the chance to make her happy . . . I'd feel richer than any Hollywood money could have made me.

But first, she was probably going to want to punch me in the face.

CHAPTER 24
ELLIE

I pulled into the parking lot of Gianni's apartment complex a few minutes before ten. I thought I remembered his unit being over toward the left, so I headed over to that side and looked for a spot.

I snagged one labeled Visitor, put my car in park, and texted him that I'd arrived. He replied right away.

Hey. My flight is delayed an hour. Want to come in?

I groaned. The *last* thing I wanted to do was spend more time with him. But what choice did I have?

Fine. Which one is yours again?

It's the last one in the building to the right of the circle drive.

Oh. For some reason, I thought you were on the left.

Nope. On the right.

I moved the car to the other side of the circle drive and found another Visitor spot. As I walked toward his door, I looked around in confusion. This was not how I remembered

snowing hard, and I'd been distracted that night for sure.

I knocked on the last door on the right, and he pulled it open. "Hi," he said, and as always, I found myself slightly out of breath at the sight of him—the combination of those blue eyes and that dark hair always got to me.

And that mouth . . . would I ever forget the way he kissed me?

"Hi," I said. Then I noticed what he was wearing. "You're flying to L.A. in your Pineview Motel sweatshirt?"

He glanced down and chuckled. "It's my favorite. I'm hoping it brings me luck—like your hedgehog socks."

"Right." My eyes traveled over his shoulders and chest, remembering the day he'd bought those shirts for us and how we'd spent the night wrapped in each other's arms.

"Come in," he said, pulling the door wider and stepping back.

I entered his apartment, and the first thing I noticed was that the layout was different. The living room was on the wrong side. And there was a staircase ahead of me—that was weird. "Did you move or something?" I asked as he shut the door behind me.

"Yes."

"No wonder." I glanced around. "I thought I was—" Then I gasped. Chills blanketed my skin. "Oh my God."

On the wall to my right were blown-up photographs of Gianni and me—at least a dozen of them of just the two of us, ranging in age from five or six through high school graduation.

In a daze, I moved closer to them, putting a hand over my mouth. My pulse was hammering. "What is this, Gianni?"

He came to stand at my side. "This is us," he said quietly as my eyes took in each picture.

The first day of school. Standing side by side at our First

Sitting side by side drinking hot chocolate afterward. Awkward with braces (me) and shaggy hair that needed a trim (him) before a middle school dance. His arms around me at high school graduation.

"But—but why?" My voice trembled.

"When I asked you, 'what about us,' you said, 'There is no us. There's never been an us.' I wanted to show you it wasn't true. That there's always been an us." He took me gently by the shoulders and turned me to face him. "I'm not going to California, Ellie."

"You're not?"

He shook his head.

"Why?"

"Because my job is here. My life is here. My family is here," he said, and I recognized my words from the day I'd refused his offer to move to Hollywood with him. *"You're here. I want to be where you are."*

"You do?" Tears filled my eyes.

"Yes. Even before you told me you were pregnant, I could not stop thinking about you. Something about leaving wasn't sitting right with me, and I didn't know what it was—but I knew that I was going to miss you and Etoile and working together. I was just too stubborn to admit it. And I was worried you'd laugh at me for thinking there could be more between us."

"But what about those things you said at the motel? About never wanting to sit still or settle down? About being bored with one person and craving the rush of a new thing? I thought you wanted to go wherever life took you."

"Stop." Gianni reached for my hands. "I've always believed in following my gut, and in the past, yes—that's meant moving around, changing things up, looking for that next adventure. But life led me to you, Ell. And my gut is

What do you say?"

The sobs that had been building in my throat all morning finally erupted, and I dropped my chin to my chest and bawled. Gianni gathered me in his arms and rocked me gently, stroking my back.

"Is this a trick?" I sobbed. "Are you going to make me drive you to the airport after this?"

"No." He laughed softly and hugged me tighter. "No more tricks. This is the real thing, Ellie. I'm here, I'm staying, and I'm yours—if you want me."

"I want you." It felt so good to say the words out loud. I looked up at him and said them again. "I want you."

He crushed his lips to mine, and I threw my arms around his neck, clinging like I'd never let go. Without breaking the kiss, he swept me off my feet and carried me up the stairs and into his bedroom. Gently, he placed me on the bed, then braced himself above me. "Is this okay? I don't want to hurt you or squash our baby lime. It deserves a chance to become a plum."

I laughed and kicked off my shoes. "We're both fine."

"I'll be gentle," he said, but he was already ripping off his sweatshirt and T-shirt, then my sweater and camisole, then wriggling out of his jeans and yanking mine down my legs.

When I was naked under his gaze, I felt a moment of self-consciousness. "My body is already changing. Maybe you can't tell, but—"

"Your body is even more gorgeous than it was before," he said, his hungry eyes traveling over my skin. "Which I didn't think was possible."

I smiled. "Thank you."

"I'm serious, Ellie. I don't know if it's the pregnancy or what, but I've never felt like this before."

"Like what?"

wanting to build a tower to keep you safe from filthy-minded beasts like me down below."

Smiling, I reached for his broad, sexy shoulders and pulled him closer. "You are the only beast I'll let in," I whispered. "I promise."

"Do we have to hurry?" he asked, burying his face in my neck and kissing his way down my chest.

"I have to be back at work by one at the latest," I told him, arching my back as his tongue stroked one hard nipple. "But it's only ten, right? We have plenty of time."

"That's only three hours, Ellie." He switched his mouth to my other breast. "And there are so many delicious places on your body that I've missed."

"Well, guess what?"

"Hm?" He filled his palms with my tender breasts, teasing the tightened peaks with his thumbs, and I slid my hands into his thick, dark hair.

"We can always come back after work tonight."

He picked up his head. "Would you? Come back and stay the night with me? Not because you have to because there's a blizzard or my car is dead, but because you want to?"

"Gianni, sweetheart." I tightened my hands in his hair so hard he winced. "Your car was never dead."

He laughed as he moved down my body, pushed my knees apart and settled between my thighs. "I'll make it up to you," he said, giving me one, slow stroke up my center. "For three hours straight."

He definitely didn't last three hours, but he did go slow, using his mouth and his fingers and then his cock, both of us moaning with pleasure as he slid inside me completely bare. "Oh God," he whispered. "I forgot how good this feels. No wonder we didn't stop in time at the motel."

"Good." He moved deeper inside me. "Because I never want this to end."

"So wait a minute," I said. "You've known for how long that you weren't going to leave?"

"Six days."

I picked up my head from his bare chest and looked down at him with my most menacing glare. "Six days? You let me walk around miserable and sad and pining for you for six days?"

"I didn't know you were pining for me," he said, pulling me close to him again. "You just kept pushing me away and telling me to leave."

"That's because I was scared." I snuggled up against his side again, breathing him in. "I didn't think you wanted me like I wanted you."

"I did. I just didn't know how to get you to believe it."

"You nailed it today." I kissed his chest.

"I had help," he confessed.

"From who?"

"Your favorite person—my dad."

I laughed. "You're my favorite person right now. But I do like your dad. And your mom."

"They both adore you." He paused. "I also told your parents."

I sat up again. "You did?"

"Yes. I had to tell them because I want to keep the job at Etoile. Which I love, by the way. The minute I quit the show, I was relieved. It was so obviously the right decision."

magazine."

"What?" My jaw hung open. "What are you talking about?"

"I reached out to Fiona Duff and pitched a story about the two of us. I had to spill the beans about the baby—I swore her to secrecy—but she absolutely loved the idea of a power couple cover. We'll shoot it next week, if you say yes."

"Yes," I said, laughing. "But it's so annoying the way you can just talk people into anything."

"Well, I also had to agree to let her daughter design and sell merch for me for her economics class project." He exhaled. "I'll probably regret it, but soon you will be able to purchase a Too Hot to Handle hot pad with my face on it."

"Serves you right." I thumped his chest. "But speaking of classes, what would you think about some cooking classes at Etoile?"

"Kids or adults?"

"I was thinking adults, like as part of a weekend package, but you know what? Kids' classes would be fun too! Like in the summertime? You'd be so great at that."

"I don't know anything about kids. Except how to act like one. You think I'd be good with them?"

I laughed. "Yes, I do. I think it will come naturally to you. By the way, my mother confirmed what you told me—that it was you who carried me into the house after I bloodied my knees."

His grin was smug. "Told you."

"I was wrong. But I'm right about you being great with kids. What do you think?"

He put his hands behind his head. "Yeah. I like that idea. Let's do it."

"I'll talk to Winnie and we can start planning." I started to get out of bed, and he grabbed my arm.

day." Although looking at him, lying there naked and tousled and giving me that look, it was tempting.

"Five more minutes?"

I gave in and let him pull me back into bed next to him. "Okay. Five more minutes. But in exchange, you have to promise me you're not going to keep big secrets anymore."

"This wasn't really a secret—it was more like a surprise. And I love surprises."

I groaned as I snuggled up to him once more. "I feel like that does not bode well for me."

"They will all be good. I promise." He wrapped his arms around me and kissed the top of my head. "All I want to do is be good to you."

"Oh! I almost forgot! I have something for you." We were just about to leave his apartment and head to Abelard when Gianni tugged on my arm. "Come sit on the couch."

"Gianni, I'm already late," I said impatiently. "I gave you five more minutes, which turned into twenty."

"Please just sit," he cajoled. "One minute, I promise."

Sighing with exasperation, I let him pull me over to the couch and sat down. "I don't know why I keep believing your promises, but okay."

"Close your eyes."

I did as he asked, and a moment later, he placed something in my lap.

"Okay, you can look."

I opened my eyes and saw a rectangular package clumsily

"Yeah," he said sheepishly. "Sorry. It was all I had."

"It's okay." Carefully, I slid my fingers beneath the tape and peeled away the paper. Then I gasped. "Oh my God!"

It was a photo frame with the ultrasound picture inside it. On the wide white matting beneath the picture was written *love at first sight* in lowercase cursive letters.

"It's our baby," he said proudly, as if I might have thought he'd stuck some stranger's ultrasound in the frame.

"I can see that. It's adorable." I looked at it for a moment, then hugged it to my chest and looked up at him with misty eyes. "I love it. Our baby's first photo."

"I got it at Target," he said. "And I almost bought a ton more stuff. I've never even been down those aisles before. They've got *everything* for babies. It's crazy!"

"It is." I stood up and hugged him. "I'm sure we'll be spending a lot of time and money there, but this is the first baby gift I've gotten. Thank you."

"You're welcome," he said, wrapping his arms around me and kissing the top of my head. "It's the first of many. I want to give you everything."

And even though I was in a hurry and would probably be a little late for my first tasting, I stayed right where I was, in his arms, chest to chest, our baby cradled between us.

It felt like home.

CHAPTER 25
ELLIE

LATE JULY

"Ell! Are you ready to go?" Gianni called from downstairs.

I was in our bedroom, trying to get my shoes tied, but it was a challenge now that my belly had grown bigger. Our little plum had grown to the size of an eggplant, according to the books, but my stomach was already the size of half a watermelon. Bending over also made me dizzy.

I sat on the bed and tried to bring one foot up and grasp the laces, but the baby—it was a girl we planned to name Claudia, for Gianni's mom—decided to throw a tantrum about it and kicked me vigorously. "Oof," I said, dropping my heel to the floor and putting both hands on my abdomen. "Okay, okay."

Gianni appeared in the bedroom doorway, looking impatient. "Hey, I should be there already. Can I help you with anything?"

"Yes." Leaning back on my elbows, I stuck my feet out. "Tie my shoes. Your daughter beat me up when I bent over to do it."

"Thank you."

"Don't kick your mother," he said to my belly as he tied one sneaker, then the other. "It's our only night off this week, and we're going to the Cherry Festival."

"It won't be that big a deal if we're late," I said. "Felicity is manning the Etoile booth, and Winnie is with her. My parents are both there too." Since it was Monday, Etoile was closed tonight, so everyone would be at the festival.

"I know, but . . ." He finished and stood up. "I'm just excited."

I laughed. "You're like a kid."

"Can't help it. I still like the rides. And remember how awesome I am at the dunk tank?"

"I remember." I held out a hand, and he took it, gently pulling me to my feet. "Even though sometimes I'd like to forget."

He kissed me. "How are you feeling?"

"Fine," I said. "She's just been extra active today. Can't sit still, just like her dad."

"Uh oh." He grinned as we left the bedroom and headed down the stairs, still hand in hand. "I hope the universe is not going to get back at me for being such a rowdy kid by giving me a little fireball daughter."

"Maybe she's going to be a Rockette," I said, putting a hand over the swell of my stomach, where she was currently practicing her kick ball change.

"That would be cool." We reached the bottom of the stairs, and Gianni grabbed his keys from the little table by the front door.

I glanced at the living room wall, where all the photos of us still hung. I knew it was sort of obnoxious to keep them up, but I couldn't bear to take them down yet—I'd just moved in here a few weeks ago. He'd been asking me to live with

"Ellie, come on," he'd said insistently. "We're ready." We were lying in bed, still breathless, our heartbeats slowing. Always nervous about the baby, he'd rolled to my side and gathered me close. "I want to be with you all the time. I know it's more convenient for you to live right at Abelard because of work, but I promise there are *lots* of benefits to living with me too. Like orgasms when and how and wherever you want them."

I laughed. "That *is* tempting."

"I got this bigger place because I was hoping to share it with you one day. And I hate going to sleep without you next to me."

"Me too," I admitted, propping myself up so I could look at him. "I just lie in my bed and wish I was here."

"I love you, Ellie." His voice was soft and serious. "I have never said those words to anyone before. And now that I know what it should feel like, I'm glad I didn't, because it would have been a lie." He looked at me the way I'd always dreamed of. "You're everything to me. You're the one."

I'd smiled as my eyes filled. "I love you too. And yes—I'll move in."

Gianni had offered to take the photos of us down, but they made me so happy to look at. There was a new one too—our *Tastemaker* cover, which had us dressed in black tie with Gianni seated at a table in Etoile and me standing next to him, pouring a bottle of sparkling wine over his head. It was sexy and irreverent and fun, just like the piece inside about us, and it was fantastic publicity for Abelard.

Every time I saw those photos on the wall, I remembered him saying, 'There's always been an us.' It made me shiver with joy every time—including now.

"Are you cold?" he asked me. "Want me to grab a sweater for you?"

Festival together in a long time. Since we were seventeen, to be exact."

"I know," he said, glancing behind me at the photos. "You'll have a better time tonight. I promise."

"Are you finally going to kiss me in a closet?" I teased.

"I will kiss you anywhere you want." Even though we were running late and he wanted to get out the door, he put his arms around me and pressed his lips to mine. "I love you."

I shivered again. Hearing him say the words was always a thrill. "I love you too."

"Come on, let's go." His blue eyes were bright with excitement.

If I hadn't been so distracted, I might have seen the mischief in them.

Several hours later, I walked over to the small Etoile tent, where Felicity was grilling mini paninis with gruyere, greens, and cherry bourbon jam. I grabbed one from the tray, and she laughed. "You like them?"

"Can't you tell? I've already had like five of them. They're delicious."

As I ate it, I slipped into the booth and dropped into a chair behind my mom, who was pouring Abelard wines into clear plastic cups. My dad was there too, talking with someone at the next booth. I'd lost Gianni somewhere, which wasn't surprising, given the way he was determined to play every game, ride every ride, taste every food.

"Hey," said my mom. "How are you feeling?"

"No clue. I lost him somewhere between the Ferris wheel and the bounce house."

She laughed. "Sounds like Gianni."

"Ellie!"

I looked up and saw Winnie heading for the booth. "Hey, Win. Have you seen Gianni?"

"Yes. He's talking to Dex over by the dunk tank. But he's looking for you."

With difficulty, I rose to my feet and wiped my fingers on my shorts. "I'm coming. I hope he's ready to go. I'm beat."

As we headed for the games area, I yawned. "Everyone said there would be an energy boost during the second trimester. Where is it?"

Winnie laughed. "I don't know. But I don't think Gianni is quite ready to leave yet, so I hope you get a burst of energy."

We'd reached the dunk tank, and I saw Dex and his two little girls standing there, but no Gianni. "Hey," I said, smiling at them. "Are you having fun?"

Dex nodded, and the girls giggled and jumped up and down. "We want to see this!" shouted Luna, the little blond one. If I remembered correctly, she would be in first grade this fall.

"Luna, shhhh!" Hallie, older by about three years, poked her sister's shoulder. "We can't give it away."

"Give what away?" I asked. "And where the heck is Gianni? I thought he was—"

"He's over there!" Luna burst out, pointing at the dunk tank.

I looked up, and my jaw dropped. There was Gianni, seated behind the blue bars on the dunk tank platform, dressed in his swim trunks and grinning madly.

"It's your turn!" he shouted. "I figured it was time for payback."

"I bought you fifty," he yelled. "Then we're even-steven. And if you can't dunk me in that many throws, it's not my fault!"

"Step right up," said the guy manning the tank. At his feet were five buckets of balls, and he picked one up and held it out.

Eagerly, I went over and took the bucket from him, then set it on the ground at the white line on the green turf runner about twenty feet from the big red circle I had to hit in order to dunk him. I picked up the first ball and stared at that red circle, concentrating hard.

"Come on, Ellie!" I heard the girls cheering. "You can do it!"

I took a breath, said a prayer, and threw.

I missed.

Then I missed again.

In fact, as the crowd gathered—including my parents, the Lupos, and much of Winnie's family—and Gianni continued to taunt me, high and dry on that platform, I managed to miss with all ten balls in that first bucket.

The guy brought me the second bucket, and I pushed up my sleeves, blowing my hair out of my face. "I need help!" I scanned the crowd. "Can anyone give me some advice?"

"Turn sideways more," shouted Gianni's dad.

"Don't hold your breath!" yelled my dad.

"Release a little sooner!" offered Dex.

"Get someone else to throw for you!" hollered Winnie.

I looked over at her. "Now that's good advice." My eyes skimmed over everyone who'd gathered around and landed on Winnie's cousin Chip—who happened to be a newly retired MLB pitcher.

A grin broke out on my face.

"Oh, shit," I heard Gianni say.

life as many times as possible. Trust me when I say that he will deserve it."

The crowd went nuts as Chip grudgingly allowed me to pull him onto the runner. Happily, I set the bucket of balls at his feet. "Here you are. Have at him."

Chip picked up a ball and looked at the red circle, then at me. "Should I move back or something? This doesn't seem fair."

I shook my head and patted his arm. "Trust me. It's fair."

He shrugged, wound up, threw, and nailed it. Gianni went into the water like a bag of bricks.

Then he did it thirty-nine more times.

The crowd continued to gather, Gianni continued to climb up there again and again, and Chip continued to throw with an accuracy that astounded and delighted me. When he got to the last ball, he pulled it from the bucket and looked at a soaking-wet Gianni.

Gianni didn't say anything, but Chip seemed to get a message anyway, because he nodded and handed the ball to me. "I think this one's yours."

I looked down at it. Written on the side was THIS ONE LAST. And I realized it didn't feel exactly like the other base-balls I'd thrown. The outside was white leather and the stitches were red, but there was a seam along the middle, as if it would open up.

I glanced up at Gianni, who gave me his signature grin. "Come on, open it up! It's easier than throwing it!"

My heart was racing, and the baby was kicking up a storm inside me. Taking a breath, I opened up the baseball, and discovered it was a ring box in disguise. Tucked into black velvet was a gorgeous three-stone ring, with a round center diamond flanked by two smaller ones, set in a platinum band. My eyes blurred, and I worried I might pass out

"Well? What do you say, princess?" Gianni called. "Will you marry me?"

I looked at Gianni again and thought I might burst with excitement. "Yes!" I shouted. "Yes! Yes! Yes!"

The crowd cheered, and I thanked Chip with a quick hug before letting him hurry back to the sidelines. When I turned around again, Gianni was coming toward me. He was drenched, his wet hair a mess, his feet bare, his swim trunks hanging low and clinging to his skin. But I'd never been more in love with him as he got down on one knee, took the ring from the box, and slipped it on my finger. "I know I'm probably the last guy you thought you'd end up with."

"The very last," I confirmed, smiling through tears.

"But I promise to make you smile every single day of your life," he said, clasping my hand in his. "And I will put all my energy into taking care of you and our family."

"That's a lot of energy."

"It is." He grinned up at me. "I think that means we're going to have a big family."

Laughing, I let my tears spill over as he rose to his feet, wrapped me in his arms and picked me right up off the ground. The people surrounding us cheered, and in a moment we were engulfed by friends and family who wanted to hug us and wish us well.

I'd only been back on the ground for a minute when I was grabbed by my mom, then my dad, then Uncle Nick and Aunt Coco, then Winnie, who was crying and laughing just like I was. "That was so romantic!" she squealed.

"Did you know?" I asked.

She shook her head. "Not until five minutes before it happened! Someone must have warned him I'm no good with surprises."

"I did," said Felicity, who appeared and gave me a quick

"Well, he pulled it off," I said, glancing down at my ring.

"I did," Gianni said behind me. "But there's just one more thing."

"What?" I turned around to face him, and *splat!*—

I took a whipped cream pie to the face.

Stunned, I stood there for a moment, blinking through the fluffy white whipped cream while everyone around us roared. I wiped my eyes and heard one of Dex's daughters squeal, "We got that whole thing on video!"

I started to laugh, and Gianni kissed me, getting whipped cream all over his face too. "We weren't *quite* even-steven," he said.

"And now?"

"Now we're good."

I threw my arms around him and kissed his lips once more. "So good."

EPILOGUE
GIANNI

"Gianni."

It was Ellie's voice whispering my name in the dark. Soft and sweet, the way she did when she was feeling in the mood. Lately, that hadn't been too often—and I got it, she was nearly nine months pregnant—so even if it was in the middle of the night and I'd been sound asleep a moment ago, I was up for this.

"Mmmm." I rolled over and reached for her. And reached. And reached. And reached again. She wasn't there.

"Gianni." Her tone was less soft and sweet now, more insistent and annoyed.

I sat up and opened my eyes, her body taking shape in the shadows. She was standing at the side of the bed, dressed. "What? What's wrong?"

She switched on the lamp. "I'm in labor."

My heartbeat kicked into a gallop. "It's not time yet! You have ten more days!"

She laughed. "Babies don't always arrive on a schedule. When they're cooked, the timer goes. And my timer went."

I swung my feet to the floor and took her by the shoulders. "Are you sure? What time is it? Did you call the doctor?"

"It did?"

"Yes. I got up to go to the bathroom and that was that."

"Okay. Okay." I got out of bed and started barreling around the room like a tornado. "Get dressed."

"I'm dressed."

"I was talking to myself." I was opening and closing drawers, yanking things out and putting them on without even caring what they were. I shoved my feet into some shoes. I stuck a hat on my head. I remembered at the last second to put on deodorant, reaching beneath the sweatshirt I'd thrown on.

"Gianni, relax. It will probably be hours before this baby is here. And I need you not to panic, okay?"

I turned around and saw Ellie standing there, her belly huge, her hands braced on her lower back. Her long, dark hair hung loose around her shoulders. She looked so young and beautiful, my heart hurt. I tossed the deodorant aside and took her in my arms. "Are you scared?"

"Yes." She smiled nervously, her brown eyes shining with excitement. "But I have you, right?"

"You have me. I'll never leave your side."

"Then I'm okay."

I kissed her forehead and held her close for a moment, willing myself to be braver than I felt. She needed me to stay calm and reassuring, so even though I felt like a thousand bulls were fighting inside my rib cage, I had to remain still. "Got your bag?"

"I got it."

"Then let's go."

had been over a month since I'd covered the seafoam green walls in one of the bedrooms with several coats of soft ivory. That had pretty much been my only job until it was time to put the crib together. Ellie, her mom, and my mother had filled the room to bursting with furniture and pillows and stuffed animals. I mostly just stood to the side and watched as the nursery came together, but I had to admit it turned out nice. I liked that it wasn't too girly—no frilly lace or bubble gum pink, just neutrals like ivory and light brown and moss green. My favorite thing in it was this giant stuffed giraffe that I'd bought on a whim one day. Ellie had rolled her eyes and sighed, but gamely set it up in one corner next to the bookshelf.

I helped her down the stairs, through the kitchen, and into the garage. Opening the car door for her, I was overwhelmed by it all. "Ellie!"

She looked at me with alarm. "What?"

"Do you realize that the next time we pull into this garage we'll have a baby in that thing?" I pointed to the infant car seat I'd installed in my SUV last week.

She laughed. "I certainly hope so. Because I'm evicting this child from my body today. Enough is enough."

I held her hand the whole way to the hospital. "So what will we do if she doesn't look like a Claudia Lupo?"

"She would not dare to come out looking like anything else," Ellie said confidently. "She and I have had many chats about this."

I chuckled. "Good."

"And I promise, as soon as I can think about planning a wedding, I'll change my name to Lupo too."

I brought her hand to my mouth and kissed the back of it. We'd gone back and forth about when the right time to get married would be—before the baby or afterward—and finally

She deserved the wedding of her dreams, not an emergency affair, and even though our mothers swore up and down it would be elegant and stunning, and they could handle *everything*, Ellie and I had stuck together and defended our right to do things on our own terms. It was enough for me that she'd said yes and wore the ring on her finger.

"It's okay," I said. "We'll get married when we're ready. We don't have to do things in a certain order or the same way everyone else does—that's *boring*."

She looked over at me and laughed. "We'll *never* be boring."

I smiled and felt like my heart might actually explode—had I honestly ever imagined life could offer a better adventure than this? Starting a family with the person you loved more than anything else in the world? Being so happy there weren't even words to express it? Feeling so alive you thought you might jump right out of your skin?

My eyes teared up, and I kissed her hand again. I'd never stop being grateful for her.

"Look at my daughter. Isn't she the most beautiful baby you have *ever* seen?"

"Gianni, you have to stop saying that to everyone who comes in here," said Ellie from the bed. To the nurse who'd come in to check her vitals, she said, "Sorry. First-time dad over there."

"No problem," the nurse chirped. When she was finished with Ellie, she peeked at the little bundle I held in my arms

"Thank you," I said to the nurse. I gave Ellie a triumphant look. "See?"

She sighed.

"Don't listen to her, Claudia." I looked down at my daughter's little face with its chubby pink cheeks and tiny perfect lips and dimpled chin. "You're the most beautiful baby in the world, and no one will ever convince me otherwise. You're almost as beautiful as your mommy."

Claudia looked up at me with those wide blue eyes, blinked once, and went back to sleep. I was tired too—the books weren't lying about the exhaustion of becoming a parent.

Claudia had been born just before noon yesterday. I'd spent the first night here at Ellie's side while she labored, and last night I'd spent in the chair by the window. Ellie had told me to go home and get a good night's sleep in our bed, but I hadn't been able to leave. Not only did I not want to be separated from them, but I didn't want to miss anything. I'd already changed my first messy diaper (totally and utterly disgusting), learned how to swaddle (I was actually pretty good at it), and rocked her to sleep (my new favorite thing in the world). I'd stood by while Ellie struggled with nursing, wishing I could be more help, but the nurse reassured Ellie that lots of moms and babies found it a challenge in the beginning and to keep at it. The next few times had gone better.

"If the doctor gives the okay, we can go home later this afternoon," Ellie said. "I can't wait to sleep in our bed."

"Me neither. But it's kind of weird they're just going to let us walk out of here with her."

Ellie laughed. "Why?"

"I don't know. How can they be sure we're qualified? I

She smiled. "I am. Come here."

I brought Claudia over to Ellie and sat on the side of the bed. "I'm totally obsessed with her, Ell. Is this normal?"

Ellie laughed. "I am too. And yes, I think it is."

"The dad books don't tell you about this, you know?"

"About what?"

"Just . . . this." My eyes got watery, and I cleared my throat. "How much love it's possible to feel. How protective you'll feel. How you can't imagine there was ever a time in your life you didn't want this."

"Gianni Lupo, are you *crying*?"

"*No*," I said, although I was totally crying.

She laughed again and tipped her head onto my shoulder, brushing her thumb over Claudia's cheek. "It's okay. I feel it too. And she *is* the most beautiful baby in the world."

We sat there together for a few minutes in silence, looking down at our sleeping child. "It's kind of incredible, isn't it?" she asked quietly.

"What is?"

"This whole thing. A year ago, I would never have believed this was possible."

I shook my head. "Me neither."

"It was just a blizzard bang," she said, laughing gently. "And now look at us. We're a family."

"We're a family," I said. I kissed the baby's head and then Ellie's. "Forever."

THE END

BONUS EPILOGUE

"Can I look yet?" I asked Gianni.

He'd blindfolded me the moment we left the house, and for the last ninety minutes I'd been trying to guess where we were going for the weekend. All I had for clues was the hum of the tires on the highway and a rough estimate of the distance we'd traveled, although I wasn't sure what direction we were heading, and for all I knew, Gianni had been driving in circles just to keep me confused. He still loved to mess with me, even after ten years together and nine years of marriage.

"No, you can't. And stop asking." He reached over and thumped my leg.

I tipped my head back far enough so the barest sliver of light appeared at the bottom of the black satin sleep mask. "This is kidnapping."

"You're thirty-three, Ell."

"Then it's *adult*-napping. Wife snatching. Abduction!" I risked lifting up the bottom of the mask slightly. "It's got to be some kind of crime."

"Hey." He tossed me one of his grins. "No peeking. You'll ruin the surprise."

"Almost, princess. We just have one stop to make first."

My phone vibrated in my lap. "Am I allowed to answer this?"

"Yes." My husband laughed. "You get one phone call."

"I can't even see who's calling," I complained. "How am I supposed to know if I want to pick up?"

"Give it here." He took the phone from me. "It's your mom. Here, you're on."

Feeling the phone in my hand again, I brought it to my ear. "Hello?"

"Hi, honey."

"Hi, Mom. Everything okay with the kids?"

"I'm sorry to bother you on your weekend away, and everything is totally fine, but Benny had a little accident on the playground after school."

Panicked, I whipped the mask off. Benny, our eight-year-old, was always injuring himself. He'd inherited his dad's reckless, daring streak along with his blue eyes and dimples. "What kind of accident?"

Gianni glanced at me and frowned.

"Mom, I'm putting you on speaker," I said, touching the screen. "What happened to Benny?"

"It's nothing to worry about," she soothed. "He sprained his wrist, but he's okay."

"But what *happened*?"

"He fell off the top of the spiral slide."

Gianni harrumphed. "He didn't fall. He jumped."

"He *may* have jumped," said my mother. "Claudia says he did. My back was turned because I was pushing Gabrielle on the swings and chatting with Coco."

Poor Claudia. She was only a year and a half older than Benny, and *so* protective, but she could never talk him out of all the dumb, impulsive ideas he had. Instead, she was the

rarely told on him because she hated seeing him get in trouble. I often wondered if that would last. "But he's okay?"

"Yes. He's fine. I was going to run him over to Urgent Care, but he can move it a little bit, and it doesn't look too swollen. Your dad says he'll be fine, but I thought you should know."

"Thanks, Mom. How's everyone else?"

"Fine." Her voice brightened. "Claudia is helping me with dinner, Benny is resting on the couch, and Gabrielle is practicing her French with Dad."

I smiled. Our youngest was only four, but her ear was amazing and she was picking up French quickly. My dad wouldn't speak anything else to her. "Good."

"Okay, you two have fun. We'll see you Sunday."

"Bye, Mom. Thanks."

I hung up and sighed. "That kid is going to drive me crazy."

"He gets that from me."

"He certainly does." I poked Gianni's shoulder. "Do I have to put the sleep mask back on?"

"Nope. We're nearly at our first stop." He signaled and exited the highway before I had a chance to read any signs.

Eagerly, I sat up taller in the passenger seat and looked out the window. It was mid-January, and everything was covered in snow, but it wasn't quite dark yet. Craning my neck, I glanced to the right and left, but didn't see anything resembling the fancy resort I'd been hoping for. All I saw was a gas station, and I was surprised when Gianni pulled into the parking lot. "Do we need gas?" I asked. "I thought you filled up before we—"

It hit me.

I started to laugh as Gianni put the SUV in park outside the door to the little convenience store. "You didn't."

"Room thirteen awaits us. Come on." He unbuckled his seatbelt and jumped out of the car.

Laughing, I followed him into the store. "What do we need here?"

"Provisions. I'm going to cook dinner for you tonight in our room. Tomorrow night we have a reservation at a nice restaurant in Harbor Springs—and we'll stay the night there too, in that resort you always want to go to and never book."

"Because it's not a place for kids, and we always have them with us!"

"Well, this weekend is just for us." He kissed my forehead and tugged my elbow. "I confess, I did pack some ingredients from home, but I also wanted to honor the tradition of gas station spaghetti."

I grinned. "Gas station spaghetti" was what our kids called pasta with tomato sauce too. We'd told them the story of how we'd gotten stranded together years ago during a blizzard.

"Was that when you fell in love?" Claudia once asked.

Gianni and I had exchanged an amused glance.

"Definitely," he said, his blue eyes alive with the secret of what had actually gone on at the motel. "After that blizzard, I knew she was the one for me. I just had to convince her of it. She didn't believe me."

"Is that true, Mom?"

"Sort of," I told her. "He used to tease me a lot and that made me mad. But that blizzard definitely changed everything."

Gianni gathered what he needed from the shelves and we made our way toward the register. Behind the counter was the man who'd been there ten years ago, portly and grizzled, his beard more white than gray. "Milton!" Gianni said. "How the heck are you?"

"We met ten years ago. We were stranded here because of—"

"The blizzard," Milton finished with a nod. "That's right. Now I remember. I'll be darned."

Gianni put the groceries on the counter. "We're back for a little anniversary celebration."

Milton cocked his head. "As I recall, you two weren't married. Fact, you said you didn't even like each other. I always remembered that."

I laughed and tucked my arm through my husband's. "We *didn't* like each other much back then. But all that changed during the snowstorm."

Milton chuckled. "Mother Nature had that one up her sleeve, didn't she?"

"She did," said Gianni. "And it's a good thing."

After paying for our groceries, we made our way to the Pineview Motel. The big old sign was the same, but there had been a couple improvements. "Look, they replaced the L!" I said with a laugh. "It's a swimming pool again!"

"Good to know, although I don't plan on giving you time for a polar bear plunge tonight," Gianni said, pulling up in front of the office. "I never get you to myself these days and I'm gonna make the most of it."

"Fine with me," I said. "Is Rose still here?"

"She is, and she knows we're coming. I'll be right back with the key to our favorite knotty pine oasis."

I giggled. "I'll be here."

Five minutes later, we stood outside the door to our old room while Gianni fumbled with the key. "Rose said she refuses to switch over to keyless entry. She likes to be old-fashioned."

"We knew this about her."

I laughed. "Thank you kindly, Mr. Lupo."

Entering the room sent a warm tingle up my spine. Everything looked exactly the same, right down to the red and black buffalo plaid curtains and bedding. "Wow. It's like a time warp, isn't it?"

Gianni shut the door and came up behind me, wrapping his arms around my shoulders. He kissed my head. "I take you to all the best places, don't I?"

Turning in his arms, I faced him and looped my hands behind his neck. Looking up at him still gave me butterflies. "I just want to be where you are."

He lowered his lips to mine and kissed me softly. "What should we do first? Walk in the woods? Some wine and a drinking game? Skip right to the good stuff?"

I started unbuttoning his black wool coat. "Let's skip to the good stuff."

He gave me his old grin. "Princess, your wish is my command."

The following morning, we slept in and stayed curled up beneath the blankets. "God, I forgot what life was like before kids," I said, my cheek on his warm, bare chest.

"Me too."

"We should do this more often."

"Hey, I ask you to run away with me all the time—you're the one who always suggests bringing the entire brood along."

I laughed. "I know. I just like it when we're all together.

Gianni turned his head. "Right over there against that wall."

"Why haven't we ever come back here before?"

"I've thought about it. But life gets busy and, you know —kids."

"Right. Kids." I sighed.

"But we *do* have awesome kids," Gianni said, his voice full of fatherly pride.

"We do."

"I mean, Benny's an idiot, but he'll learn to rein that in."

I laughed. "He's such a charmer too, just like you were. He can talk his way out of anything."

"Thank God Claudia is so sweet," Gianni said. "And Gabrielle is so smart. At least two out of the three won't give us heart attacks."

"Until it's time for them to date," I reminded him.

"Oh, I'm sending them to a convent before they hit puberty. Are you kidding? They're too beautiful to just walk around on the street with regular people." He rolled over, stretching out above me. "Just like their mama. I don't know how I convinced you to let me have you to myself for good."

"You knocked me up."

"Oh, right. Fucking genius of me."

I laughed, wrapping my arms and legs around him. "Speaking of knocking me up . . ."

His eyes popped. "You're pregnant?"

"No, not at the moment."

"You mean you *want* to get pregnant?" He sounded surprised, but not unhappy.

I bit my lip. "I've been pondering the idea. I thought I'd be done after Gabrielle, but I've been thinking maybe one more would be nice. What do you think?"

and repainting that bedroom for the fourth time in eight years."

"Good." I smiled seductively at him. "Want to get started?"

"What the princess wants, the princess gets." He buried his face in my neck and kissed my throat.

"Are you ever going to stop calling me that?" Against my thigh, I felt his cock growing hard, stirring up desire within me.

"Never." He picked his head up and looked down at me. "Not as long as there's an us."

I smiled again as my whole body hummed. "There will always be an us."

JOIN MY READER GROUP!

For exclusive behind the scenes information, access to ARCs, early cover reveals, and sneak peeks to what's coming, join my Facebook reader group, Harlow's Harlots, using the QR code below!

The Frenched Series

Frenched

Yanked

Forked

Floored

The Happy Crazy Love Series

Some Sort of Happy

Some Sort of Crazy

Some Sort of Love

The After We Fall Series

Man Candy

After We Fall

If You Were Mine

From This Moment

The One and Only Series

Only You

Only Him

Only Love

The Cloverleigh Farms Series

Irresistible

Undeniable

Insatiable

Unbreakable

The Bellamy Creek Series

Drive Me Wild

Make Me Yours

Call Me Crazy

Tie Me Down

Cloverleigh Farms Next Generation Series

Ignite

Taste

Tease

Co-Written Books

Hold You Close (Co-written with Corinne Michaels)

Imperfect Match (Co-written with Corinne Michaels)

Strong Enough (M/M romance co-written with David Romanov)

The Speak Easy Duet

The Tango Lesson (A Standalone Novella)

Want a reading order? Click here!

ACKNOWLEDGMENTS

As always, my appreciation and gratitude go to the following people for their talent, support, wisdom, friendship, and encouragement...

Melissa Gaston, Brandi Zelenka, Jenn Watson, Janett Corona, Kayti McGee, Laurelin Paige, Corinne Michaels, the entire Social Butterfly team, Anthony Colletti, Rebecca Friedman, Flavia Viotti & Meire Dias at Bookcase Literary, Nancy Smay at Evident Ink, Julia Griffis at The Romance Bibliophile, Erin Spencer at One Night Stand Studios, narrators Ava Erickson and James Cavenaugh, the Shop Talkers, the Sisterhood, the Harlots and the Harlot ARC Team, bloggers and event organizers, my readers all over the world...

And once again, to my husband and daughters, who make me smile every day. You're the greatest adventure ever.

ABOUT THE AUTHOR

Melanie Harlow likes her heels high, her martini dry, and her history with the naughty bits left in. She's the author of the Bellamy Creek Series, the Cloverleigh Farms Series, the One & Only series, the After We Fall Series, the Happy Crazy Love Series, and the Frenched Series.

She writes from her home outside of Detroit, where she lives with her husband and two daughters. When she's not writing, she's probably got a cocktail in hand. And sometimes when she is.

Find her at www.melanieharlow.com.